Port Mungo

BY THE SAME AUTHOR

BLOOD AND WATER AND OTHER TALES

THE GROTESQUE

SPIDER

DR HAGGARD'S DISEASE

ASYLUM

MARTHA PEAKE

Port Mungo

PATRICK McGRATH

BLOOMSBURY

First published in Great Britain 2004

Copyright © 2004 by Patrick McGrath

The moral right of the author has been asserted

Bloomsbury Publishing Plc, 38 Soho Square, London W1D 3HB

A CIP catalogue record for this book
is available from the British Library

ISBN 0 7475 7019 1

10 9 8 7 6 5 4 3 2 1

Typeset by Hewer Text Ltd, Edinburgh
Printed by Clays Ltd, St Ives plc

All papers used by Bloomsbury Publishing are natural,
recyclable products made from wood grown in
well-managed forests. The manufacturing processes conform
to the environmental regulations of the country of origin.

http://www.bloomsbury.com/patrickmcgrath

FOR MARIA

I

When he first came back to New York, and that would be twenty years ago now, my brother Jack was in a kind of stupor, for it was shortly after the death of his daughter Peg. What can you say about the death of a child? She was sixteen when it happened, and the impact on all of us, Jack of course in particular, was devastating. When I glimpsed the extent of his grief, after the first shock wore off, and he awoke to the grim slog of flat empty days that yawned before him – all meaning, hope and pleasure drained from life – I called out to him from across what seemed a chasm, and got back only the faintest of answers, which might have been no more than an echo; I mean I did not know what to say to him to bring him back into living contact with the world, and more immediately with myself, his sister. I don't suppose there's very much you can say.

I never feared for his sanity however. I never feared that he would attempt to do harm to himself, and for this reason: he had his work. And with the first, weary, reluctant attempt to pull himself together came a return to the studio, a loft I had rented for him in an old warehouse building on Crosby Street. I remember watching him silently building stretchers, the very mindlessness of this familiar activity giving palpable relief to a soul in pain. I sat in that loft drinking tea and trying to make conversation as he nodded and grunted and nailed his stretchers, and the next day he cut canvas, and began to staple it to the stretchers, and again I was the one who sat there with him, talking or silent, whichever he seemed to prefer, simply a familiar body in the same bleak space during those slow wretched days. I was there too when he mixed paint in a bucket, Indian red and black pigment, and thinned it with turpentine to the consistency of soup, and I remember how he turned the brushes over in his fingers, running the fibres across his palm. He had discovered second-hand paintbrushes in a hardware store a couple of blocks east, in Chinatown, big floppy decorators' brushes softened by long use by working men.

And as I watched him I saw what the years in Port Mungo had done to his hands. Jack's hands were once like mine, our best feature, I used to think: thin, and long, with slender tapering fingers, elegant white bones intricately assembled for fine work with the violin, perhaps, or the fountain pen. Mine were as white as ever, Jack's by contrast had become purely functional entities, and like any tools put to daily work they showed the marks of use: scarred and chipped, horny-nailed, the skin burnt brown, old paint baked into the beds of the nails and the backs matted with bristles pale as straw. And as he nodded and grunted I began to see that the cast and temper of the *man* was similarly coarsened and scarred, and it struck me that he had spent too many years working in the harsh sunlight of that shabby town.

Then one day quite without warning he told me he didn't want me to come to the loft any more. He said I was suffocating him – me suffocating him! I was wounded by the abruptness of this rejection, also by his lack of gratitude, though not entirely surprised. For it confirmed that the years in Port Mungo had done nothing to civilize him, in fact I had the distinct impression that he'd deliberately destroyed in himself all remaining traces of a social decorum learned as a child in a country he no longer called home. It wasn't until six weeks later, and with no word from him in the meantime, that he called me up and suggested we have a drink.

We met in a bar on Lafayette Street, and I have to say I was dismayed at the state of him. In six weeks the man had turned into a husk, no flesh on his bones at all. I subdued the gust of irritation his appearance provoked in me, and aroused the familiar dull wave of rising concern. We sat at an obscure table at the back of the bar, he took off his glasses and I saw in his eyes what I can only call an extinction of the spirit; and I strongly suspected it had to do with something other than grief. I waited for him to speak. He played with his cigarette. There was a trembling in the yellowed fingers as he lifted his drink to his lips. He tipped back the vodka in one movement.

– What's the problem, Jack?

He said something about not being able to eat, or sleep, or work, or *think* properly any more –

– Why not?

He flung a look at me, then turned his head away. I knew the gesture well. He'd mastered it years ago, it was meant to suggest depths of torment no average mortal could be expected to comprehend, such sentiment being reserved for a certain few select chosen souls. It had intimidated me once.

– You're not using needles, are you?

For a moment it looked as though he'd rise from his chair in a towering rage and sweep out into the night to do more damage to himself because nobody understood him. He was forty years old! But he hadn't the juice in him to make such an exit. A bit of a sigh, sardonic and private, and he rubbed his face. I wondered if he wanted money, if that's what this was all about. I paid his rent and gave him an allowance, this we had organized immediately on his return to the city, but perhaps he had a habit and his habit had outrun it.

– No, Gin, I'm grieving.

Then it all came out, how lonely he was without his girls, for not only had he lost Peg, but his younger daughter, Anna, had been taken away from him and was now living in England with our brother Gerald. He said he felt utterly friendless and bereft

3

in New York, it was too much for him, he couldn't stand to be by himself in the loft any more – could he come live with me for a while? I had thought this might be what he was after. I wanted to say yes but something prevented me, and I think it was connected to this intuition, or intimation, rather, that he had drifted far from civilization's ambit down in Port Mungo, and had much to conceal from me. But it broke my heart, him coming to me in need, and me prepared to give much, but not everything, no, I had to keep some distance from him, and I said this. I'd sort him out if he wanted me to but I couldn't have him in the house.

– You can't have me in the house.

The way he said it, I might have been speaking to a dog.

– No.

He nodded, he accepted it without argument. I think he heard it in my tone, and understood that I was not the compliant adoring uncomplaining sister I had been once, and he said yes, that was just what he needed, a good sorting out, and he grinned at me, which created such creasing and cleaving in the taut flesh of his bony head that I realized he hadn't grinned at anyone in quite some time. It warmed me to see it, and I grinned back, and there we were, Jack and Gin, just like old times.

We got drunk and talked about Peg, also about Vera – Vera Savage, the painter, the mother of his girls. He wept a little, and I did my best to comfort him. The depth of his emotion impressed me, but he had squandered much of his strength and had few resources left with which to cope with his grief. We parted warmly, and with various resolutions made. I told him to go straight home, no drifting about in the night. He said he would. I didn't altogether trust him. Jack's will, once roused, was fierce, but he was weak, and he was drunk, and drink undoes the will like nothing else. But when I got to Crosby Street the next morning he was clear-eyed and alert, having slept, so he told me, better than he had in months. I was gratified to know I had some

4

influence over him still. Nobody else could have turned him from the trajectory he was on, even if I did apparently suffocate him.

So we got the loft organized, we put his work table in some sort of order, and talked about what he wanted to do. All rather dark and bleak, his ideas, but this was not the point. Work itself was what he needed, and if his brief season in what he regarded as hell was the engine of fresh creativity, then so be it. I left guardedly confident that he was once more on course.

I visited him again the next day, and for several days after that, and I saw him steadily resuming his old habits, the long hours of daily work, I mean, the deepening immersion. A corner had been turned, and having begun to work he never again sank quite so low as he had in those first weeks. Of course he never properly recovered. To the end of his life there was a chord in Jack's character, softened with the years to a kind of melancholy drone, but once a howl of misery: Peg's death created it, and Peg's death sustained it. But Peg's death did not stop him working, and working, for Jack, generated a kind of stamina which dissipated the worst of the grief.

As to what he was painting, it was disturbing because so strongly pervaded by what I understood to be the emotional residue of loss. Tones and values were heavy, laid thick on splintered armatures of black brushstrokes, and the dominant impression was of heat, sickness, darkness, decay – he referred to them as his 'malarial' paintings, and certainly they aroused in the viewer ideas of dank swamps steaming with disease and such. To me they lacked the force of the paintings done in Port Mungo, being sombre where they were vivid, but of course I did not say this.

When he stopped work, and came away from the canvas, and flung himself on to the couch, he would talk about Port Mungo, and his thoughts emerged so disjointed and fractured I would have thought him psychotic had I not understood the state that the act of painting put him in. I remember him talking about the night when Vera in her rage seized a kitchen knife and attacked not Jack but their *bed*, tearing and slashing at the mosquito netting, stabbing the mattress and ripping the sheets to shreds, this insanity not exhausting her fury but inflaming it, rather, and then she went for his canvases, and he had to disarm her, and this, he said, was not the first time she had attacked his work, far from it. Peg was woken by the noise, she was screaming, it was all about alcohol, of course – I was appalled, I wanted to know what happened next. He had to throw her out of the house, he said. For an hour she hammered at the locked door, but he was so angry he refused to let her back in, so she went off somewhere else, to her lover, most likely –

I believe it was matter like this, drawn from events still raw in his mind, which fuelled the passion evident at least to me in the dark pictures he painted that spring: his tempestuous relationship with Vera, and of course the death of their daughter. And I think he was punishing himself, for more than once, late at night, when drink had cleared the way for honest thought to come through, he hinted as much, and I tried to tell him that he'd done all he could, no man could have done more, though in fact I had no evidence that this was so, and given the mystery that still seemed to enshroud the girl's death I admit I did occasionally imagine other scenarios, though I took none of them seriously.

A year later he was ready to show the canvases from Port Mungo, as well as several from Crosby Street, the so-called malarial paintings. Dealers visited the loft, and the following autumn he had his show at Paula Cooper. It sold out. It was a critical success. How proud I was. Jack Rathbone was on the map, and if he allowed his star to fade in later years then that, as he himself said, was his choice. In fact it was always his choice, everything he did, though I seem to be the only one who remembers that now. This was not a man who ever lost his moral compass, as Vera seems to believe – and certainly not a man who would take his own life! It's unthinkable. It makes a mockery of everything.

One last incident from this period, which for me expresses the pathos of their failure perhaps more vividly than any other – Jack and Vera's, I mean, and the culmination of that breakdown in the tragedy of their daughter's death – came in the stifling summer of 1982. In those days if you lived in SoHo you had to go to Chinatown for your supplies, and Jack had acquired a large black bicycle with a basket on the front and a pair of saddlebags behind. His building had a steep set of iron steps, and one day that August, as he came wobbling along the cobblestones with his groceries, he saw a woman sitting beside a suitcase at the top of his steps energetically fanning herself with a newspaper.

Poor Vera, Port Mungo had not been kind to her. The tropical sun had destroyed what had once been a porcelain complexion, and she had been struggling for some time with alcoholism. But Jack later told me that she had kept alive the flame he first glimpsed in London when he was a youth of seventeen, and herself a woman of thirty, and this, he said, despite the fact or possibly, perversely, *because* of the fact that she had been so thoroughly battered by life. Listening to this, I knew the sexual charge between them was far from dead, it was not even dormant! Down the steps she came and then she was in his arms, and the bicycle went clattering into the street and groceries spilled everywhere – broken eggs, spilt milk, apples rolling along the gutter, and the eggs, he told me, actually starting to fry on the sidewalk, that's how hot it was.

They climbed seven floors in dusty gloom to reach Jack's place, twenty-five hundred square feet of high-ceilinged, brick-wall loft with large windows over the narrow street below. Vera made no effort to conceal her curiosity, she was at once sniffing about, one painter in another painter's space, an animal event, a canine activity. She was envious, and what painter wouldn't be?

7

It was a good studio. I'd found it for him, I knew what he needed. He wasn't short of wallspace, nor of light. A little later they were settled under the fan in what passed for Jack's living area, which comprised a smelly mattress and an old couch dragged up from the street. She told him she was living up the Hudson now but was on her way to London, where someone had given her a show.

– But I think I'll move in here instead, she said.

– Like fuck you will.

That got him a flash of the old Vera, the old trouper who'd got him out of England and taught him how to be a painter. The mother of his girls.

– I'll give you three nights on the couch.

– You call that a couch?

It was a good time, a sweet time, but it was outside of time, Jack said later, outside of everything, a cocoon in which they gave themselves over to a reunion that could not be sustained nor even prolonged beyond those five days and nights. Time turned torpid, tropical, sluggish as the Mississippi River – they slept till noon, and stayed up till five because it was cooler in the small hours. The city sweltered and stank, there was a heavy, humid stillness, a silence in which they seemed the only living souls. People say that Manhattan breaks down the separation of inside and outside but it was not true of Jack's experience, I think because he was an artist. When his door closed he was not in New York he was in his own head, or in his own *guts*, he would say, and the joy of it, when he was a younger man, was in leaving his work and opening the door and stepping back out into roaring humanity. He had two standing fans on either side of the mattress. They ate, slept, had frequent sex on that mattress, leaving the building at midnight to sit in some bar and drink beer. Mostly they talked about Peg, and after weeping alone so often for his dead daughter, how good it was to weep in Vera's arms. They talked about Port Mungo, and about Anna, Peg's little sister, who was now eight. For three years she had been

8

living with Gerald's family – he and his wife had three children, all older than Anna – and Vera planned to visit them. This was how the time passed; and in that still, quiet interval Jack's hectic creative momentum slowed to a standstill and briefly, through Vera, he made spiritual if not actual contact with the family he had lost.

Her proposal came the night before she was to leave for London. I think she knew it was hopeless, but it had to be done. That was Vera all right, if a possibility occurred to her she was not the one to suppress it, the fact of its occurrence demanded at least an attempt upon it; she is the same today. So she told him they were going to rebuild a life together, not as it used to be but in a new way, a better way. They would buy a barn upstate and make two big studios, each with a view of the river – Mungo-on-Hudson, what about it?

– But I don't want to live up the Hudson!

– Then we'll live in New York. We'll live here.

He regarded her fondly. He didn't say, you're only after my loft. She was serious, and at the same time she knew it was hopeless.

– No, darling, he said, and sweet Jesus it cost him – he would have been angry with her for putting him through it, but he'd known she would, she had to, he'd known it the moment he told her she could sleep on his couch. He didn't go out to Kennedy with her, she wouldn't let him. They hadn't slept. He went out onto the fire escape and watched her emerge from the building. She looked up at him, shielding her eyes from the early morning sun. She stood in the middle of the street and gave him just a little of the flowery bow he'd first seen on the Charing Cross Road when he was seventeen, sweeping her Panama down close to the sidewalk – a quotation, yes, from the Book of Better Days. She made him sad. Off she tottered up the street with her suitcase, shabby woman in a tight skirt, over fifty now, quite alone, penniless, to catch a bus to the airport to go to a show in a nothing gallery in London. Jack thought: her

9

promise is all behind her and her talent all burned up. What is to become of her? What happens to painters who run out of talent – spent painters? He stood on the fire escape watching her up the street. She had lost everything, all except her eye. She still had her eye, and when he had hauled out his canvases, the work he had done since coming back to New York, how generously she had spoken of his accomplishment. There was much of her in them, it's true, but he who had recently come to the city and was just starting to know success, at Vera's praise he had swelled and glowed as he had swelled and glowed for no other. Reflecting on this later I realized he painted for her, he painted *only* for her, hers was the judgement, hers the approval that counted.

Ten years ago Jack left the Crosby Street loft and came to live with me on West 11th, this at my suggestion. I saw him change during his last years in New York, but the changes were superficial. A certain wild shyness, that famously *farouche* quality – it became more tempered – he began to guard his fire, hold his best energies for the studio. He stopped going out and his appearance grew distinctly odd, as he came to resemble a kind of urban Apache, with his hair turned silver and bound up in black headscarves, and the baggy clothes flapping about his lanky frame, all dark blues and blacks, and his long bony face, burnt and weathered from the tropics, ever more scraped and taut and hawklike. He restricted himself to wine, apart from the one cocktail at six, and managed to give up cigarettes. Superficial changes, as I say; what remained constant was the discipline of work, the daily return to the studio, the finality of the closing door –

In his later years, then, my brother lived like a recluse and towards the world sustained a posture of indifference and even outright hostility. By day he painted, and I did not disturb him. His studio was at the top of the house, with a window from which he could look down into the garden, one of those narrow city gardens condemned to perpetual gloom because sand-wiched between taller buildings which hogged the light. I let it grow wild, rather like a Russian garden, though on a smaller scale of course. I thought of it as pasture. But Jack was high enough to get good light from the north, and he also had a view of the street, and when he closed the door behind him no telephone rang, no voice spoke unless it was his own; here he could think. I remember saying this to him once, and – think? he said – no, not thinking, Gin – I can still hear the bite in his tone, that hint of the fang – *sinking*, rather, into regions of the mind – and here he paused, I remember, and made a steeple of his fingers, and set his chin there, frowning, as he uttered this solemnity – 'where I submit to imperatives alien to all worlds but art'.

They hung trembling in the air a few seconds, those por-tentous words, and then with a bark of laughter he scattered them to the winds. He was not a pompous man.

But a large part of my brother's life was spent in creating precisely the conditions in which this 'sinking' could occur. And he did this despite the demands of other people, I mean the clamour of domestic responsibility and the claims of intimacy. I now believe he paid a terrible price for his daily turning away, but I also know it was as necessary to him as oxygen. Deprived of it too long, and he became a nightmare. He needed to sink, he said – to *immerse* – so as to grope towards some primitive understanding of what he was about. What *was* he about? Impossible to say, exactly, but Jack once told me he believed art to be primarily a vehicle for the externalization of psychic injury. Certainly a great part of his own activity was the attempt to master the disorder aroused by the emotional turmoil he had come through – loss and pain, guilt, failure, rage – master all that, yes, and in the process find a little truth. Which I suppose is what I am after too.

As for the pattern of our days, at six we would meet down-stairs and talk. That's what we did of an evening, Jack and I, when he'd finished in his studio, and I'd mixed us a nice cocktail, we would sit in the big sitting room and talk, largely about the past. I say the past, I should say Jack's past, for his life was a good deal more eventful than mine, in fact the most remarkable event of my life has been Jack himself! He travelled more than I did, he accomplished more, and he certainly suffered more – in short, he had more memories than me. Almost all his stories I had heard rather often but I mustered an interest every time, and occasionally I even made him see himself afresh, which provoked in him a kind of affectionate sarcasm. He liked to say that he'd known a number of women like me, bohemian kinds of women, dilettantes, he'd say, dabblers, wary of experience but at the same time curious about life: women who would rather think about life than go to the trouble of actually living it.

This stung but I did not argue with him, there was a grain of truth in it. I am a tall, thin, untidy Englishwoman, I drink too much and yes, I suppose I am rather – oh, detached – distant, aloof – snobbish, even, I have been called all these things, also cold, stiff, and untouchable, though those who think me untouchable never saw me when I was perfectly touchable indeed! I should also say that I have an independent income, which has been quite adequate for my own needs and also, I should add, for Jack's. Which is why it always impressed me that until the very end he continued to work. Not with the fervour of his youth, of course, nor with the sustained intensity of his middle years, but he worked, he worked every day, and I took a close interest, inasmuch as he would let me. I admit this was partly out of concern for his health. He was plagued by arthritis, and while through willpower alone he could usually ignore the steady grumbling ache of it, and the sporadic stabs of pain, the restriction of movement in his knuckles was a sore trial. At times it was debilitating. We were told the cause was uncertain, but that it might have been a sustained allergic reaction to his own tissue, which was ironic, to say the least. Curiously his old malaria medicine from Port Mungo would control the inflammation when it got too bad.

I have perfectly healthy hands, in fact my hands are my best thing. I used to say to Jack that if there were some way of making a hand exchange, I would do it at once.

2

It is probably true of most children that they are not aware of the character of their upbringing until much later, when they can look back and regard it with some objectivity. This was never the case with Jack and me. We were born into an old family, and we knew at the time that our childhood was privileged, also that it was eccentric in its lack of structure, largely because our father, emotionally speaking, was almost entirely absent. My mother died when I was three years old, and Jack just an infant, so neither of us had any real memory of her. My father did not remarry, nor could he ever speak of that 'perfect woman' without becoming maudlin and tearful, which Jack and I found embarrassing and faintly ridiculous. Gerald was five years my senior, but we never saw much of him as he always seemed to be away at school, or off on a trip.

When I think of my father now I am ashamed how little I appreciated him when I was a child. He may have been distant but he was kind and gentle and tolerant, and I was surprised after his death to discover how well-loved he was by those who knew him. He had a special affection for me, I suppose because I was his only daughter, but I don't remember that I returned it until much later, being in thrall as I was to Jack, who had nothing but scorn for the old man. I think children are uncomfortable with sadness, Jack certainly was.

It was a foible of my father's not to send Jack and me away to school, but rather to employ a series of private tutors for us, the most memorable of whom was a young woman with the improbable name of Helen Splendour. Miss Splendour taught us German literature and Irish history, though her real achievement was to awaken in us a passion for art. She was a small, slim woman who dressed in brown worsted stockings and neat earth-coloured tweeds and brought an intense earnestness to every activity she instigated. She was interested in the history of our family, and it became great sport with us, as we hiked along deserted Suffolk beaches on blustery autumn days, and then sat shivering in the dunes making watercolour studies of the sky, to see who could invent the most outlandish tale to tell her about our ancestors, many of whose portraits hung in dusty galleries back at the house.

It was Jack who invented the Curse of the Rathbones. This was an ancient malediction which he claimed had afflicted successive generations of our family for several hundred years. Jack had a precocious sexual imagination when he was a boy, and he could always bring a blush to Miss Splendour's soft cheek with stories of rapacious Rathbones of unbridled appetite and an utter dearth of moral fibre, whose exploits were sanctioned by the family's wealth and standing in the county. He would describe some brutal deflowering in a barn, or in the woods, and the catastrophic consequences which ensued; all of which would have Miss Splendour shuddering with delight, to think of such ravages being perpetrated on the local women.

At night we lay in front of the fire on the schoolroom floor with books of reproductions from my father's library spread out on the carpet. I remember we loved Hogarth for his grotesques and Blake for his flea. For a short period we venerated the pre-Raphaelites above all others. Then we discovered the German Expressionists – a painting of Kokoschka's gave us special delight, *Murderer, Hope of Women* – and we decided that this was it, this was our calling, one day we would attend art school in London and live unorthodox lives and become real painters.

And as the years of our childhood passed the dream did not fade, but grew stronger, driven as it was by Jack's determination and the enthusiastic encouragement of Miss Splendour.

Every summer my father took us to the west of Ireland, where he made his annual pilgrimage to the grave of William Butler Yeats. We were left to ourselves, Gerald always being off on some school trip to the continent, so with Miss Splendour leading the way in her stout brown brogues and brown worsted stockings we climbed the hills of Corraun and Achill, settling on windy outcrops of rock, where we attempted to render the sweep of the coast, and the bay beyond, and the holy mountain of Croagh Patrick in the distance. Jack had a real talent, this became apparent early on, while my own abilities were more modest. But under the bright eye of Miss Splendour I became proficient, more or less, at sketching and watercolours.

One summer my father bought a small boat with an outboard motor from a local fisherman. I can see it to this day, or rather I can *smell* it, for whenever I think of the boat I seem all at once to have petrol fumes and seaweed and peat smoke in my nostrils. There was one condition attached to our using the boat, which was that Jack was never to go out in it without me. Jack was known to be reckless, while I was the sensible one. There was a narrow shingle beach half a mile from the back of the house, and that's where we kept the boat, chained to a tree.

I retain one incident from those years with a clarity that I now regard with some suspicion, for I fear it may be a compression of a number of incidents involving Jack and me and the boat. But one day, when the sky was threatening rain, and the wind freshening from the west, Jack for perverse reasons of his own wanted to go out in the boat but Miss Splendour said it was not a good idea and I supported her, for Jack was often foolishly contrary simply because he was thwarted. I can still see the three of us standing on the beach beneath a dark, spitting sky, and Jack saying loftily that he's going out whatever anyone says about it, and Miss Splendour in passionate tones – practically in tears! –

telling him not to, and me shouting at him, calling him a bloody idiot. He didn't listen. He dragged the boat to the water's edge as Miss Splendour tried to hold him back, and I looked on in a state of mounting consternation. Jack soon had the boat in the water, and as he started the engine I ran into the surf and climbed in with him, so compounding the poor woman's distress.

There was an island in the bay about a mile off the south shore of Achill called Ghost Island, nothing on it but a roofless derelict croft where we'd build a fire and squat beside it smoking cigars stolen from my father's study. This particular day we went out in light rain and reached the island without mishap. But an hour later we were huddled by the sodden ashes of the fire, cigars extinguished and ourselves soaked to the skin by the rain now driving like nails through the rafters. Jack gazed up at the black clouds rolling low overhead and confidently declared that any minute now it would clear.

An hour passed, or what seemed an hour, and by then it was starting to get dark. Jack said the storm was almost over, and the wind did seem to be dying down, so we scrambled across the rocks and dragged the boat into the sea. Almost at once we were bucking and plunging in black choppy water. I was sitting up in the bow, chilled to the very marrow of my bones and never so miserable in all my life. Through the rain I could just see the house a mile or so across the water, a long low whitewashed building partially obscured by a scrim of rain and with grey smoke blowing horizontal from the chimneys. Jack hauled at the cord, cursing it to hell, but the engine only sputtered as the boat rocked helplessly in the waves.

Then, with a roar, and a belch of smoke, it caught, and began to chug, and Jack shouted that we were all right now, and I can see him now, bolt upright in the stern, all lit up with excitement, his hair plastered to his skull and the rage of a second ago quite gone and forgotten. So I sat up and tried like him to believe that this was a grand adventure we were having, and for a while I almost succeeded. But Jack didn't even have to try.

The sea grew rougher as we pulled away from the shore but what with the wind and the rain I couldn't hear the chugging of the engine any more, and as our progress was almost nonexistent, the black waves coming at us from all sides, and Jack steering into them so we wouldn't be swamped, I never knew from one moment to the next if we had stalled. Then came a huge wave, and I remember a sudden panic rising into my throat, and I closed my eyes and hung out over the side of the wildly rocking gunwale praying to God to see us safe home, as we somehow climbed over the wall of water and plunged down the other side. I knew I was going to be sick and so I was, quite violently sick, and it was terror as much as the motion of the boat. It was horrid, the sensation of choking, and my hair all over my face, and my stomach heaving again and again until there was nothing left in it, and my eyes running, my nose running – and in the course of all this becoming aware above the roar of the wind that Jack was howling with laughter, and it was because I was being sick! And the more I was sick the louder he howled, he was like a madman, streaming with water and shrieking his crazy laughter into the sky, and I have never forgotten it. Then he began to sing.

We were two hours crossing a stretch of water that normally took us no more than fifteen minutes, and Jack later declared that had the engine cut out we'd have been swept clear into the Atlantic. He said it was the best afternoon of his life so far. I do remember that as we drew near to the beach behind the house we saw the small wet figure of Miss Splendour waiting for us on the shore, and I have never seen anything quite so pathetic in my life.

I have one other memory of that time which I feel must be included here. One evening I went upstairs to get a book and as I came along the corridor I heard voices inside the schoolroom, though no light showed under the door. When I opened it I saw Jack on the carpet in the gloom, leaning back on his hands, his legs stretched out in front of him, and Miss Splendour lying beside him, on one elbow, a few strands of hair drifting free of the neat tight bun at the back of her head. They turned towards me, Miss Splendour abruptly sitting up, startled and alarmed, as well she might be: my brother's penis was up out of his trousers, emphatically erect, and I'm quite certain that a second before I opened the door Miss Splendour had had it in her hand or in her mouth, or both. It was huge, this I do remember from the glimpse I had of it as I went in to get my book. When I left the room I banged the door very loudly behind me.

Miss Splendour never said a word to me about what I'd seen that night, and behaved the next day with her usual brisk bright-eyed energy, quite as though nothing at all had happened. In fact she left us within a few months, though whether the two events were connected I never did find out. Jack on the other hand was eager to talk about it. He would have been about fourteen at the time, and me sixteen or so. I told him to keep it to himself, but this seemed only to egg him on, and with devilish grinning persistence he demanded to know what I'd thought when I opened the door and saw him there beside Miss Splendour with his thing out. I told him I thought it was pretty bloody silly. What if I had been Daddy, or Mrs Croke? This was our housekeeper. Jack laughed loudly at the idea of old Mrs Croke finding him with his thing out with Miss Splendour.

– You think it's funny, I said, but I don't.

– That's because you're a girl.

– So what?

He had no answer to that. But what I am trying to suggest is that my brother's sexual curiosity, or *appetite*, rather, while it may have been active at an early age still had a certain, oh, frank wholesome openness about it, at least as it pertained to our relationship. There was nothing furtive there. He always showed me his erotic drawings, which were very graphic indeed, and we talked about sex as we might talk about what we'd had for dinner, such was the easy intimacy we enjoyed throughout our childhood, and which persisted until the day he ran off with

20

Vera Savage. Nor were we the least self-conscious about it. We were brother and sister, Jack and Gin, why would we hide anything from one another? That came later.

Jack by this time was seriously committed to becoming an artist, and it was far from an unrealistic ambition. His early promise showed every sign of maturing into a solid talent, and he had begun to paint in oils, the bold streak in his character evident in the way, at times, he practically *attacked* the canvas with a loaded brush. But he could also be quiet and slow, as though the act of painting stilled or soothed the emotions of his turbulent young heart. My own enthusiasm was meanwhile on the wane, though I said nothing of this to anyone, not even to Jack. I had recognized that he was a far better artist than I would ever be, but I didn't want to be left behind. I suppose in a way I was in love with him. We were impatient to get to London, and my father, having resisted this plan of ours for some time, at last gave in, relieved, I think, to be rid of us, for we had become troublesome to him through various alcoholic escapades. He settled a generous allowance on us, which was mine to administer as I saw fit, about which Jack fulminated, naturally, but to no avail.

Then came London, and St Martin's. We had spent so much of our childhood with only each other for company that I was apprehensive about what our fellow students would make of us. We were tall, beaky youths, rather birdlike in appearance, like pale storks, I used to think. Our hair was the colour of damp sand and we spoke in strangled county accents, and despite our best intentions we gave off an air of supercilious arrogance which I suspect they found rather objectionable. Jack set about changing all that. He intended to conquer the metropolis, and by his dress and behaviour soon erased any impression of superiority. He formed opinions quickly, shouted them loudly, became frequently drunk on beer, and within a few months had gathered something of a coterie about himself. As for me, I had decided soon after our arrival in the capital that the best part I could play in this drama of conquest was that of the sage and silent sister. I accompanied him everywhere and, ever watchful, wasted no opportunity to murmur my counsel in his ear. I dressed plainly and affected an owl-like inscrutability, hoping in this way to mark out for myself a distinct and unassailable position in his retinue.

3

When I first met her, Vera Savage was an established artist of thirty who alone of her generation had had work shown in America. Two of her paintings Jack had declared to be masterpieces: one was called *Spirit of the Blitz*, a caustic and irreverent picture which had caused something of a scandal when it was first exhibited. The other, *Vandal at the Gates*, was remarkable for its hugeness if for nothing else. Both were figurative – this itself an oddity in the heyday of abstraction – and both were executed in loud clashing tones and with a kind of insolent brash energy which owed nothing to pictorial understatement or linear decorum or tonal restraint or any of the other qualities traditionally favoured by the English artist; though in fact Vera was not English, she was from Glasgow. But Jack had confidently declared that this was the only way one could possibly paint any more. It was 1957 and he was seventeen years old, and Vera Savage was coming to St Martin's to lecture us on modern art.

So there we were, one damp Thursday evening, milling about on the pavement outside the college with various other students when we heard raised voices, there was a mêlée of sorts, a scuffle, and we glimpsed a grinning dishevelled figure in black stockings and a shabby cocktail dress being escorted on tottering stilettoes into the building. Jack liked the look of her at once, this was clear, and for this reason: she dressed like a prostitute. She

23

stood there at the podium, a loud, bosomy woman in a tight dress and pancake make-up, one hand cocked akimbo on her hip and the other flapping the air as she spoke to us with a kind of hoarse nervous bravado, and I remember thinking her opinionated and not very clean, nor entirely sober. Her hair was the colour of coal, her lips were scarlet and she had lost a tooth, whose absence lent her a distinctly menacing aspect when she grinned. What was it she talked about? Much of it I have forgotten, but I know she told us how pointless it was to attend art school, which raised a cheer, and then she spoke about *inspiration*, and how travel, drink, the colour black, bodies of water – passion – these were the sorts of things that inspired her. It was our duty, as artists, to find what inspired each of us. She also told us we should be able to work anywhere. Her own studio, she said, was a disused operating theatre in the basement of an old fever hospital. She also declared that a real artist would sooner let her children starve than work at anything but her art, at which Jack jumped up and loudly applauded, producing laughter throughout the hall. After the lecture she sought us out and attached us to the group she led next door to the pub. Seven weeks later Jack ran away with her to America.

Seven weeks. In seven weeks he abandoned everything: his family, his home, also what I thought of as the bohemian life we shared in an untidy flat in Kennington, where we threw wild parties – at least they seemed wild to us – and never washed a dish or made a bed or swept a floor. I think Jack did not sleep at all, the night we met Vera. At one point, finding himself seated next to her at the back of the pub, and having said something that caught her attention, and having then sat with lowered eyes and sunken head as she spoke energetically to him, to my horror he took her face in both hands – pronounced some kind of blessing on her – and kissed her on the forehead. Then he screamed.

She was amused. She promptly seized him by the hair and kissed him back, hard on the lips with her mouth open. Jack was flushed but not with embarrassment, with a sort of brazen excitement, and he looked about him, he caught my eye, glorying in his own audacity. I was standing at the edge of the group, quite sober, and staring at him with palpable dismay. For the rest of the evening the pair of them talked to each other in low tones, occasionally shouting with rude laughter and both drinking a lot. The last I saw of Vera Savage that night she was in the middle of the Charing Cross Road and producing for Jack's benefit a sweeping bow with copious baroque flourishes of the wrist. He shouted to her that he would see her tomorrow, as hissing I dragged him away.

The next day at lunchtime we walked into the pub and there she was, by herself, waiting for us. Or rather, waiting for Jack. Why? Beneath a façade of studied eccentricity he was still very much the earnest art student, his limited experience of the world lending him the merest patina of sophistication with which to conceal the depths of ignorance within. But he was ambitious, and he was bold, and he took himself extremely seriously, and perhaps this was what attracted her. A day or two later, when she saw his work, and liked it, apparently, the thing was cemented. I believe she recognized a dim echo of her own style, albeit immature and unformed, and was flattered. As for Jack, he was in love, he had told me so the night before. It had happened in the pub, he said, and although he had never experienced such an emotion before he was in no doubt at all as to what it meant. He knew the precise moment: at one point in the conversation, in fact just before he planted his lips on her forehead, she had put her hand on his for several seconds, and that was it. It was as simple as that. I knew it had more to do with the loud, slutty aspect of the woman, and the fact that she painted as he wanted to paint, but I also realized that no matter how tarty her clothes, no matter if they reeked of cheap scent, when Vera Savage was aroused, which was often, for she contrived arousal with alcohol, she seemed to possess a life-force to which men were irresistibly attracted. Jack was no exception, in fact he responded with immediate enthusiasm to her vitality, in particular to her louche talk and her expressive, tactile behaviour.

We talked soberly, the three of us, in the pub that morning. She was wearing the same old cocktail dress from the night before, but she had scrubbed off her make-up and looked much younger, almost girlish in fact, her skin so pale you could have traced the faint blue veins beneath. Also, the Glasgow accent was much less broad, clearly she modulated it to suit the occasion. We talked about painting, and I was astonished to discover, in the clarity of daylight, and herself at ease, and not in front of an audience, that she was without dogma, in fact she was without conviction of any sort at all. We spent an hour together, and as I remember it now Jack bombarded her with questions which to her ears must have sounded laughably naïve, for he held to his ideas with no little intensity, believing with all the ardour of his youth that art had to be cleansed of the corrupting influences of the past, though quite what those influences were I cannot now recall. But to all his impassioned certainties she responded with mild shrugs and worried frowns, and discovered exceptions to every broad sweeping law he proposed, and seemed uncomfortable with anything that smacked of theory or abstraction. Finally she apologized – I'm awful sorry, Jack – and laid a hand on his arm and said she supposed she was a practical sort of an artist, and if a thing worked, it worked – she supposed he must think her very stupid –?

That stopped him in his tracks. That shut him down all right. That with his flood of talk he should elicit from Vera Savage an apology for her own stupidity – in that moment I think he jettisoned every idea he had about painting and started again with a clean slate, for he was young enough then that such a shift was possible. Personally I considered it not unlikely that she *was* very stupid, but at least we now understood why, in her lecture the evening before, she had resisted generalization, and had worked her way back to certain painters, Kandinsky in particular, and what she had learned from each of them.

26

This was as far as we got that day. Almost as an afterthought, as she rose from the table, she said she was going to a party later, would we like to come? Yes, we would; and I scribbled the address on the back of a beermat.

We had fetched up in a small house in a shabby street in Camden Town. We had found Vera in a smoky kitchen surrounded by a group of men, and the serious thoughtful woman of the morning was gone. This was Vera out on the town, with her face painted, and more than a few drinks in her, and she was telling them loudly that it was all over with Europe, that the war had done for Europe, that the future of art was not in Paris – certainly not in London – no, it was in *New York*. The men groaned and sneered, but all the same it was an impressive spectacle: there she stood, or swayed, rather, a fake leopardskin coat draped about her shoulders, and a glass in her hand, shouting that she was sick of the English and their hypocrite ways, at least with Americans you knew where you stood, and some wag, a poet called Julian, I think, said that if she knew where she stood how come she fell down so much? There was loud laughter at this, hoots of it. I was exhilarated by the whole scene and thought Jack would be too, but oddly he hung back, maintaining an unsmiling reserve amid the hilarity.

Later the three of us sat on a window-sill in the yard at the back of the house and Vera talked more about New York. She was quiet now, serious, maudlin, very drunk. She repeated herself, she made grandiose claims, she declared New York the greatest city in the history of the West and produced several reasons why. Jack listened intently. Impatiently he cut in, he asked her questions about the city, about the art that was being produced there, and became ever more thoughtful as he pondered what she told him. Then he asked her what New York *looked like*, he wanted her to talk about the architecture, and there was more in this vein – he wanted to know what things *cost* – and when at last we left the party, the damp streets of Camden

Town, the industrial brick chimney towering black against the night sky, and the rain slanting through the lamplight – it all seemed as grey and mediocre and *finished* as Vera had earlier said it was. It was an important night, largely because of this idea of New York as a shimmering, dynamic focus of restless energy, of unfettered creativity, of artistic freedom, and limitless aspiration –

Vera took my hand in both of hers and warmly told me we were going to be great friends. Jack she took by the lapels of his overcoat, and for several embarrassing seconds they kissed noisily on the doorstep, him with his hands rummaging round inside her coat until I loudly coughed.

I will never forget the fevered conversation we had on the way home, a conversation which continued for most of the next thirty-six hours. It was momentous, and it changed the course of all our lives, this is no exaggeration. When Jack met Vera two days later it was just the two of them. They were in the back of the Salisbury, in Covent Garden, at a small brown table with peeling varnish and black cigarette burns all over it. The pub was quiet, late morning, and a beam of sunlight full of swirling smoke came shafting down. Vera sat with her hands clasped about a large gin-and-tonic and told him she was a married woman.

– I know that, he said.

Up came those sleepy eyes, thick with smudged mascara, small gods of humour sporting about the painted mouth.

– I know all about Gordon, he said.

He was apparently a piece of work, this Gordon she was married to. We'd done a little research.

– I don't care about him, he said, I care about you.

The gods of humour allowed the grin to split open, so the black slot showed, but only for a second. I realized she must have heard this before, and it was one of her games, it was as if she said to all her men, all right, you be the one to take me away

28

from him, go on, do it. The difference, I'm afraid, was that Jack *was* the one.

– I know you don't love him.

Apparently this provoked laughter. She pushed herself back in her chair and regarded him with some amusement and also, I think, no small amount of affection. I think by this time she was well taken with him.

– Here's what we're going to do. We're going to have some more drinks, then we're going to a hotel.

– To do what?

– What do you think?

He certainly had her full attention now. All this he had planned out beforehand, and discussed with me in detail. She leaned forward, put her elbows on the table, interlaced her fingers and set her chin there.

– And what are we going to do after that, Mister Rathbone?

– After that we're going to a travel agent in the Strand and book passage to New York.

I don't believe any of her men had come up with a strategy like this one before. It seems she let out a loud shout of surprise. She slapped the table. She was intrigued. In some ways she liked being told what to do. She was a strong artist but a weak woman. The trick was knowing which was which.

– But I've agreed to spend six months in England.

– Then I'll go by myself.

At this point Jack, frowning, thrust his hands in his trouser pockets. Vera was staring at him, squinting and smiling at the same time. She was amused, perplexed, threatened by this intense young man. She was also tempted. She liked the sound of this. It was mad enough for her, wild enough, it was dramatic, and Vera was easily bored. Now came the *coup de grâce*. From out of a pocket Jack produced a roll of ten-pound notes fastened with a rubber band. He tossed it onto the table where it came to rest in a patch of smoky sunlight.

– That should do us a few months.

From the bank account set up by my father to see us through our first year of art school, that morning I had withdrawn half the money: Jack's share. Vera fingered the tight roll of banknotes. He told me later that watching her touch the money he knew he had her. It was not that he'd bought her, exactly, but he had made the decision, made the plan, she need only acquiesce and the adventure was hers, and it wouldn't cost her a penny. She pushed her chair back and rose to her feet. She stood over the table gazing down at him, the sunlight streaming around her from the top of the pub window, and her breasts – he modelled their roundness with his hands – swelling up under her cardigan till he was *giddy* with desire, he wanted to have sex with her there and then, on the floor, in the sawdust, in the spilt beer and fag ash, and he told her so. Dear god, but how young he was, to be acting so boldly! – but that was Jack. He said she bit her lip when he said it.

– Did you want another drink, hen? she said.

They had more drinks – he could go one for one with her even in those days – and then went to a hotel. Back then you had to go somewhere seedy if you wanted a room for an hour or two and had no luggage. There was a place off Russell Square she knew, and she preferred to go there rather than to our place in Kennington, or the old fever hospital. They went by bus and sat on the top deck holding hands. Afterwards, when it was all over, they went to a pub round the corner. They were ravenous with hunger. They had pork pies – and god, he said later, how good they tasted! – and were in a dizzy mood, side by side on a bench at the back of the public bar, the pub transformed into a theatre and the two of them, he said, the only audience – life a comedy performed for their benefit alone – they were silly with love, or at least with sex, and drunk already on the American plan, the beer and the gin having nothing of the potency of this fierce happiness which had sprung up between them.

For it had gone well in bed. Jack told me all about it later. I listened with mixed emotions – hard not to think of little Miss

Splendour in the schoolroom that night – as he described in some detail the dowdy, cramped room with the grubby lace curtains on the window, and a large dark wardrobe at the foot of the bed with mirrored doors of tarnished glass, and yes, it had gone well. Slow and cautious at first, the pair of them had clambered from opposite sides into a musty bed and lay between cheap sheets, holding hands, Vera whispering that this was enough, they need do no more than this. They lay there for a few minutes, there was some tentative stroking, then a kiss – and that woke them up. That got the blood moving, and somehow they discovered how – or their bodies did, rather, for it was their limbs in their shifting negotiations under the sheets that found a fit, and the fit of their bodies, convex to concave and thigh upon thigh led them without difficulty and with sudden growing pressure of passion to the moment when Jack flung back the sheet and rose up on his knees to pull off his shirt, as did Vera in manner more demure, and it was consummated then; and they clung whimpering to each other for many minutes afterwards. Vera was really rather a reticent lover, Jack once told me, her libido weaker than her personality might suggest, but bed, in the early days, served to instil in them the sense of fusion that set them apart from the world, and rallied them to the cause that swept them clear across the Atlantic, that cause being – them against England!

So they sat in the back of the little pub off Russell Square, eating pork pies and drinking beer and talking about America. He never wavered for a minute. He later said he had seen it all quite clearly the night of the lecture, that he'd known then that he wanted her, but that he could never have her in England. The plan had been formed that night, he said, and by the time she was making her idiotic bow in the middle of the Charing Cross Road he was certain they were bound for New York.

This was not strictly true, and I was there, but this was how Jack liked to remember it.

It was a fraught time for all of us, those last few weeks in London, as Vera disentangled herself from Gordon the Terrible, as we now referred to him, and we waited in a state of breathless suspense for the great day to dawn, I mean D-Day, Departure Day. My own position was delicate: put bluntly, I disliked Vera, and I disapproved of her, but I couldn't risk alienating Jack by saying so. And though I was learning more about the woman every day – Jack talked of nothing else, of course – none of what I saw or heard aroused my sympathy, much less my affection. She was more complicated than she appeared, this I did admit, and she was possessed of a powerful original talent, but she had little control of that talent, nor did she seem to want to control it, in fact at times she seemed determined to trash it, for there was a self-destructive quality to her drinking even then. I saw vulnerability and isolation in her, and of course there was the damage done by her upbringing, which was a Gorbals tenement building, violent father, alcoholic stepmother, too many children in too small a space. None of her deep damage would manifest for a while yet, but what did alarm me was that she had an impulsive streak every bit as unpredictable as Jack's: they were too much alike, and what they saw in each other was little more, I believed, than a reflection of themselves. And while I hoped that because she was married she would back out of their arrangement at the last minute, I could not be confident about this.

The decisive encounter came ten days before they were to leave for New York. Jack was meeting her in the Salisbury, which had become their trysting place, being close both to St Martin's and to her various haunts in Soho. She was late, thirty-five minutes late, he remembered glancing at the clock over the bar just as she came through the door. She looked grim indeed, he had never seen such an expression on her face before – more than her face, her whole body seemed to have been battered with a plank. She sank down on the chair opposite him and pushed her hands through her hair, sighing and groaning as she did so. Jack went to the bar and bought her a gin. She took a long swallow then stared hard at him, and he was apprehensive, he did not understand what was going on.

– Well, she said, that's done.

Her fingers closed on his. He said nothing. Then he knew it was all right. Her teeth bit down on her bottom lip, it was the wicked schoolgirl expression, she wore it when she'd got away with something.

– You told him?

– I bloody did. I told him.

– And?

It happened in the kitchen, she said. Gordon had been cooking their supper. After the word 'divorce' came up he began to cry, but when she repeated it he flew at her like a thing possessed and she'd had to push him down onto a chair. Then he threw a plate at her.

– Then what? Jack whispered. He threw a *plate*!

– I threw a plate at him.

– Christ almighty.

Jack was flabbergasted. He was not afraid to steal the man's wife, but he was shocked that they would throw plates at each other; as was I – clearly we had thought the thing through with insufficient imagination. It seems there was a good deal of plate throwing, and shouting, and swearing and weeping, before she was able to get out of there, and it was her opinion that Gordon would continue to refuse even to discuss the idea of divorce, but that he could not stop her going to New York, how could he?

– He knows about New York? cried Jack.

He did. This at once cast my brother into a state of acute panic, for he feared Gordon would find a way to wreck their plan. It was for precisely this reason that I had been ordered to tell my father nothing about it, and not a word to our brother Gerald either, who was bound to make a fuss if he caught wind of it. But with regard to Gordon's potential for inter-ference Vera was sanguine. She told Jack that he expected her to come back after she had had her 'squalid little fling', and

33

that when she returned he would be waiting for her. It seems this was far from her first squalid little fling. Apparently Gordon too had flings, and I think Vera quite enjoyed being caught between the two men, each formidable in his own right, and herself unsure which of them would prevail in the end. I do know she shared Gordon's bed right up to the day she left.

I learned in the days following that Gordon had broadcast Vera's 'outrage' to half of Soho, and that Jack had acquired a certain infamy. This he could tolerate, and even savour, provided Vera got through the last days in London without vacillating or, god forbid, changing her mind. It was a period of excruciating tension, and only my own staunch support sustained him. My misgivings I kept to myself. He had told her that if she didn't come to New York with him he would go alone. He had meant it when he said it, but the prospect of going without her filled him with dread. Our plan was that if she didn't go then I would. What would happen after that I hadn't the faintest idea.

Came the day of departure, and we found ourselves under the clock in Victoria Station. He had his suitcase, his passport was in his pocket, also his roll of ten-pound notes. It was a miserable wet morning in October and he was wearing a black raincoat with the belt cinched tight and the collar turned up. He wore a black hat pulled low over his eyes, but he spoiled the effect by taking it off every five minutes to wipe his forehead with his handkerchief and push a trembling hand through his hair. There he stood, smoking a cigarette, staring off into the middle distance, a tall, nervous, long-haired young man making the first large dramatic romantic gesture of his life. I thought of Manet's *Gare St Lazare*, all vaporous iridescence, a fragile web of glass and iron, figures dissolving in steam – and dear god, I thought, much more of this and Jack too will dissolve in steam. They were to travel by rail to Southampton and board the *Queen Mary* in the late afternoon.

I had become fatalistic. I knew she wouldn't come, and that I would be forced to travel with Jack to New York to face a future of – to put it mildly – some uncertainty. I glanced at him as I paced about the crowded station hall, and he was quiet and abstracted now amid the steam and flurry and din, and then I scanned the crowds for some sign of Vera. The big clock ticked overhead, and the departure of the Southampton train grew imminent. Curiously I felt a kind of sadness, as well as relief. I understood well enough my own resistance to Jack's departure, I wanted him in London with me, and I passionately resented this painted creature from Glasgow who was taking him away from me. All the same, I remember thinking that Vera would not find with Gordon, nor with anybody else for that matter, what for all his immaturity she would find with my brother – I knew his strength, I knew his drive, and I knew she needed him, if she were to grow, and flourish, and be fulfilled as a woman and an artist, though I was not certain that *she* understood this, I couldn't be sure she *knew* she needed him, and that he would solve the problem of her existence. What a waste, I thought. What a sad, foolish waste, what a waste of *Jack* –

Then – a shout – my heart sank – and there was Vera, coat flapping open, weaving through the crowd, colliding with a man in a bowler hat, not pausing to apologize, and her friend Julian hurrying behind with her suitcase, and Jack was running towards her and then they were in each other's arms in the middle of Victoria Station on a damp Tuesday morning and it was all theirs, it was all spread out in front of them –

No time to lose; and a few minutes later they were squeezed into the window of their compartment, with me and Julian on the platform, and we were all talking at the same time, and then the whistle, and clouds of steam billowing up in the damp air, and the train was moving –

They collapsed into their seats. The compartment was full, five each side, but no person in it permitted a flicker of human interest to cross their face, nor their eyes to meet the lovers' eyes: the last of England indeed. Without turning to her my brother punched Vera in the arm and murmured, 'Beast.' He knew she was grinning because the woman opposite suddenly jerked her head to the window and rigidly stared out at the wet dreary streets of south London.

A week later they were in New York.

His first visit to the city was not a happy one, but despite that my hard-headed unsentimental brother was never able to think of Manhattan other than with a kind of blind grateful affection, and hold it in his imagination as a place of refuge for lovers in flight. They were on deck with the other passengers when through a misty rain he saw the skyline rear up before him, a close-packed mass of old-fashioned skyscraper buildings huddled at the tip of a mythic island. They stood at the rail, wrapped in their overcoats, as Vera explained how the streets ran east to west, and the avenues north–south, and the Brooklyn Bridge spanned the East River, and the subway cost a dime – or was it a nickel – and on and on, but after a while it was too wet for them on deck so they slipped down to the bar for the last drink of the voyage.

They were disembarked at 42nd Street, and came down off the ship into a great damp shadowy shed with steel rafters and a hubbub of voices, crowds of milling men and women, suitcases and cabin trunks piled everywhere, laconic American officials. Having cleared customs they found themselves and their luggage on a pier on the West Side just as the rain eased off and the clouds parted. The sun was going down over the Jersey shore in a haze of smoky reds and greys, and they had a place to go to, a small hotel on 26th Street called the Madison where Vera had stayed before. They found a cab and sped off crosstown. The midtown skyscrapers stood out against the darkening sky with their lights all ablaze, symbols, surely, of, oh, hope, I suppose – aspiration – power, glory, success, and Jack said that during those minutes in the cab he experienced an intense excitement, so intense that it aroused him sexually, and with it as powerful an intimation as he'd ever felt that *greatness* lay within his grasp; and he could see no earthly reason why, with Vera beside him, he should not achieve all he knew he had it in him to achieve.

4

My brother could never be called a wistful man, but there was more than a whisper of nostalgia in him when he spoke about their first days in America. They were glorious, he said, he could *taste* it, the feeling of those days, as though it were a piece of fruit he'd just bitten into and the juice still wet on his lips. Everything they saw and did seemed to amplify the outrageous joy they had in each other, a pair of bold young painters flushed with the flame of their new romance and shaking the dust of old Europe off their boots. They had got away with it! – this was the feeling. Down Fifth they'd stride at night, he said, the collars of their overcoats turned up against the wind, the city throbbing round them like a living heart, and warm light spilling out from bars and restaurants on every block. They would push through the doors of some smoky saloon with gleaming brass rails and dark wood panelling, the jukebox in back and large mirrors behind the counter such that every bottle had its double, and find people who remembered Vera from her first visit, and with affection too, how could you not? With her ceaseless talk and her wild, gap-toothed laughter, how could you not want to draw close, said Jack, and share the light of that abundant spirit?

Abundant spirit was certainly the theme of their first nights in New York, he would then say wryly, and of the many that followed, for whatever the company Vera assumed she had

39

more to offer it than anyone else, and she did not hold back. Instead she held forth, and when propped up at a bar with a glass in her hand she could dominate any group. How she loved to tell the story of dumping Gordon and leaving England, all for the love of this beautiful boy, who had carried her off with such purpose, such gallantry! – and how the crowd applauded when she lifted her glass and declared Jack Rathbone the last of the great lovers, the last true romantic, and Jack, poor Jack, clutching her close to him, bewildered and intoxicated by it all. The talking and drinking would run on into the small hours before he could at last go home with his genius, and if no one was able to recall much of the conversation the next morning, what did survive was the feeling of being privileged to be taking pleasure of such a rare and elevated kind, to be out carousing, I mean, with artists at play with their wits at full stretch, their tongues unfettered and winged –

But as the days flew by, each much like the last – an endless round, it seems, of bars and parties among people he later came to regard as phonies and losers – Jack said he became aware of the first flush dying, and it was dying because he was beginning to feel a deep unease that they had not yet made any *work*. I understood his impatience, of course I did, and his frustration too, because I knew how intensely ambitious he was, and it never occurred to me to doubt his account, I suppose because it confirmed what I already suspected about Vera, that she was a slut and a lush and *lazy*. In time I came to regard her differently, and even grew to like her; and after Jack's death I leaned on her heavily, when for a while she was the sole pillar of strength in a house of shattered women. But in those early days I felt only disdain, which was simply the mask of my jealousy. A studio with a bed in it had been promised by a guy called Herb who was about to leave for the Cape. He would let them have it for nothing, he said, and given their limited resources this was important, but they saw him in the Village night after night, in one bar or another, and he always had a reason why he must be in the city a few days more.

Jack became convinced he was Vera's lover from her previous visit, and that he didn't leave the city precisely because she was there, but it meant that they had to stay on at the Madison, where they could not work. So as they tramped the city streets by day it became clear to my brother that while he grew increasingly anxious, Vera was untroubled by their idleness. Every morning he woke early with a hangover, and lay in bed seething with impatience as it grew ever more clear to him that if they carried on this way they would one day be without any money, and worse, that Vera did not care – that she was content to let that day dawn, and would not worry about the prospect *until* that day dawned. Which meant that it was up to him to make sure they didn't go broke, but without involving her at all. That seemed to be the deal. He had thought the deal was they were going to set up a studio together and work side by side. Vera was certainly looking at art, and talking about art, but she wasn't *making* any art. She said she needed to charge her battery.

He asked her how long this took, and I imagine from what he told me that they were in bed for this conversation, that it was late morning, and that they had had a late night. Another late night.

– It takes, she said, as long as it takes.

I see her sitting up on her elbow, licking her dry lips, groaning, pushing her hair off her face, reaching for a cigarette. Jack was unsure whether such behaviour was to be expected of an artist like Vera Savage, and therefore accepted, or to be resisted, to be challenged. All his instincts told him he was watching not creative gestation but waste. He said this. She turned to him, squinting, then her face changed, she stretched out a hand and took his jaw in her fingers, and angled it towards the light, what little they had of it in that poky room with its one small window, and his pale hair flopping over his forehead.

41

– Just look at you, she whispered, and with so much tenderness, and the tears standing out in her eyes!

How then to berate her for her shiftlessness? But he tried.

– Darling, we've got to *work*!

Still she held his jaw. Then she was astride him.

– You've got to work. Go on, work.

Then she sank onto him, closed her eyes, lifted her chin.

– Not just me, he said, or murmured, rather, as he lost control of the conversation.

Or so I imagined it. He thought he might try again later, when they were out on the street. There was the chance of a more serious conversation when they had their clothes on, but there were so many distractions! Here was the new Guggenheim Museum, extraordinary spiral going up on Fifth Avenue, here was Central Park, the park, yes, all that wildness and water and silence at the heart of so much congestion and *din* –! He would talk to her seriously when they were in the park.

So they talked seriously when they were in the park. They went in at 86th and tramped south in their overcoats, hands plunged deep in their pockets and Vera's head sunk low as she frowned and he poured out the thoughts that woke him each day at dawn and cast an ever-lengthening shadow on his happiness. And she nodded, and agreed that yes, it was time they made some work, and she understood, yes, that he was eager to get on, and so yes, tonight they would decide one way or another about this studio of Herb's, and if it wasn't going to work out, why then they would look for something else – and then all at once a large shaggy hound was padding towards them and she cried out with pleasure and sank to her knees to make friends with it – and he saw it meant nothing to her, what she was saying. She was trying to make it mean something, she was trying to share his compulsion to work, but it simply was not in her.

This rocked him. He had to stop and sit down on a bench.

They sat under a tree, and dead leaves drifting down around them. The day was cool and misty, the park was empty. They sat smoking by the Bethesda Fountain and he could not explain how rocked he was by what he'd just seen in her. He didn't know her any more. How she worked, this was a mystery to him now. Whatever it was, her working process, it bore no resemblance to his own. He did not know what this would mean for them.

Jack said he saw then that the idea of them properly living and working together would only become a reality if he made it so. He knew he had it in him to settle to long sustained bouts of work, but he wanted to have her working beside him, in an adjoining studio, and for them to come together at the end of the day, to talk of what they had done, to criticize, to learn, to encourage, to develop – this had been the idea, but he now saw he had been deceived. She was a stranger to the long sustained bout of work. How she had become the painter she was he didn't know, but he now suspected, and it was awesome to him, that hard work had not been the key, rather some kind of innate talent: it had come easy to her. But what evidently did not come easy to her was the will to exercise that talent, and Jack didn't know how to ignite it in her.

Facing this, facing the ruin of the dream that had driven him to abandon England, and landed him in a city where he was a stranger, with a woman he now felt he didn't know, he sank, for a day or two, into something approaching despair. A black cloud attended him, and this I know well from my own experience, that when my brother had a black cloud attending him no joy was possible for anybody else. Apparently Vera did not under-stand what had happened. She assumed he was anxious about money. She attempted to reassure him. She told him she could always get money from London if she had to. He asked her how. From Gordon, she said, and Jack lifted his head and laughed a bleak hollow laugh.

That night they were in a bar as usual and Jack was still

43

deeply absorbed in his predicament. What could he tell her, when she asked him what was the matter – that *she* was the matter, that the future she had seemed to promise him was an illusion? She would have denied it vehemently. She would have passionately reasserted her commitment to the idea of a partnership of artists – the American Studio – an idea first formulated late one night in the back of a Soho pub and embellished in the weeks since. But now Jack feared that the American Studio would never materialize, not in the form he had imagined it, and this fear left him adrift, uncertain where to go next, what to do – dear god he was only seventeen years old!

It was a strange, violent night in New York. As though a spirit were abroad, or a posse of demons. There were jangling discordant energies wherever they went. Shouting cops, restive crowds, snarled traffic. Saturday night, a full moon, madness in the city: in one bar an enraged man picked a fight with a stranger and when they tried to throw him out he tore the washroom door off its hinges and hurled it across the counter, bottles, glasses and mirrors shattering, and they all had to run for the door.

An hour later, in another bar, Vera's friend Herb turned on Jack, irritated by his silence.

– What are you doing here, man? he shouted, over the hubbub of talk and jukebox, and in a tone of sufficient hostility that the rest of the table fell silent and looked on with interest. They all knew Herb's history with Vera. Jack shrugged. He was burning, he told me, with rage and embarrassment, but all he did was lift his glass, lift his cigarette, as if to say – nothing, drinking and smoking like you.

– Yeah, but what are you doing? I mean, taking up space, that it? You give me nothing, man, you're like a plant.

– Shut up, Herb, shouted Vera.

– A house plant.

Herb turned grinning to the table.

– Better a plant than a Herb, shouted Vera, but it was too late

44

for Jack. It hadn't occurred to him that anything was expected of him here. These people were older than him, they were Americans, they knew Vera from before, their talk gave him no openings. He was not an artist, not yet, he was not an American, he had nothing to contribute. He bought drinks, he assumed that his position was understood. Now this. The rage all at once boiled over and he lunged at Herb, swinging wildly with both fists. His mood was brutal to begin with. For several weeks his existence had had meaning only in relation to Vera. He was baffled by her friends, he hated bloody Herb – he was sure there was something between them still, and it preyed on him – he felt there was no solid ground under his feet, nothing familiar to cling to. He needed me, but me of course he had left far behind. Now this. Herb scuttled away and stood panting and growling and shouting at him to settle *down*, man, be *cool*, man, and Jack slumped back on to his chair, wiping his face where he'd spilled beer in his brief assault. Then he pushed his chair back and in the sudden silence the legs scraped loudly across the boards of the tavern floor. Without a word he walked out into the night.

For several hours he walked the streets, thinking of nothing but how good the cold air felt on his skin, and seething still with jealous rage. He didn't know that Vera had rushed out after him, but that he'd walked away so fast she didn't see where he'd gone, nor in the loud, mad city did he hear her shouting for him. He tramped the city streets, his thoughts in utter turmoil, alone in this alien place, and Vera a part of a world which offered no place for him, which rejected him. He tramped the streets and allowed the anger and misery to boil up and rage unchecked.

Midnight, and he found himself down at the Battery, sitting on a bench, smoking a cigarette, gazing out at the harbour where just a few weeks before he'd stood on the deck of a liner and felt the limitless promise of the city. The night was cold and clear. The crisis was on him, and he must make a decision, to go back

45

or go on. To go back was unthinkable. But how to go on? He had to get out of New York. But he had to get out of New York *with Vera* – and that simple thought shed all the light he needed. It was a decision not to abandon her.

I believe he made other decisions that night, or rather that certain ideas crystallized in his mind. He told me he waited for sunrise, for the first light of dawn to touch the Statue of Liberty and burn off the mist on the water. He said there had been other times in his life when the early morning hours seemed to open new avenues in his mind, something to do with the edginess, the febrility that comes of not having slept, something to do with the sense of an empty world out there, a sleeping world, the space for one's thoughts not contested but free, rather, for expansive movement, for the sweeping perspective. Gazing out at the harbour Jack at last found some clarity. He said he understood that what lay ahead of him were years of obscurity while he became a painter. He would suffer humiliation and neglect, but this he could endure: he would grow the hide of a rhino and become impervious to the opinions of others. Better by far, he thought, to spend those years elsewhere. He would come back to New York but only when he had something to *offer* New York, he would return a mature painter with a body of work. The city was no place for an aspirant, for a beginner. New York was full of aspirants and beginners, and they all seemed to be Vera's drinking buddies. He would stagnate if he stayed, he would grow sodden and lazy, and delude himself into believing he was an artist when he was nothing of the sort. He needed rigour, he needed routine, he needed somewhere he could live cheap and work without distraction. Above all he needed Vera beside him.

And then, as yet another stray beam of enlightenment came shafting in with the sunrise, all at once he felt with a sense of rising wonder – and he was still young enough that such sudden dramatic shifts of mood were possible – that the paranoia was

46

lifting, that the knot of sexual suspicion he had been harbouring, and worrying at, obsessively, was dissolving – it was all in his imagination, of course it was, and he had to communicate this to Vera without delay, sweep away all the bad feeling, sit down and talk to her, consider their options, make a plan –

When he got back to the hotel she was waiting for him in a state of great distress. They clung to each other and she told him how she had scoured the Village for hours, and so had Herb, but it didn't matter now, none of that mattered, and they fell on to the bed, she wrapped her legs around him, and responded with joy to the love newly started from some secret spring inside him during the hours he'd been alone by the harbour. Afterwards they didn't sleep, they sat up talking, and this he called the Rising. Later he made a painting inspired by that long dark night of the soul, as he thought of it: *The Rising*, probably the rawest of what I regarded as his phallic paintings.

They talked about the future, and he told her he had to get out of New York, that he could no longer live the life they were living. He was moving on, and she could come with him if she wanted or she could stay where she was and drown her talent in whisky. She did not argue. She was languid with sex.

– Where do you want to go?

He told her he wanted to go south.

– How far south?

As far as he had to, until he found a place where he could work. He told her that more than anything in the world he wanted her to come with him. He begged her to come with him.

Later they sat in a coffee shop down the block. It was almost noon. She was wearing dark glasses. Beyond the plate-glass window the rain was gently falling. She was more awake now, and worrying at this ultimatum of his, delivered earlier when she was still soft and tender from the sex. She cranked up her engines of dissent. Rusty and spluttering at first, she soon had her theme and Jack allowed her to run it out. The general drift was, he was asking her to turn her back on her friends, all that was familiar to her. First London, now here – what was wrong with New York?

Nothing was wrong with New York, he told her, it was how they *lived* in New York that was wrong: they stayed in bed all morning, he said, then they wandered the city for three or four hours, then it was time for cocktails.

She took off her sunglasses and rubbed her eyes. She spoke about being dragged far from civilization. She said he was leading her deep into a jungle she would never find her way out of. But Jack knew, so he said later, that as she grumbled and rambled she was at the same time coolly examining his proposal, and that even as she argued, the idea of going south began to rouse her, for she was always susceptible to the prospect of flight, she was far more the drifter than he was.

– Where is it you want to go, Jack?

She was properly awake now, she had drunk enough coffee, the hook was in. He shrugged. He was cool, offhand.

– Mexico.

– Mexico!

– Cuba. Honduras.

She had her sunglasses on again, he couldn't see her eyes. But she ran her tongue round the inside of her mouth as she reached for the cigarettes and murmured the names. Mexico – Cuba – Honduras – poetry!

– Go by water, he said.

– By boat, yes.

– Look for a town on the coast.

– A river town.

Is this how the conversation went? A river town may or may not have been suggested, and Vera may or may not have been so easily persuaded. But she knew that without Jack she was sunk. She had no plans, no money, nothing. And she was still very much in love with him. And so, in this fashion, or in a fashion similar to this, the decision was made. They would pack up and go south. She grew excited later, this Jack did remember clearly,

48

she decided that here was one of the moments of grand pathos in an artist's life – a moment of heroic self-sacrifice – a moment when a woman lifted her eyes and glimpsed her destiny, understanding, yes, what must be done, no matter the cost, for Art to be served. She called it 'The Leaving of Manhattan'. She described, over drinks, to the usual crowd, the epic canvas she intended to paint, a vast thing of colour and movement, allegorical figures in the sea and in the sky, with Manhattan a kind of radiant heart in the centre of the composition, and pulling away from it a great white ship with four slanting funnels and Jack and herself alone at the rail with their eyes on a future where Art and Art Alone would rule, and their friends on the dock weeping and dancing –

How they laughed. Let her mock herself, thought Jack, let her set herself up as a ridiculous figure, the woman who left Manhattan so she could paint in peace –

But just let me get her to that quiet river town and she will be painting pictures of real importance. More to the point, so will I. No, she wouldn't let him go without her, he knew this, she wouldn't miss this adventure, and besides, there was real spirit in Vera Savage, an old deep spark of the unquenchable stuff. And Manhattan – Manhattan could wait. Manhattan wouldn't go away.

For much of the next year they drifted. They didn't leave New York in a great white ship with four red funnels, they took the train to Miami. I believe there was a sexual crisis of some kind, Vera told me about it years later, the first infidelity, if you don't count Gordon, which she didn't. They weathered the storm through my good offices: the money arrived the next day, and it came as a shaft of grace for it allowed them to move on and, more important, to buy clothes which were appropriate to the climate.

I next glimpse them in Havana – this was before the revolution – living in an apartment at the top of a crumbling pale-blue building with a balcony from which they could see the Caribbean tossing over the seawall if they craned out far enough. There was a covered courtyard, a place of cool shade dappled with sunlight before you hit the glare of the street, a riot of bougainvillea crawling over the peeling walls, the whole a study in texture and tone that Jack was soon attempting to paint, this with the active encouragement of the neighbours, who had at once taken to the young *pintor grande*, him and his *pirata* both.

They slept on a huge bed beneath a headboard of dark carved hardwood and kept the shutters open so as to gather up any breeze that found its way down their narrow street, *Calle de Placencia*. Jack remembered the vast shining moon that bathed their bed in silver, and always, he said, somewhere near by, a loud, rapid conversation punctuated by shouts and laughter, or weeping, or screams, or a radio playing dance music, or a streetcar clanking by below, and for a while they were happy. They would lie propped up on pillows, smoking cigars, listening to the night, then fall asleep and dream about painting. They rose early and by eight they were at work.

For several months they lived in the apartment near the seawall. He said he worked hard and came on rapidly. Vera too was working, and Jack watched her closely. At first she painted without interruption, at all hours, for days and nights on end. She painted what she saw on the streets of Havana with a free, loose hand on remnants of cotton duck they picked up cheap in the fabric houses of Havana Viejo, using large brushes and powdered pigment in bright primary colours they mixed themselves in buckets. Decayed colonial buildings baking in the sunlight, their roofs eaten away by grass. Towering palms with massive finned automobiles gliding by. Plazas and foun- tains and statues, grand boulevards, gaily dressed *habaneros* gathered on street corners to pass a bottle and dance. Shouting women hanging out of windows, hauling up groceries in a basket. Wretched *campesinos* asleep on benches. Parrots, skulls, fields of sugarcane swaying in the moonlight, sun gods, rusting tankers, and baroque movie theatres featuring American movie stars, all found their way onto Vera's big canvases.

So he learned from her even if she did not teach him, and just as well because she could not articulate what it was she did. It's a mystery, Jack, she said, art's a mystery, OK? – and laid one finger on her breast and another on her eye. This gnomic gesture was followed by a solemn silence, then a gust of chesty laughter. They got out a few weeks before Batista fled the country, and missed the spectacle of Fidel Castro entering the city after a triumphal journey the length of the island, and his rousing oration to a crowd of half a million in front of the Presidential Palace. Apparently it turned cynics into romantics and romantics into fanatics, and I almost wish I had been there myself. Was that why they moved on? Because of the deteriorating political situation, the escalating violence, the hardening antagonism of the people of Cuba towards the brutal oppression they had so long endured – was that it?

But no, it was all much more banal than that. Jack told me it was because Vera couldn't handle it any more. After the productive month or so there came a period of inactivity when she lay on the couch in her studio all day, smoking cigars and gazing at the ceiling. Then she started going out. Soon she came to prefer the street to the studio, the nights to the days, it was all just as sadly predictable as that. They were subject to much stress at the time, partly to do with money, partly to do with the irritability that came of sustained daily drinking, and partly to do with the mischief that came of Vera's idleness.

– Mischief? I said, catching a whiff of something in his tone.

He nodded. He laboured at his canvas every day, and in the empty apartment her absence would work its mischief at the back of his mind. He would push the thought down, he would employ the full resources of his will to remain concentrated on the work at hand. At noon he stuck his brushes into a jar of turpentine and wiped his hands on a rag, put on his cotton jacket and straw hat, and descended the echoing stone staircase to the arcade below to buy cigarettes, knowing that he was really going down to see if Vera was about, assure himself that she was not in some room with a man. If he didn't find her it would not be a happy afternoon in the studio, and he would rage in his mind until he heard her footfall on the staircase. Then they would fight.

– How, fight?

But he would not be drawn out, he would not tell me if their fights were merely verbal, the same shouting and screaming they heard every night coming from other apartments in the building, or if it went further, if there was actual physical violence.

Then came the night they heard gunfire close by. Jack had for some weeks been finding it more and more difficult to control his suspicions of Vera, and his work was suffering as a result. She refused to talk about what she did in the hours she spent away from the apartment. She told him it was no way to live, this trying to account for each other's movements at all hours of the day or night. Her line was: why can't you trust me? He tried to banish the jealous thoughts, but no sooner did his head clear than the small voice started up again. He thought he might be going mad.

But he was not mad! These thoughts came for a reason! He was picking up signs without being aware of what they were, he must have been, there was some subtle way she was telling him what she was doing, only he couldn't identify it, but the message was coming through all the same, and he thought it was probably as simple a thing as how she touched him, or perhaps how she didn't touch him, a telling but almost imperceptible falling off in her physical behaviour towards him that could only be the effect of a divided sexual attention.

He asked himself why it mattered so much, but that got him nowhere, it mattered because it mattered, and he was far from complacent in this regard, far too fiercely committed to this union to be indifferent to the casual diversions of the body. But it also occurred to him that if she was indeed innocent then his constant suspicion would soon drive her into some man's arms and create the very situation he was so desperately trying to avoid. Who could he talk to about this? Nobody. Me he had left behind. And I remember thinking that it might have been just this, I mean his isolation in the midst of people for whom Vera was the main attraction, and his dogged insistence on long hours alone each day in his studio, that aroused such jealousy and suspicion in him, or at least created a kind of morbid condition of the spirit in which these emotions could flourish.

He grew to hate Havana. He grew to see its loose easy life as the enemy of his bond with Vera, and of his work.

Then came the gunfire in the night. It woke them up. They knew what it was, no question of fireworks or backfiring automobiles. Jack went out onto the balcony, Vera following him, hissing at him to be careful. He stood with his hands on the balustrade, peering all around, but there was nobody about, nothing to be seen. The moon was low over the sea at the end of the street. He came back in, and they sat in his studio smoking, waiting for more gunfire, for whatever was going to happen next. Nothing. The usual sounds of Havana late at night. The sea, the trees, the insects. Vehicles on distant streets. No voices though.

At last Vera got up and stood at the table, frowning, pouring them each a drink, a cigar between her teeth. Her hair was damp with the warmth of the night and her bare shoulders were bathed in moonlight.

Jack said he hated guns.

– They're getting them from Russia, she said.

– Where did you hear that?

– Someone told me.

And again the small bitter voice, seizing on this oblique reference to her life out there in the city, the life he knew nothing about –

– So many friends you have.

He knew what he was doing when he said it, he hated that he was doing it, but he seemed to have no choice. What was the impulse – intensify the crisis, push it to the breaking point, get the thing finished and resolved one way or the other – was this it?

– Oh christ, Jack, don't start.

But he had started, and within ten minutes she was dressed and out the door, out into the dangerous dark streets, and he didn't see her until the morning, by which time he knew it was all over with Havana.

So they left Havana, and with them the battered cabin trunk with the brass studs in which they'd packed their painting gear, their sketchbooks, their journals, their clothes and books, as well as a bottle or two for emergencies. Vera's canvases they shipped back to London. I see them on some smoky old coaster with rusted rivets and welded patches on the hull, the pair of them leaning on the rail, in dark glasses and Panama hats, as they moved on to the next island, the next coastal town. Jack's experiences, recollected in drunken tranquillity, by this time would have downshifted through nuanced grada-tions into a mild and rather maudlin memory of himself as a very young man drifting about the Caribbean with this difficult woman with whom he was engaged in a torrid and complicated love affair. The steamer belched oily black smoke into the sunlight and the captain stood on the bridge trying to shoot dolphin with a rifle. Off to the west the mangrove gave way to sandy beaches, an unbroken backdrop of dense palms with mountains in the distance and every few miles, just visible across a hazy, shimmering sea, a cluster of wooden shacks on stilts, and a rickety jetty, and the faint stench of seaweed drying in the sun. It was well into the afternoon when they learned that they would soon be docking for a couple of hours, and the prospect of a cool cantina and bottles of iced beer was welcome indeed.

– You had an idea, I said, what you were looking for.
– Oh yes.

Port Mungo: a once-prosperous river town now gone to seed, wilting and steaming among the mangrove swamps of the Gulf of Honduras.

5

I visited the place only once. I spent ten days there. On the waterfront I saw rough bars built of concrete blocks run by hard-faced Chinese and patronized by prostitutes and mean-looking men from off the boats. I remember dusty streets and alleyways, and canals, which stank, being open sewers, and disgorged into the river, which was visible from almost any-where you looked, glittering in the sunlight behind the stilted shacks, or from the end of an alley where chickens pecked in the dirt and a collapsing dock occupied a few feet of frontage. I retain a vivid memory of the open market, where I saw a man split a live iguana down the belly with a machete, that reptile's flesh being a local delicacy. There were flies everywhere, noise, blood, the stench of butchered meat mingling with the fragrance of papaya and mango.

I will not pretend I wasn't devastated when he left me. Isn't every man a hero to his sister? Jack was certainly a hero to me, and I had diligently kept his image shining like a beacon before my eyes, the image of a brother resolute in his identity and ready to overcome every obstacle in the pursuit of his ambition. I cannot be certain exactly what happened in New York. Much of what he told me has since been contradicted by Vera, though I do know that they got through the money in a matter of weeks and then moved south, and this I know because I had to wire them funds to a bank in Miami Beach. I suppose I was a fool, but for years I thought about him constantly, my devotion sustained by the very occasional letter, usually a scrawled thing on onionskin paper with drink smears and cigarette burns all over it, and the margins alive with sketches and doodles. How I treasured them! – I wrote back copiously, and subjected any man who showed an interest in me to a withering comparison with Jack, and never, of course, did any of them come close.

I hadn't seen my brother for more than ten years. Much had happened in the meantime. After Jack left England I had grown close to my father, and when he died I was surprised how deeply it affected me. He left the bulk of the estate to me. Jack got nothing, nor, to his astonishment, did Gerald, who by that time had become a doctor and was set up in a good practice not far from London with his wife and children. I knew exactly what I wanted to do. I sold the house in Suffolk and a year later moved to New York. I, too, had been intoxicated by Vera's description of the city that long-ago night in Camden Town, and with every subsequent visit I paid to Manhattan – this was after Vera and Jack headed south, of course – my feelings for the place grew stronger. I bought the brownstone on West 11th Street, and quickly established the kind of quiet, bookish existence I had always wanted. There were a number of desultory love affairs, but through it all Jack was never far from my thoughts, nor absent from my innermost heart. I attempted to invite myself down to Port Mungo several times, particularly when I heard that they had a child, a daughter – Peg – but each time Jack had put me off. Then had come a letter in which his need of me was so nakedly apparent that I began to organize my travel arrangements the same morning.

And so I made the long, hot, arduous journey south, culminating in a four-hour trip down the coast on a slow ferry. I was profoundly nervous, and at the same time giddily excited at the prospect of seeing my long-lost brother again. He met me off the boat, at the jetty. He was almost thirty now, and what I saw advancing on me was an unkempt, sunburnt man in faded canvas shirt and pants, his long hair bleached in strips by the sun and tied back in a ponytail. He greeted me in his familiar manner – clasped me to him stiffly – while Peg, barefoot and brown-skinned, hid behind him and watched me intently with dark, wild eyes. He murmured to me as he held me in his arms.

– Gin, how really good of you to come. It's a vile journey.

– I've missed you, I said, and then, to myself: more than you will ever know.

We made our slow way, in fierce heat, with Peg pushing the wheelbarrow in which my bags had been stowed, along dusty streets, between listing shacks, to the warehouse district. Everybody seemed to know Jack and Peg, and much interest was shown in me. Jack grinned as he watched me shake hands with old black men with rheumy eyes and gold teeth. I understood not a word of what was said to me until Peg shyly translated. We eventually fetched up at a vast ram-shackle wooden structure built out over the river. This had apparently been their home since the day Jack and Vera first arrived in the town.

Later we sat out on the deck over the river and drank rum. We watched the sun go down behind the western mountains as the Mungo turned black, its surface alive with flickering insects and flashes of silver. Sounds both human and animal punctured the silence, and on the far bank I saw children splashing about in the shallows, and behind them, against the gathering sunset, broken-down shacks with tin roofs and crooked chimneys from which woodsmoke drifted into the rain forest beyond. Jack took a strange pride in this primitive place he had come to, and in particular in that great sagging barn of a house. It had once been a banana warehouse, though it was empty when they'd got there. Buildings left empty in the tropics deteriorate fast, he said, but it was big and also so cheap that enough money remained from what I'd last wired for them to lease it for several years. It was more a ruin than anything else, no question; but it was their ruin, and it was here, he said, that he properly learned to paint. The dirt road out front was called Pelican Road, and that was the name the house had acquired.

They'd found a woman called Radiance to cook for them, and she brought three of her sons to rid the house of spiders and scorpions and various other unpleasant creatures which had taken up residence. They had all set to work with brooms and mops, and later with buckets of whitewash, which they'd slapped on to the silvered old boards so as to make the inside of the building as light as possible. They replaced the rotting floor-boards, installed a simple kitchen, and slung hammocks. They bought a few sticks of furniture and as many oil lamps as they could lay their hands on, and after a few days the place was more or less habitable. A large teak bed was brought in by water then carried into the house in pieces and put back together on the top floor.

The rolls of coarse burlap were unpacked, and enough of the powdered paint they'd purchased in Havana to last them half a year, and then at last they'd stepped out on to the deck, the two of them, into the sunlight, and gazed out over the river, and the harbour, and the sea beyond, and clinked their beer bottles and toasted their great good fortune. And so began their days in Pelican Road, the old banana warehouse that would be my brother's home for almost twenty years.

All this he told me in a tone of quiet satisfaction, and I realized that he regarded the acquisition of this shabby place as a real accomplishment. I was troubled by this. I asked him if Vera was as proud of it as he clearly was, and he said he remembered her stamping across a vastness of wooden floor, peering up into the gloomy rafters, sweeping her hand across what seemed acres of wallspace, and declaring that *ten* painters could work here and not get in one another's way! She apparently liked the tropics, and for a year or two at least she'd liked living in this wreck of a house that lurched precariously out over the river –

There was no sign of her now.

All this he told me that first evening, in tones, as I say, of profound satisfaction. I was more interested however in the man himself. The changes in Jack were dramatic. Most striking was the absence of that reckless energy which had been so irresistible in London, and not only to me. For it had been replaced by a kind of abstracted introspection, in fact it seemed as if all the flamboyant energy with which he had once come at the world was now turned in on himself. Why should I have been surprised, much less saddened? The last time I'd seen him he was a youth – a strong, splendid, wilful youth, but a youth all the same – and now he was a man. And if he had once been a romantic, he was now, I guessed, a realist, or perhaps a cynic: Vera had made him so. We were both silent for a while. Something screamed in the jungle. Then he spoke again, and his mood had shifted.

– I'm usually all right on my own, but this time I just felt so bloody cast down. She's gone off again.

I saw the self-pity rise in his throat, then get swallowed. I waited for more but that was all. It was of course impossible for me to say that I had guessed this would happen, that I had seen clearly what sort of a woman Vera was in those first heady days in London. So I asked the question that had been on my mind ever since I stepped off the ferry. I asked him why, of all the godforsaken spots on the face of the earth, they'd chosen this one?

A bit of shrugging here, scratching of the head, a glimpse of teeth. Oh, one got used to it, one even grew fond of it, and besides, he had a good place to work, and Peg was happy. And he had friends, yes, not gringos but locals. He liked the easygoing Creoles, their openness and generosity, which had sustained them in the early days. It seems it had been another of their impulsive decisions. When they saw the sleepy waterfront, the fishing boats, the painted wooden houses leaning out over the slow green Mungo – he flapped a hand dismissively at the river, and also, I thought, at the idiot romanticism of his youthful self – he said they just had a *feeling* about the place, so they got off the steamer and had their trunk unloaded on to the dock. And the rest – sardonic bark here – is family history. Curse of the Rathbones.

My brother was indeed cursed, I remember thinking, but not by a family malediction, but by the woman with whom he'd thrown in his lot. It became clear as he talked that Vera was a chronic alcoholic, just as I had long suspected, and that her drinking had grown worse during the years in Port Mungo. Jack also gave me to understand that she was often unfaithful to him, and this I could see was more painful to him even than the drinking. The damage she'd done him could be read in his eyes, in his body, in his gait and posture: he was a bowed and harrowed man, where once he had been straight and fierce. But he had his work, and he also – and here again I heard the quiet pleasure in his voice – he also had his daughter. Peg was born a couple of years after they'd got to Port Mungo, and when he spoke of the girl it was with such tenderness that I knew his life was blessed at least in this regard, that the joy she had given him had gone some way to compensate for all the pain Vera had caused.

And his own sex life? In response to Vera's infidelity, had he found – comfort – himself, elsewhere –?

Here I discovered another change in my brother. Ten years before he would have launched at once, and with some gusto, into an account of his adventures. Now he was reticent. The question disturbed him, and I did not press him. But I continued to worry at it, for my brother had a powerful sex drive, and it was inconceivable to me that he now channelled all his libido into his work. I asked myself whether he had a mistress he was being discreet about, for I wouldn't have been in the least surprised. The girls of Port Mungo were pretty creatures, what I had seen of them, slender, green-eyed young beauties with delicate brown skins, and possessed of an enchanting physical grace – wouldn't any white man wish to claim one of these shy things for his own, set her up in a stilted shack on the other side of town, there to receive him whenever his loins were stirred –? I suggested as much but Jack said no. He shook his head. He was not interested in the local girls.

I let this statement hang in the air for a few moments. One of the gringo women, then? An explosive snort of laughter in response to this. Have you seen them, Gin? None of them under sixty. Hides like rhinos, pickled in spirits. I was pickled in spirits myself by this time, and so was he, but all the same I abandoned the topic, and what Jack did for sex remained a mystery. Perhaps, I later thought, he had indeed undergone some kind of Damascene conversion. Perhaps in the face of Vera's flagrant serial infidelity he had resolved to act in direct contradiction of her ethos, almost as a rebuke – to be faithful to her, I mean, and celibate in her absence. Perhaps his own infidelity in Miami Beach, early in their travels, had sufficiently traumatized him that he no longer went after other women, being one of those rare men who make only one sexual mistake in their lives, and resolve never to stray again –?

In fact I now believe that in spite of his wildly nonconformist life my brother did possess the moral fibre to control his appetites and sublimate them into his art; and I believe too that he never repeated the clumsy sexual error he made early in his relationship with Vera.

She told me about it once. This was much later, when she was on one of her periodic visits to New York, and for some reason the pair of us had been left alone after dinner, sitting at the kitchen table with a bottle or two and an overflowing ashtray. Over time a cautious intimacy had developed between Vera and me, and I had somewhat relaxed my stern disapproval of her. I suppose the years permit one a more complex perspective on things. I don't remember how we got on to the topic, but I remember the sly glance she flashed at me, the lift of an eyebrow, as though to say: so that's what you're after – and then she launched into the story. It happened in Miami Beach, she said, filling her glass for the umpteenth time, and lighting yet another cigarette. She blew smoke at the ceiling. They were staying in a cheap rooming house a block back from Ocean Drive, she told me, this of course after their departure from New York. They were waiting for me to wire them money so they could get to Havana. Jack was not doing at all well, she said, and she described to me not the fearless young man I had known but a lost and frightened boy, adrift in the world and uncertain of his direction, clinging to his lover because he needed her but at the same time resisting and resenting his dependency. He was miserable in Miami Beach. The weather was hot and they couldn't afford to replace the clothes they'd brought with them from London. Nor could they afford anything better than a tacky room away from the beach, sharing a bathroom down the corridor with some old men. Their window looked on to an alleyway where garbage was going bad, but they couldn't close it against the smell as they needed the breeze.

She was content to kill the time reading, she said, old paperbacks or whatever magazines and newspapers she could scrounge up. She would lie on the bed in her underwear, in the stale, heavy heat, and for hours she smoked and read. Jack would pace the floor and then invent for himself some mission, the purchase of cigarettes or yet another fruitless trip to the bank to see if the money had come.

She did not share his restlessness. She was like a cat, she said, languid for hours, indifferent to time, she liked the heat. Not so Jack. He chafed. He seethed. He hated the heat, the stasis, the paralysis – and suddenly I saw him as a kind of chrysalis, a creature waiting impatiently to emerge from its cocoon. Vera remembered that one afternoon she had fallen into a light doze when Jack slipped quietly into the room and went to the dressing table. He was perspiring heavily. His shirt was sticking to his back. He did not realize she was awake. She lay on the bed in the warm gloom and through half-closed eyes watched him in the dressing-table mirror, saying nothing, because he was being furtive, which naturally made her curious. He had undone several of his shirt buttons and was bending forward to examine his neck in the mirror. All at once he froze, aware now that she was watching him. Their eyes locked in the mirror. Overhead the heavy wooden fan turned sluggishly, to negligible effect.

– What is it you're doing, Jack?

– I think I got burnt, he said, buttoning his shirt again.

– Let me see.

– No, it's all right. Go back to sleep. I didn't mean to wake you. I'm going out again.

– Give us a kiss then.

This provoked no small alarm but what could he do? Trust to his luck. But it was not his lucky day. She smelt cheap perfume even before he reached the bed. She had not expected this from him, and she had no idea how to deal with it. She simply told him, with the first kindling of angry disbelief, that he'd been with a woman. She was sitting up now, and wide awake.

– No I haven't, he said.

The room stank of perfume not her own, so his denial was not only useless it was insulting. She was duly insulted, at the same time experiencing a sick weary feeling that the banality of the row they were about to have was no different from that of the tens of thousands of infidelity rows being conducted in America at that very moment. She had thought they were different. She had thought they were transparent to each other. Now this. Vulgar perfume and vulgar lies. She was suddenly desperately sad. Jack sat on the bed, he made some sort of a sound intended to be comforting, and touched her. She rose up in a rage and at once he was out the door, leaving her alone with her breaking heart, without a friend in this pastel-coloured city.

Vera sat at my kitchen table gazing into her wine. Then she looked up at me and said a curious thing. She said she'd felt as though she'd lost her virginity. I understood exactly what she meant.

When he came back two hours later he found her in front of the mirror putting on her make-up. He was ready to face the music and take his punishment like a man. He had bought her a bottle to ease the pain. He had prepared a speech. What he had not anticipated was her icy indifference, her tacit refusal to participate in some tawdry guilt-and-reconciliation scenario, nor did he know what to make of her evident intention to go out. She silently revelled in his confusion. For an hour she had allowed herself to be utterly ravaged by this calamity. Then she had risen from the bed a different woman, initiated, so she said, into the ways of Jack Rathbone's shabby heart. It only remained to act on her resolve and do to him exactly what he'd done to her. He had tried to come with her when she left the room, and that's when she'd showed him a truly poisonous contempt. She told him she did not want him with her, she was going out by herself. He attempted to ask her where she was going and she was able without uttering a single word – not a single word, Gin! – to convey to him that he had lost the right to ask her any such question. She told him not to follow her, and then she left.

It was all depressingly easy after that. In a bar on Ocean Drive she sat next to a plausible man and asked him for a light. He asked her if he could buy her a drink. It was just beginning to get dark. The palms along the beach were black against the deepening blue of the sky. The waves were hissing on the shore, huge open cars cruising down the street, bursts of music drifting from the beach. She'd sat on a high stool in a cocktail bar just off the lobby of a turquoise hotel, a woman with a breaking heart, determined to seduce a stranger to make a point.

She did. And actually, she said, giving me a large slotted grin, she liked it. A lot. This was a new kind of American for her. He was a salesman. His name was Richard. He came from Long Beach, California, and was in the swimwear business. When they lay side by side afterwards, smoking cigarettes, he showed her snapshots of his children. He wanted to see her again, but she told him no, it would just be the once. But to leave his room was not easy. Three times she tried to get dressed, and only the last time succeeded. He took her down in the elevator and they had a last martini at the bar. She said she had no idea what they talked about though he paid her compliments, and he must have considered himself a lucky man, I thought, to have pulled a good-looking woman like Vera with such ease.

She was walking up Ocean Drive at midnight in the direction of their fleapit rooming house when a figure stepped out of the darkness and spoke her name. He had been wandering the streets looking for her. He was sober, miserably hangdog, but sober. She had never seen anything so pathetic in her life. Never before had he seemed so young, and it occurred to her that she had had a far better time of her infidelity than he had had of his, which made her generous, though not so generous as to tolerate anything resembling interrogation. He would have to use his imagination.

– Do you want to walk on the beach? he said.

She'd tried to be distant, to affect a kind of condescending detachment, feeling herself still the wronged party. She'd asked herself: does it matter, sex? Or is it utterly inconsequential? Sex doesn't matter, she thought, but the effects of it do. She allowed herself to savour her recent encounter, and smiled a private smile – and dear god, I thought, there can't have been a lot *left* to Jack's imagination! But she couldn't keep it up. He moved her, she said, this wretched boy struggling by her side. She turned to him and there by the seashore they clung to each other like the lost souls they were. Then they kicked through the surf with their shoes in their hands. He had prepared a new speech, one from the heart, the real thing. He would never do it again, he said, he truly meant it, and it was clear to her that nobody had ever dealt him so bald a retort as she had, and that it had stung him to the core. He was badly frightened of losing her, and he would never again take her for granted.

All this she heard as they trod the damp sand, car horns and music drifting faintly across the beach, and Jack working hard, rousing as much moral purpose as she believed he had in him. But she didn't care about moral purpose, she was just so relieved that this dreadful day was over and they were once more at peace.

I asked her if she thought he'd really meant what he said, that he would never again be unfaithful to her. She shrugged. She said she supposed he might have meant it. She had given it no thought, nor did she then, I mean the night she told me about it at the kitchen table. And I thought: you may shrug, Vera Savage, but to keep such a promise when your partner is as rampantly unfaithful as you have been, what kind of morality is that? A superior kind of morality, no? And that's why I believe Jack told me the truth when I asked about his sex life in Port Mungo. I believe he had resolved not to ape Vera in her promiscuity, and I believe he held to that resolution.

Their money came through the next day. They had slept well, orphan children clinging together in the night, and in the morning they were pathetically grateful to find themselves in the same bed. The arrival of the money was like a shaft of grace.

Two days later they moved into a small hotel in Havana. As they walked the streets in their new lightweight tropical clothes America had seemed a bad dream, a long night of excess in New York followed by a diabolical Florida hangover. But they had got away, they were together, they had a plan. Their hearts were light as they strolled arm-in-arm through the old town, Vera with a large cigar between her teeth, greeting the old men, the children, the prostitutes in her dreadful Spanish, and Jack thinking about studios, already searching.

He never once spoke to me about his infidelity in Miami Beach, though I hinted at my knowledge of it often enough. He was, I think, in a way, a sort of monk.

It became one of the few welcome features of the days I spent in Port Mungo, the conversations Jack and I had each evening when the sun went down, as did the level of rum in the succession of bottles without labels he produced from the kitchen cupboard. It was the beginning of the hurricane season, and by my third day the air had become oppressively sultry and charged with electricity. I yearned for a storm to relieve the tensions in the atmosphere. There were mountains to the north, south and west of us, and at night the lightning flared and flickered against these distant great barriers. The air grew unbearably hot, and I would feel the perspiration break out constantly on my forehead and beneath my shirt. Later the storm moved in across the gulf and the sky was lit by sudden wide sheets of lightning which threw up in stark relief angry black fists and knuckles of stormcloud, and bright jagged flashes which hissed into the sea. The trees across the river flapped about in the rising wind, their broad leaves languidly enfolding one another, and then the blessed rain came.

I was curious about Vera's pregnancy, and asked Jack how she had responded to the prospect of motherhood. Had she been happy she was expecting a child? A flare of amusement from my brother. He would not belabour me with a detailed account of it, he said, except to say that waddling, emburdened, in a tropical climate would try the fortitude of any woman; and he did not need to add, never mind a woman like Vera. He told me they moved the big teak bed into her studio, and when the time came Peg was born amid a clutter of brushes and pots and jars of turps, and one of the infant's very first sights was an unfinished canvas whose theme was fertility. Painful, cumbersome, messy fertility.

The local doctor was an Englishman called Johnny Hague. Lying on her back with her shirt unbuttoned, and that man's cool fingers delicately probing the bulge of her belly, this was one of the few pleasant memories, Jack said, that Vera claimed to have had of that time. I caught something in his tone. He was sitting forward, his elbows on his knees and his head sunk forward, staring at the deck so I couldn't see his features. Then up came his face in the lamplight, and with it a most baleful expression, as he gazed straight at me, his mouth working with resentment and distaste.

I understood what he was telling me.

Silence here.

Apparently she lost interest in motherhood rather quickly. Jack had anticipated that a child would draw them closer together, but within a few months she was up to her old tricks again.

What old tricks?

She'd developed a habit of wandering onto the docks in the early morning, and if there was a boat going down the coast she'd be away all day and come home drunk as a lord. Before Peg was born he had been making progress, he told me. The drinking was less grandiose in scale than once it had been, less apocalyptic in its effects, and she had even begun to voice a guarded enthusiasm for the relative moderation he was impos-ing on their lives. But after Peg was born all at once she saw him as a man tethered to an infant, and less able to oversee her activities. This provoked a bitter laugh as he talked about it, but it was not comic then, there was nothing comic about it at all. The first time he appeared in the doorway of a waterfront bar with Peg asleep in his arms – by god was she surprised! She was drinking beer with men from off the boats, and being dragged out of the bar, this cost her dear for the assumption that he could not handle Peg and her both. For she did leave the bar, she knew better than to defy him, and after a short explosive row she sank for several days into a black sulk.

But she went back to work, she stayed in her studio, until one night at supper, in the early gloom, by the light of the kerosene lamps, he put a bottle of rum on the table and suggested they celebrate.

– Celebrate what? she said, for she was still sulking, despite the fact that at the sight of a bottle of rum and Jack being friendly her heart would have lifted in her breast.

– God and all his works.

– Oh fuck off, Jack. Why can't you let me be?

– I do let you be! Have a drink and don't make trouble.

So she had a drink, and when she drank with him now she drank like a normal person, she knew he would not tolerate the gulping of drinks. Then she talked about what she was doing in her studio, and at last he began to see the real Vera, the painter, that is, not the drunk. Her hair was stiff with salt from swimming in the sea, and she hadn't brushed it for a week, this in protest at being hauled out of the bar, and the front of her shirt was smeared with paint. But filthy though she was, she looked like an artist, whereas after a few nights in the bars she just looked like a slut, despicable.

Down to her studio they went and she stamped about in front of various canvases and spoke in a quick passionate flood about what it was she thought she was doing. When she faltered he came in with his questions and soon had her plunging forward again, and all the while he saw that she was *working*, rather than losing herself in alcohol, and knew he could take the credit for that.

But as time passed his influence steadily weakened. She grew more and more restless, and then one day she announced that if she didn't get out of Port Mungo she'd go stark mad. Jack was certainly unsympathetic to the spirit in which this ultimatum was delivered – hostile, defiant – and he responded with anger. The ensuing row only confirmed her in her determination to get away, and they parted unhappily. She'd spoken vaguely about 'having a look at Mexico' though he strongly suspected she wanted to get back to Havana and see if she could have as much fun under Fidel as she'd had before the revolution.

– How old was Peg?

– About two.

– Was she fond of her?

– She resented all the attention she got.

Silence as we pondered this. Various flashes out on the

horizon, a distant boom of thunder. We were still on the deck with our rum. Something bit my ankle and absently I slapped at it.

– Does she have no maternal feelings *at all*?

Again he sat forward and pushed his hand through his hair, frowning, groaning slightly, I presume because the question aroused such bitter emotion. He looked at me, he looked away, he muttered something under his breath. All this theatre. At last he spoke.

– None.

– Oh Jack.

I leaned across and took his hand. He gripped my fingers hard for a few seconds. Then he said he believed he could have held her had she not been unfaithful to him. She was not at root a promiscuous woman, he said, rather her sexuality was stitched into her emotional dependence on the man taking care of her. But her affair with Johnny Hague created a disturbance which seriously damaged the connective tissue between them. She realized, unconsciously, he believed, that by destroying their sexual bond she could destroy his power over her.

He sat there in the darkness after telling me all this and busied himself with the lighting of a cigar.

– Your power over her, I said.

– Christ, Gin, somebody has to control her!

6

Jack's revelations shocked me but they did not surprise me, I suppose because I had made my mind up about Vera in London, and my antagonism towards her, which I deluded myself into thinking was based on a cool assessment of her character, was in fact shot through with the resentment of a rival: she had taken the man I loved. Absurd and irrational, of course – I was Jack's sister. What we had was not a romance, though it was a relationship of a profound and intensely intimate nature, and I did not recover quickly. My own move from London to New York a year after my father's death was partly an attempt to draw closer to him, and I must acknowledge the pleasure it gave me at the time to think that I had been right about Vera – that she was no good. She was a bad mother, a faithless lover, a drunkard, a spendthrift, a drifter. I am not proud of this, but it did at least allow me to empathize with Jack in his constant worrying at what had gone wrong, why things had turned out as badly as they had. She grew increasingly restless, he said, and the time came when she was more often absent than present.

– But why?

He said he supposed she never felt she had a duty to stay at home. To stay at home when she wanted to be off, that would have seemed to Vera a kind of death, he said, a strangling of some vital impulse, and this was all tangled up with her idea of herself as an artist, which was the only part of herself that mattered to her. Mother, lover, teacher, muse – she cared nothing about her performance in any of these roles, none of it had anything to do with what she thought was the point of her. Anyone could be a good wife or mother, this was her argument, but nobody could be the artist she was, nobody could make the paintings she had it in her to make. Therefore anything was justified if it served the work, and if that meant setting off at two days' notice to tramp across Chiapas it would serve the work, then the hardship suffered by those she left behind was of no real consequence.

– Does she love you?

Eyes down, shake of the head. Knotted silence.

– God alone knows, Gin. After her fashion.

– So what happens when she comes back from one of these trips?

We were out on the deck, it was late in the evening, we were watching the Mungo. Lightning flickered in the distant mountains of Guate. All at once Jack became animated. His line was – not so fast, lady! He had no time for any of her barroom philosophy, if she wanted back in his house she must earn it. First would come the row. She shouted and sulked, she refused to admit she had done anything wrong, she insisted she had never promised to be other than she was, she tried the sanctity-of-the-artist line, but it did her no good at all, she knew in the end that the only thing that would suffice was a sustained, sincere apology, and until she some-how found her way to the place inside herself where sus-tained sincere remorse could be awoken then her life would be hell, Jack would make it so.

So they would hole up in Pelican Road and after a day or two she was forced to acknowledge what Jack had suffered by her absence. He did not rest. He said he scraped away at her denial like a sheet of industrial sandpaper. There was little sleep for either of them, there was much shouting, there was even – rich one, this! – the throwing of plates. She would threaten to go off again and never come back and he told her to go ahead, did she think she was the only woman he could *procure* if he wanted one? What was the point of a woman anyway? Someone to drink with, someone to take to bed, otherwise a distraction from the work.

This sort of argument Vera could understand, of course. They shouted their existential slogans back and forth, they trumpeted their manifestoes of artistic self-sufficiency, but in truth it was all bravado, though Jack knew it better than she did. And she was the one who'd come back. She needed him. And if, once, he had missed her badly when she went off, he had learned how to live alone, he had had to –

When he said this I lifted a sceptical eyebrow. Far from learning to live without her, he was plunged into such distress by this latest absence that he had been forced to send for me. Even his tone of voice belied what he was saying, for it was with a smile on his face, and a kind of fond nostalgia in his tone that he spoke of her homecomings, as though he actually took pleasure in these ghastly fights. I assumed this meant he was always glad to see her again, which was incomprehensible to me. What possible justification could there be for loving a woman who behaved like this?

After the row, the sex. Stripped raw by two sleepless nights of ego-battering insults hurled back and forth across a battle-field of broken crockery and beer bottles, apparently they fell upon each other with ravenous appetite. I believe she crawled all over him like a frog on a branch, Jack hinted as much, and several drawings pinned to the wall of his studio suggested that this was how they went about it. A day or two in bed, and then, still smarting from their wounds, they were more or less back to normal. It was during those hours that she'd tell him where she'd been, and out would come the dusty sketchbooks, the tequila-stained notebooks, the photographs, the maps, the stories. He said these were happy hours. He may have hated her abandoning him, but he seized eagerly on the records she brought back of her adventures. Then he would show her the work he'd made while she was away, and how he liked to hear her talk about his painting! I watched his face grow soft at the thought of it.

– What then?

Then she'd remember Peg, and off she'd go to find her daughter, shambling, barefoot, rootless woman, her hair spilling out of her headscarf, and looking in her canvas trousers and bleached shirt like nothing so much as a sailor fresh off a pirate ship, lacking only a parrot for her shoulder and a hoop ring in her ear. A silly fond smile on my brother's face as he told me this. Off she'd go across the white sand with a bottle of beer hanging from her fist, and despite everything, he said, he loved her.

I let this pass without comment.

So Jack raised Peg almost entirely by himself. He was at the same time pursuing his work with a ferocious discipline, and a pattern emerged, him pouring more and more of himself into his painting – her coming and going, and doing less painting with each passing year – and Peg growing up a careless free spirit: running wild.

I have vivid memories of Pelican Road. I was of course very curious to know Peg, having heard so much about her in Jack's letters. When I was down there she was a shy girl of eight with the long limbs and narrow pointed features of a true Rathbone, and already quite a character. My first evening, after I'd had a wash and then warily settled myself in an old cane chair on the deck over the river, she hung back in the doorway, peering at me, shifting her weight from foot to foot and frowning.

– You're very white, she said at last.

I detected the faintest trace of an English accent, but it was almost totally submerged in the lilt of the patois. She seemed to decide I was harmless, and approached me. Gingerly she touched my hair.

– Aunt Gin?

– Yes, Peg.

By this point the child had quite overcome her shyness and got herself half-seated in my lap, and was picking at my earrings with her long, brown, dirty fingers. I worried there were lice in her hair.

– You want to go out on the water?

She pronounced 'water' like 'matter'.

Jack appeared on the deck with a bottle of black liquor, the local rum.

– Darling child, Gin does not want to go out on the water, in fact I don't think I want you going out on the water.

He turned to me and said they'd recently lost a child to a crocodile. Peg grew excited at this and with her strong dirty fingers she forcibly turned my face away from her father and towards herself and told me about the boy being seized by the croc *right near this house, man*! Her face was inches from mine, her eyes wide.

– That boy, she whispered, he one bloody mess.

– Peg, why don't you bugger off now, said Jack.

– OK, Jack, she said, in a weary tone she must have learned from her mother. I'm going to bugger off now. Later, Aunt Gin.

– Later, Peg.

Then, quite deliberately, watching me as she did it, she took a cigarette from her father's pack, lit it, and let it hang from the corner of her mouth as she exhaled smoke through her nose. Jack appeared not to notice. She left the deck backwards, still with the cigarette hanging from her lips, holding my eye and making peculiar wriggling gestures at me with the fingers of both hands. Once in the gloom of the house, with a shout she darted off, and we heard her bare feet pattering down the stairs.

– Remarkable child, I said.

– I worry about her in that boat.

We gazed out at the sluggish river, which gleamed in places

77

in the last of the sunlight, and probably harboured hungry crocs at that very moment. I rather enjoyed watching my brother being a father. He seemed good at it, rather like our own father: affectionate, distracted, indifferent to petty matters like smoking, watchful in a vague sort of a way, and Peg, I thought, seemed to require no more than that. Later that same night, undressing for sleep in my shed of a bedroom at the back of Vera's studio, I suddenly became aware of a figure standing in the doorway. An oil lamp gives out only the weakest illumination, and I was startled to see a motionless figure where a second before there had been none. I gave a little scream. It was her of course.

– Peg! What are you doing there?

– I want to see your white skin.

I was astonished.

– Well, I'm sorry, my dear, but I'm rather modest in that department.

– Can't I watch? Jack doesn't mind.

– I'm afraid not.

– OK. Later, Aunt Gin.

– Later, Peg.

She melted into the darkness. Jack doesn't mind what? It was another world down here, and I had no idea how they lived. I decided to jump to no conclusions about any of it.

The next day Jack took me down to his studio. I remember it vividly. All his work was there and much else besides, all the junk he'd accumulated, plus the work of local painters and others passing through who'd heard of Jack Rathbone's studio in Port Mungo and come to visit. It was a vast cavernous space with wooden walls and lofty rafters and huge doors giving onto the dock through which flooded light reflected off the river, with a wooden scaffold on wheels for getting at the high parts of large canvases. Amid the quantities of stuff in there I remember the jaws of a shark mounted on a beam, and the figurehead of an old sailing ship, the wooden head and torso of a goddess with red hair. In those days it was a social place, Jack's studio. Local people moored their boats at his dock and squatted in the sunlight, smoking and murmuring to one another as they watched him work. Children scrambled up onto the dock, and clustered dripping wet and grinning in the doorway. Others came by with objects for the artist, in the hope of earning a few cents. Men he drank with dropped in, and occasionally some grizzled native of the town would approach the canvas, peer at it closely and murmur a word or two about the colour of the sea, or the plumage of a tropical firebird flying over a volcano, or the figure of a lost girl rooted in the trunk of a ceiba tree –

He introduced to me various characters sitting on his dock and then took me to the back of the studio and hauled out the work he'd been making. Dear god they were strange things! Untreated jute or sacking stretched on knotty sticks, the dimensions uneven and the paint itself having a kind of fatty texture, heaped up thickly on the rough surface and the imagery a raw, passionate, chaotic, primitive response to the world he lived in. Some of them were six feet on a side, and the colours, the greens and blues, the orangey reds, the greenish yellows, had a harsh and acid tone, and all the same weight, somehow, so little air seemed to get through. Perhaps it was my own immediate ambivalence towards Jack's world which shaped my reaction – the jungle, I mean, the sun, the river, the shacks, the sea, the flies, the trees – the *light* – but growing conscious of these stirrings of bewilderment I knew enough to say that it was strong stuff, although in truth I was profoundly unsure. Later, of course, what had seemed like so much bluster I came to regard as heroic, the sheer scope and ambition of what he did down there.

Years later, when he came back to New York, Jack continued to work out the imagery he first developed in Pelican Road. He told me he would never have worked with such, oh – *grandiosity* – had he not lived in Port Mungo. He found there a reflection of himself, he said, and the meaning of his life as an artist was the effort to translate that identification directly onto canvas. I thought of his repeated motifs, the rain forests and rivers, the serpents, the birds, the gleaming mythic bodies, and much as I came to admire that work I never properly understood how he saw himself in those paintings.

It was after Vera had returned from yet another of her boozy journeys – and this I did not learn about until much later, because it didn't happen until three years after my visit – that during one of their passionate reunions Peg's little sister Anna was conceived. So I missed the spectacle of Vera Savage, a woman sorely lacking in maternal instinct, and well into her forties, giving birth to her second child. Jack had no expectation that her behaviour would be any different than it was before, nor was it. Once again he took responsibility for the infant girl when Vera, after a few short weeks of half-hearted mothering, became bored with little Anna and began to treat her with what she called 'benign neglect'. Jack recognized this as the same wilful disregard to which Peg had been subjected, but this time he made no argument about it and simply took over. He employed the same wet nurse who had breastfed Peg, a large calm woman called Dolores, and for the first fifteen months Anna lived in her house, along with Dolores's seven children. During those months it was Peg who spent hours every day with the infant, and could often be seen wheeling her little sister down to the waterfront in a barrow to show her off to the fishermen. Jack told me all this without any rancour. He said it was not Vera's fault she had no interest in mothering. Fortunate thing, he said, that he could cope. And Dolores was a treasure.

A curious figure he cuts, then, my brother, this fiercely driven artist, this latter-day Gauguin, stimulated by the wealth of form and colour in the natural world down there, also by its fecundity, its exuberance, its violence – yet at the same time displaying a maternal solicitude towards his two daughters while their mother was off doing whatever she liked, mostly, it appeared, drinking and chasing men. And it later occurred to me that it was perhaps because of this sustained immersion in nature and mothering that he was losing the civilized reflexes. And he *was* losing them, of this I had no doubt at all, and I can remember various occasions when this fact was vividly brought home to me. Once, towards the end of my stay, we were sitting out on the deck at sunset, having the first drink of the day, when we heard from inside the house a series of groans and a slow uneven tread on the stairs. We turned towards the door. It was Peg, and she was in pain: always barefoot, she had trod on a thorn of some kind and could put no weight on her left foot. In she hopped and Jack briskly told her to sit on the deck in front of his chair and had her lift her leg. He leaned forward to examine the sole.

– This it? he said, prodding the ball of her foot, and Peg let out a scream.

– Oh don't be such a baby.

He then seized her slim brown ankle, and, with his other hand gripping the foot tight, applied his mouth to the sore place and began to suck. That foot was filthy! – she'd been all over town, god alone knows what she'd stepped in. I offered to go fetch the disinfectant but he said it wasn't necessary. He sucked lustily at the dirty foot, sucked and spat, and every few seconds he lifted his eyes and grinned at her. Peg grinned back as she wriggled about on the deck on her bottom. After a minute or two he sat back, picked at her foot with a fingernail, then extracted the thorn with his teeth. He held it up for us to see, then tossed it over the railing and wiped his hands on his paint-smeared trousers.

– All right now?

– Thank you, Jack, said Peg.

But before she limped off he had her stand with her back to the railing and urinated on her foot! To disinfect it, he said.

Then he sat down again, grinning at me, as he pushed himself back into his trousers.

He enjoyed my snort of disapproval, and I was on the point of telling him what a primitive he was becoming when there came a scream from the staircase.

– What is it now? he shouted, turning towards the house.

– Mummy's home!

Port Mungo boasted one grand establishment, a sagging relic of the town's former glory which despite its flaking paintwork and spreading mildew – its cellars were flooded on a yearly basis – did maintain certain of the old amenities, in particular the large rooms on the upper floor which got the breezes off the sea. For this reason the Hotel Macaw was favoured by those of the townspeople who at mid-morning or twilight liked to take their rum in the relative comfort of large rattan chairs, beneath ancient ceiling fans, in the spectral presence of dead banana moguls who drifted along the verandahs with the proud ghosts of exotic Creole women on their arms.

Jack and Vera took me there the evening she turned up at Pelican Road after an absence of several months. When Jack had heard Peg's shout he was out of his chair and down the stairs in a second, himself shouting as he went. I waited on the deck, not wanting to intrude. A minute later Peg appeared at the top of the stairs.

– Mummy says why don't you come down and say hello, you rude cow.

So down I went. There she was, sitting cross-legged in the middle of her studio among bags and baskets, rummaging about in a battered rucksack. There was a young black guy in cut-off jeans bouncing on his haunches near by, rolling a spliff, and Jack stood at the table pouring rum into tumblers. He turned with a smile as I came into the studio.

– Here she is! cried Vera, and rose from the floor. She stood before me grinning broadly, her arms wide, and there was the empty slot between her teeth: same old Vera, only more so, this was my first impression. Into her forties now and it showed, for the ravages of weather and drink were evident, but somehow, at the same time, she glowed. There was more than a little of the hippy earth mother about her – the brightly coloured headscarf, the flowing cotton garments – but more, I think, of the gypsy queen, for her skin was tanned a deep brown now, and there was much silver on her person. She took me in her arms. Her physical presence was overpowering, and I found myself hugging her close and enjoying the smells that came off her, patchouli oil, marijuana, citrus, I don't know what else. I didn't want to let her go. When we broke apart she gazed into my face with glistening eyes and told me it was a beautiful thing I had done, coming all the way down from New York to see my brother.

– And me! shouted Peg.

– And my Peg, said Vera, holding my hands and squeezing them tight. Then she turned away, abruptly dropping my hands.

– Where's the *rum*, Jack? she shouted.

It was not a typical homecoming, I believe, for the simple reason that I was there. I saw none of the resentment, none of the animosity which according to Jack usually accompanied these reunions. It was all very warm and cheerful, my brother resembling not so much the stern paterfamilias as a fond old hen with a lost chick back under the wing. Soon we were all upstairs on the deck, including the young black guy, and quite who he was I couldn't figure out. Peg was sitting on her father's lap and gazing intently at Vera as Jack asked questions about her trip, and as she told her stories I began to form a very different picture from the one Jack had given me. Instead of the restless irresponsible creature he had described I saw a woman with a genuine curiosity about the world beyond this obscure little river town, and it was an artist's curiosity, for it was as an artist that she spoke about what she'd seen. And I glimpsed too her courage in setting out into that world – no simple thing for a woman alone, not in Central America – so as to know it better. I am no sort of an explorer, nor even a good traveller, I am a woman who likes to sit in a room in a city – preferably New York City – with a book in my hand, and travel in my own imagination. So what Vera did, what she had been doing for years, was impressive to me.

And what of Jack? He had come to life with Vera's return, he animated for the first time since I stepped off the ferry, and all at once I was struck by the thought that for all his dedication and self-sacrifice and seriousness, and oh, the ponderous nobility of his artistic endeavour – every day of the past week he had been in his studio from dawn to dusk. He appeared briefly only at lunchtime, with paint on his hands, and nothing to say beyond a grunt or two, and it took a couple of large rums at sunset to tease a human response from him. Imagine that every day, for months on end, for *years* on end – and all at once I understood why Vera wandered, and with that realization my moral understanding of the household tipped on its head and I saw Jack's formidable discipline as a kind of silent brooding ingrown negative energy which must have sapped the vitality of a woman like Vera and driven her wild with frustration. No wonder they fought! No wonder she left home for months on end, and took lovers, how else could she live with my brother, whose single conversation in life – and this I had already seen for myself – was with himself? One of the paintings he had shown me was called *Narcissus in the Jungle*. I now understood what it was about. It was a self-portrait.

Vera soon got restless in the house and wanted to go out. She wanted to go to the Macaw, so after supper the three of us set off into town. Close to the dock we turned onto a street of large wooden houses which with their columned porticoes and broad staircases must once have resembled the plantation mansions of the American South. Each of these buildings, peeling and sagging now, sheltered numerous families. Washing lines and hammocks were slung across verandahs where rich men had sat smoking large cigars and pondering, presumably, the price of bananas. Near the end of the street, set back from the seawall, the lamps of the hotel spilled out on to the water. We climbed its wide stairs to a pair of double doors folded back against the wall. We stepped into the hallway, aware of voices in the bar to our left, and the desultory tinkling of a piano.

Our appearance roused the company. Stout men struggled up from the depths of wicker couches and rattan armchairs and waved cigars in our direction. Desiccated women fluttered their fans. There were bluff cries of welcome as we made our way across the room to the bar: this was the bourgeois element of Port Mungo, and it had seen better days. And here was Ector, the bartender, in a short white jacket, idly turning the pages of a month-old newspaper. He looked up and put away his paper.

– Hello, boss.

I was introduced to Ector. He was a short swarthy man with a moustache shaved thin as a hair. His smile revealed several gold teeth. Jack ordered rum as Vera moved to the other end of the bar, where a big man with a head of thinning red hair sat staring at a chessboard. The two warmly embraced, and then the man turned towards me and half rose off his barstool.

– Gin, darling, Vera said in her hoarse workingman's accent, this is my friend Johnny Hague.

– Good evening, he said.

I turned towards Jack, curious how he would respond to Vera's former lover. They nodded at each other with cool inscrutability. He had a languid upper-class slur, this Johnny Hague, and he not so much sat on his barstool as draped himself over it, long legs in baggy white flannels crossed at the knee. Vera was leaning against him, her hands on his shoulder, beaming at him, until her drink appeared. We made polite conversation. It was an ugly face, big chin, large teeth, high forehead, and the pale red hair combed back in wisps. He told me he ran the hospital. He treated mostly fever cases and machete wounds. Out of loyalty to Jack, I tried to display indifference to the man but he appeared not to notice. He was rather amusing on the subject of machete wounds, he certainly made Vera laugh. He said he lived here in the Macaw, up on the top floor. Handy for the bar, he said, and I said I supposed it must be. He then told me he knew my brother. I didn't understand.

– Jack, you mean, I said.

– No, Gerald. We did pre-med at King's together. King's College Hospital, Peckham. Still write to him every year or so.

Jack had not told me about this family connection.

Extraordinary thing, I said.

He asked if I had any news of him, and I told him what few details I had of Gerald's life. I was more animated than I'd intended to be. Vera had flung an arm round the man's neck and everybody seemed to find this all quite normal.

Jack meanwhile had moved out on to the verandah and was smoking a cigar. So I joined him, and wordlessly we gazed out to sea. I was about to mention this bizarre coincidence, the local medic being an old friend of Gerald's, then thought better of it and talked about Peg instead. Having seen them together for the first time, I said, I saw a lot of her mother in her, and Jack roused himself, and with small snorts of laughter told me how she came in for her supper at dusk every evening, and on being asked what she'd been doing all day would either reply, nothing, or untap a flood of stories so jumbled that little sense could be made of it, until she collapsed fast asleep at the table or had her attention seized by something out in the yard or on the river and lost all interest in her story, all of which he said was pure Vera. He then fell silent and glanced back into the room, where she and Johnny seemed still to be having a fine time at the bar. Suddenly I felt terribly sorry for him. On an impulse I suggested he and Peg come to New York. Come stay with me for a week or two, I said. See some art, take her to a few concerts. Give her an idea what the city's like.

– My dear Gin.

He turned from the rail of the verandah and gazed at me. In the darkness I saw his eyes shining with unshed tears. Abruptly he went into the bar, trailing his fingers across my shoulder. I hadn't realized quite how low he was, so low that a simple act of kindness, sister to brother, could affect him profoundly.

7

M any years later, when Jack was living with me in New York, he told me that he had always been a jealous man. Ironic, this, he said, producing a dry strained cough of mirth, that the lover of Vera Savage should be afflicted with sexual jealousy. I agreed. I said that to have embarked on the journey those two took, burdened with feelings of suspicion and possessiveness – surely a recipe for disaster? Jack thought so. But earlier in his life he'd thought that those feelings would pass, or rather that experience would burn them out of him, leave him tempered as though by fierce heat – but no. It became no easier. And he'd realized from observing others that jealousy died only when love died. A jealous man was no longer jealous when he no longer cared. Another irony – he couldn't not care. He couldn't not love the woman, it was beyond him, and god knows he tried. Her boozy way of living drew men to her, he said, of course it did, and while she was tough, and could look after herself better than most, a few got through. The clever ones, the good talkers – certain sorts of men had always interested Vera, he said, writers usually, articulate characters who could put an idea in flight and carry the imagination of a painter with it. Painters love ideas, said Jack, they will give their heart without a qualm to a man who can get an idea airborne and then move it around like a kite in the wind.

He said he learned not to ask too much about her trips away

from Port Mungo. Too painful, he said. Enough that she came back, even if it took her a year to do it, which it did once. Hearing this, I was astonished yet again at the sheer resilience of the feelings my brother seemed to harbour for Vera, and continued to harbour until the day he died. That his heart had not grown hard, as it would have in the breast of any other man: how was it that he had the capacity to go on loving her despite the emotional battery she'd inflicted on him? I don't know; but I do know that a love as robust as that is more than enough to keep a man alive, which is why the medical examiner's report was so distressing to me.

But this love of theirs: somehow the relationship accommodated their very different ways of living, somewhere it found the supple strength to allow love to flourish between these two unlikely figures, one of them a kind of monk, the other a buccaneer. Much of the burden fell on him, of course, as he was the one who was abandoned whenever Vera chose to wander off, but this he could cope with. But when she took up with Johnny Hague, he said, he was cut as never before. He felt that she could at least have behaved with restraint while she was in Port Mungo, and he said it with a flare of indignation which seemed to issue directly from the fiery mass of anger ignited in him when the affair began. What sort of affair was it? The sort, I suppose, that predictably occurs among white people living in hot places with time on their hands and a fondness for liquor. I had sized the fellow up, briefly, in the bar of the Hotel Macaw, and while he was a rough, red, ugly brute of a man I had glimpsed a vitality that might well have attracted Vera. Also, there was the fact that he was an educated man, and that his conversation offered a welcome change from my brother's endless deliberations on paint and its ways. For I had realized after a very few days in Port Mungo that the great problem of the tropics was boredom, and that Jack, perhaps, with his single-minded dedication to his work, alone had solved it. But for others – like Vera, like Johnny Hague – work had long since lost its allure. Time was the great problem, debauchery the common solution.

It seems they made only the most perfunctory attempts to keep the thing secret. In such a small town it would have been hard to conceal it even if they had tried to, but Jack said he would have felt better about it had he seen at least a modicum of clandestine effort. But no. Vera left the bar of the Macaw with the doctor at midnight, went upstairs with him to his room at the top of the building, and returned to Pelican Road in the early morning when people were already on the streets or on the river, people who didn't need to guess where she had spent the night, and were not reluctant to talk about it. Jack couldn't have cared less about the gossip but once he understood that he was being laughed at because of Vera's behaviour he confronted her and demanded she put an end to it.

– And what effect did that have?

A shrug. It seems they were less conspicuous after this, but it hardly mattered, the damage was done.

– How old was Peg?

And here all at once we were at the heart of the matter. Peg was an infant when it began, but Peg grew up. And as Jack told me this I understood, although to this day I don't know how, that I had touched the first link in the chain of events whose end was Peg's death. I also realized why Jack had not spoken of it to me before: it tormented him. His sense of loss was still acute. His awareness of the mistakes that had been made in Port Mungo was as fresh as it had been all those years before, when he'd first traced the inexorable movement of cause and effect whose terminus was his daughter's death. And the first cause, Jack seemed to be telling me, was Vera's affair with Johnny Hague. All else flowed from that. If she had shown some restraint things would not have turned out as they did, and Peg would still be alive. Perhaps.

So Vera had carelessly embarked on an affair with this disenchanted doctor, this Englishman in exile with his Cambridge drawl and his lazy irony, and also – Jack became convinced – a drug habit that was a distinct liability when it came to the making of medical decisions. Not that Johnny had so many decisions to make. Those of the local people who had any truck with western medicine presented him with few real problems. Fever, infection, machete wounds – as Johnny had said at the bar of the Hotel Macaw, the doctoring in Port Mungo wouldn't tax a drunken intern. What did he see in Vera? Probably what any man would – good talk, an appetite for life lived as perpetual celebration, a promise of reckless sex – and for a jaded cynic like Johnny Hague this was irresistible. His pursuit of her was not exhausting, nor did it need to be. She was amenable, in her amused, detached way, and he was soon deep in thrall.

Jack sneered when he told me this. He had seen it before, men in thrall to Vera. Men often fell in love with Vera, he said, she was the sort of woman who provoked it, hadn't he done it himself? But what he had then done was to live with the consequences, and after the first flush of intoxication had subsided he had not wandered away, no, he had understood his fate, or his work, rather, as consisting of being the man who *held on*, and this he had done as best he could – attempted, that is, to be a husband to Vera, inasmuch as such an idea was not absurd. He had learned the work as he went along, and he supposed that on balance there had been as much joy in the thing as there had been pain – does anybody do much better than that?

Not a thing I had ever really given much thought to. I said probably not.

It hardly mattered now. The point was, this was his decision, and he remembered the circumstances of its making, the night in New York when he had fled the bar and walked the alien streets and sat on a bench in the Battery till dawn, and decided that he would stand by this woman regardless, not because she necessarily wanted him to but because she *needed* him to, whether she knew it or not, for if he didn't do it perhaps nobody would, and then she would go under.

Thus my brother's thinking that distant night in New York, or his reconstruction, rather, of that thinking, which resulted, he claimed, in his extraordinary loyalty down the years: him the man who held on.

All of which gave him ample time and opportunity to watch other men fall in love with Vera, also ample moral authority, earned through suffering, with which to sneer at them. Johnny Hague had once been a confused, idealistic young physician unwilling to assume the position his family expected of him. He had not wanted a comfortable professional life in England, he had wanted to practise medicine in a place where his work would have value of a different order altogether. But the years in Port Mungo had kicked the idealism out of him, and they had also exploited his weakness by corrupting him, by wearing down his resistance to the idea of using the drugs in his dispensary to treat his own fatigue and disillusion. They worked. They eased the bitterness with which he now regarded the great error of his life, and allowed a kind of perverse romanticism to burn fitfully in a mind only truly alive in the nocturnal glow of morphine intoxication. This, then, the limping anti-hero of the Hotel Macaw, who had delivered Vera's child and ten weeks later taken her up to his room at the top of the hotel and persuaded her to betray Jack then and there.

Jack was in the bar when she came down. He told me this in such a bleak tone that I could not ask him, although I dearly wanted to – what was it like? That meeting of the eyes, the blaze of knowledge between them, as she stepped into the bar from the staircase and saw him there, and him knowing she had just come from Johnny's room, that minutes earlier – what, five? ten at the most? – minutes earlier she had been copulating – what, bent over the bed with her skirt rucked up, grinning over her shoulder at him, and him thrusting into her from behind? – and now Jack staring at her as she entered the bar: what was that *like*, for a jealous man? A most primitive moment, surely, in that no amount of – understanding – could erase the fact of a sin still smouldering in the immediate wake of its heated commission – there in the turgid, trembling air of the hotel bar, and Jack not alone in his knowledge of what room Vera had just come down from.

– What was it like?

– Very bloody horrible indeed.

He didn't elaborate, and I didn't ask him to. I presume they went home together. Did the row begin as they walked down Pelican Road, or after they were indoors? I think it did not begin in the hotel, I think he would have told me if it had. Was Peg awakened by their shouting? Or was there no shouting at all – Jack gone cold as ice, arctic and noble in silent suffering resentment – and Vera a stranger as ever to guilt and remorse and not about to begin apologizing now. But a low point however you construe it, a low point for those two.

– How long did it last?

Years. Off and on. It never really ended, not as long as they all three lived in Port Mungo. Johnny talked of getting out but as far as Jack knew he never did. Unlike Jack he seemed not to know when it was time to leave, and if he did he lacked the courage to do it.

– Off and on?

Off when Vera was away, on when she wasn't – and here another dark bark of mirthless laughter. No, it was more complicated than that, he said. The sex lasted a few years and then petered out. It was pretty much like any other physical affair in those years, when the tensions were exacerbated by Jack's fluctuating levels of tolerance. There were times the three of them coexisted more or less amicably, but at other times the atmosphere was poisoned by Jack's rage at Vera's relentless betrayal, it all depended.

– On what?

– My mood, said Jack. And what, Gin, he said – genuinely amused now – did my mood depend on?

94

– The work?

– The work. Simple as that.

– And what happened, I said, after the physical thing stopped?

A long pause here. Extended sightless gazing at the wall. He told me a friendship existed between them from which Vera was unable to extricate herself, even though he believed she wanted to. She had found something of value in this frail creature, this rather pathetic man trapped in an existence he himself had created on the basis of an error – the error, said Jack, of believing himself adequate to the stern moral challenge of doctoring in an obscure tropical backwater. He wasn't up to Port Mungo. The town was destroying him, eating away his backbone, and his plight aroused in Vera a tenderness that Jack claimed not to understand. Port Mungo was not destroying *him*, he said, and Vera showed him none of the tender solicitude she lavished on that man – this was Jack's complaint, when at last I dug it out of him.

– And was Johnny Hague never uncomfortable about what he was doing to you?

– Oh sure, at the beginning. He showed a lot of bloody discomfort when the thing started. Vera got him over that.

– How?

– She told him lies about me.

– What sort of lies?

It was like getting blood out of a stone, getting him to talk about it.

– That I hit her. And worse.

I was speechless. What could be *worse* than what she'd said? But he wouldn't say more, and it troubled me, for I could not imagine what this *worse* could possibly be. Still he was protecting her; still, apparently, he loved her.

She tired of the man eventually, and made no secret of it. Jack said she broke the bastard's heart, and he for one was glad. This of course shifted the balance between Johnny and Jack, it made for uneasy encounters in the bar of the Macaw; uneasy, that is, as far as the men were concerned. Vera acted blithely unaware, greeting Johnny with the kind of warmth you reserve for an old friend with whom relations have never been other than cordial. As she had the night I was there. Jack was at times made furious by the looks Johnny cast across the room, and threatened to go over and thrash him. Vera laughed immoderately at the idea of Jack as a barroom brawler. Then, when she was away on her travels, he caught glances from the doctor, as though to say – you and me both, brother.

Jack said Johnny had hated him from the moment he had been rejected by Vera, because while once he had been able to crow over Jack's humiliation, Jack was now witness to his. I thought of our brief encounter, and did not remember a man seething with hatred. If anyone was seething with hatred it was Jack. Reflecting on this I felt a twinge of doubt, mentally I stepped back a few paces and tried to get a clearer view of the thing.

None of it would have amounted to much, said Jack, in the normal course of events. Small towns abound in such festering hostilities, and they were members of a prickly community, the band of gringos who'd stayed on after the banana boat pulled out. No, what distinguished this particular state of hostility, he said, and shifted it from a harmless antagonism into something with much greater potential for malicious damage, was the fact that Johnny was a weak man, a dishonest man, a *vindictive* man, his judgement thoroughly distorted by the abuse of drugs.

8

He did bring Peg to New York, and for three weeks they
lived with me here in the house. I will not forget meeting
them at the airport, seeing them emerge into the arrivals hall
among a crowd of travellers, as families surged forward with
cries of joy. I didn't surge, myself. I stood watching them for a
few seconds before I stepped forward. They were certainly a
shabby pair, Peg in patched jeans, a baggy T-shirt, and scuffed
canvas shoes, heaving a battered suitcase I recognized as Jack's
from the old days. She was eleven now, and less a child than she
had been; there was a new kind of aura about her, its source, I
think, an awareness of her own dawning womanhood: the
gangling tomboy of Port Mungo was in the process of changing
into a tall slim swan of a girl with delicate features and a riotous
tangle of jet-black hair. She was distinctive too for her ringing
shouts of laughter, as for example when she saw me coming
forward in the arrivals hall. She had certainly gained in confidence.

Her father was no less remarkable. Gaunt and sunburnt, he
wore a faded cotton shirt, khaki pants and sandals, and Mayan
bracelets on his wrists. He was as brown as his daughter, and his
face and bearing suggested he might be a member of a
missionary sect just returning from the Amazon. But he was
no missionary. Tough and serious he may have been, but there
was no piety there, he was cursing as he dug through his bag for

cigarettes, and in the few moments I watched him, trying to see him with the eyes of a stranger, I found myself suddenly deeply impressed at what he'd become. I felt love, admiration – envy, even – with the recognition that he had held to his commitment and become an artist. Suddenly my own placid existence seemed a safe and cautious thing, altogether lacking in the fervour that burned in this tall frowning man who stood oblivious to everything in the arrivals hall of LaGuardia Airport and fired up an unfiltered, foul-smelling, crumpled Mexican cigarette.

It was May, the weather fine and warm, and we took a cab into the city. Peg had her head out of the window the entire trip. Jack was quiet. He must surely have been thinking about the last time he was in New York, when he and Vera were newly in love, and it could only have saddened him. There were times, he told me later, when he quite simply *ached* for the woman. Where was she now? He didn't know. He'd had a postcard from Mexico City, that was all. The house on West 11th Street is a narrow brownstone on a quiet block, with a steep flight of steps to the front door, and three floors plus an attic. It is a house I love, for it has been my haven and sanctuary, and Jack's as well, eventually. This was the first time he had seen it, and he walked inside with his arm round my shoulder, looking rather apprehensive, Peg struggling behind with the suitcase. What did he see? Sanded floors, a few framed posters, Mexican rugs, large cushions, flowers, ferns, books everywhere, wicker furniture, sunlight, cats. Lingering smell of incense.

– Lot of rugs.

– I love rugs, I said defensively.

He said nothing more, but for the first time I found myself unsure about my rugs. Peg meanwhile had made straight for the fridge and found the ice cream. I showed her the garden at the back of the house, but she wasn't impressed. She wanted to see the river, so I promised her we'd walk down to the Hudson before dinner.

It was a happy visit. We went to the Museum of Natural History, Central Park, the Bronx Zoo, the Empire State Building. Jack had never taken the boat out to Liberty Island, though he certainly had strong associations with the statue, having spent long hours staring at it from a bench in Battery Park. We went to the art museums, and I was aware of the intensity with which he inspected the recent American work. He later spoke dismissively of almost all of it. It was not a good moment for painters, he said. Not propitious. But he was deeply impressed by Rothko's work. Those great gloomy paintings held his attention for many minutes, and so fierce was his concentration that I did not dare speak to him while he stood frowning at them, and took Peg away so he wouldn't be disturbed. Afterwards I tried to discover what he thought of them, but he wouldn't tell me, and it was only much later, after he'd moved back to the city, that one night after a few drinks he said that he'd been humbled by Rothko. I never heard him say that about any other contemporary artist.

One evening during that first visit we were sitting over dinner in a quiet restaurant in the Village. We had emptied four bottles of wine between us. Peg was fast asleep in her chair. I had suggested to Jack that they come live in New York but he said no, that wouldn't happen until the work was right.

– And her? I said, indicating the sleeping girl.

– Why would I want to move her?

– She can't stay down there all her life.

– Why not?

Jack was unconcerned. He thought that if Peg ever wanted to go live in a city she would figure out how to do it for herself. But for now, why disrupt the girl's life? And as for him, when the time came he would know. Another five years, he thought. He knew he had to come back eventually. Wasn't that the point of Port Mungo, to paint in peace until the work came right and then bring it to New York? That had always been the plan.

99

We fell silent, we smoked, we were comfortably drunk. I was startled by the simple clarity of his commitment. Neither his own comfort, nor his child's future, apparently, would change the course he had chosen. Perhaps he was a kind of missionary after all: a priest of art.

A day or two before they were to leave I asked him if he had everything he needed. He thought I meant art supplies. No, I said, had he bought any *clothes*? I smile now when I think of it. He was startled by the question. I think the idea of spending money on clothes had simply not occurred to him. He was a very frugal man, but then he had to be. He had no source of income other than the allowance I gave him, the drip-feed, as he sarcastically called it. Perhaps, I said, we might go up to Bloomingdale's? Brilliant idea, why hadn't he thought of it?

I knew then that my brother was becoming a genuine eccentric. We went to Bloomingdale's and got him some jeans and shirts – he only wanted clothes, he said, that could take the smear of paint. Peg came along and soon disappeared into a changing room with a miniskirt and a few other items and when she emerged Jack and I were astonished: only eleven years old, but she was a mere whisper away from woman-hood. And what an actor she was! Far from feeling shy or uncertain in such unfamiliar garments, she minced up and down in front of us, pouting and preening and swinging her little bottom, and not for the first time I was struck by how much of her mother was in her, the performance was pure Vera.

They visited me again a year later and that was the last time I saw Peg. How sad it was. Her brief moment of grace had vanished. She had become a lanky, sullen adolescent. Things remained unstable at home. Vera was as rootless as ever. Jack had come to accept that she was flawed, irredeemably so, and he no longer held out hope of her amounting to anything as an artist. He had lost her, he said, not so much to alcohol as to a kind of chronic restlessness, an inability to stay in any one place for more than a month or two; she even found it hard to stay in bed all night, and would wake in the small hours and pace about the house, the insomnia eventually provoking the need of a drink and thus compounding the sorry cycle. He said he thought it must be an organic disorder of some kind, but she wouldn't do anything about it.

– I can't kick her out, he said, it would break Peg's heart. She worships her. She wants to be just like her. I'm the villain now.

I saw this during the time they were with me. It was not a successful visit. The tension between father and daughter was palpable from the moment I met them at the airport. Since I'd last seen him Jack had decided that he must soon move back to New York or he would sink into a kind of terminal stagnation, and all the work he had done would count for nothing. At the time it did not occur to me that he was frightened of New York, but of course why wouldn't he be? He had more than enough imagination to realize that for a painter like himself, already in his thirties, to gain a toehold in this most competitive of art worlds would not be simple. But the idea that he might have become fearful, working in the obscurity of Port Mungo – and obscurity brings safety in its train, and breeds rigidity – this I didn't consider, I suppose because I had never imagined him afraid of anything. I wonder now whether Rothko was the inciting agent.

Peg's feelings on the face of it were less complicated. She simply didn't want to be here. She was twelve now and had too much going on in Port Mungo to want to accompany her father on this trip. But it seems Jack had insisted, I assumed because he didn't want to leave her unsupervised at home, which I could well understand after seeing how the girl behaved. She got drunk several times, and affected the kind of bravado I recognized as a copy of one of her mother's performances. She was angry, she was rude to both of us, she was uncooperative, sulky, and disobedient. Her moods were erratic. For the ten days they stayed with me I never knew when she came down in the morning if she would be elated or depressed. This I took to be the standard stuff of growing up, and I wondered how Jack coped, given his sustained focus on his work. It could not have been easy, having this volatile adolescent under the same roof.

Then I saw how he coped. Or I should say, I saw an ugly exchange between the two of them which at the time I dismissed as atypical, a response to unusual stress in an unusual situation rather than an instance of how they normally related to each other. We were sitting in a restaurant one evening. Jack had been silent for most of the meal, as had Peg. Each of them was preoccupied, or angry, or both, I didn't know why, nor did I particularly want to find out, I had discovered early in the visit how unrewarding it was to attempt to winkle out the cause of a malaise that one or other of them might happen to be entertaining at any given moment. It never cleared the air, the reverse if anything, and they didn't thank you for trying. So we'd eaten in silence, and drunk several bottles of wine, though without this having any perceptible effect on anyone's mood. When the main course was cleared away Peg abruptly rose to her feet. Jack seized her wrist.

– Where are you going?
– Uptown.
– I don't think so.

Peg tried to shake free of her father's grip but she could not.

– Let go of me, Daddy, you're hurting me.

Still Jack held tight to the girl's wrist, with an expression I had never seen in him before: face set hard, like bronze, jaw clamped tight and eyes wide. Peg was a tall girl, lithe and strong, but her father was stronger. Heads had turned in the restaurant.

– Jack, I murmured.
– Shut up, Gin.
– Daddy!

– You're not going anywhere, you're coming back to the house.

– You're hurting me.

Then Peg suddenly stopped squirming and pulling. She was still. She was stiff. She stood silently staring down at her father – the whole restaurant riveted on this drama now – the pair of them like statues. The moral advantage swung decisively in Peg's favour: no longer the unruly child, she was the victim of her father's power. Jack flung the girl's wrist from him with disgust, and turned away.

He uttered a coarse epithet.

Peg stood there a moment longer as her father's ugly word fell into the silence their conflict had created in the room. I could hardly believe what I had just heard. This was Jack, my brother, voicing such bitter contempt for his own daughter! Peg allowed just enough time for the import of what he had said to register on everyone who'd heard him, and then tossed her mane of black hair and strutted out of the restaurant.

– Get the check, Gin, said Jack.

I was on the point of telling him to get it himself, and walking out after the girl, but I did not. It would not have done any good. As I say, I thought this was just an appalling aberration that had come about because he was stressed out and Peg was being difficult. But I thought later: what if it was not unusual? What if their relationship had deteriorated to the point that shabby power struggles like this occurred routinely, with Jack using physical force to subdue the girl, and snarling at her as he had in the restaurant? It occurred to me that I had perhaps glimpsed the reality of their life in Port Mungo, where Vera's constant absences had created a kind of hell in which my brother habitually indulged his anger at his daughter's expense.

The next day she came home with her head a mess of tufts and spikes, having had all her lovely hair cut off by a kid she'd met in Washington Square Park. I was very shocked by it. I saw in this angry gesture towards her father a violent rejection of her femininity, as though she were excising that part of herself that possessed the capacity to love. So much rage in that ugly gesture! – I would almost have said it was an act of injured sexuality, had she been a few years older.

9

I t was not many months after this visit that Anna was born. I
tried to discover whether Vera's pregnancy was having an
effect on Peg at this time, perhaps contributing to her anger
towards the world, and towards her father in particular, but Jack
was not forthcoming, he didn't like to speak about the period
between Anna's birth and Peg's death. But I have always thought
how desperately sad it must have been for him, that he should
have lost his daughter before they had come through this
difficult phase of her growing up, and how predictable, in a
way, that he should feel responsible for her death, as though the
anger he'd felt towards her had caused actual harm to befall her.

I worried at it often, over the years, but for a long time it
seemed it was to remain unknowable, what happened in the
mangroves, at least to me – a mystery, although I hate the word.
There are no mysteries, only people who conceal; only *secrets*.
And certainly the immediate circumstances of Peg's death were
a secret, Jack's secret, possibly Vera's, and that was how it would
stay unless one of them chose to divulge it. In the end Jack did
tell me, but for several years, in our times of greatest intimacy –
late at night, in drink, typically – we could talk about anything
but that. He would mention his own stupidity, his own failure to
prevent her death, always in such a way that it roused me to tell
him not to blame himself, he wouldn't have let it happen if he
could possibly have prevented it. But he never mentioned the

details of the thing. I used to think: what did he have to hide? He was not by nature a man to withhold his thoughts, no matter how complicated, or absurd, or shaming they were, certainly not with me, who knew him so much better than anyone. Was I hurt at his withholding? I suppose I was, also concerned, inasmuch as I disliked the idea of the thing festering in him, and I am enough of a Freudian to believe the mind must discharge toxic materials or become infected by them. I assumed Jack's silence about Peg's death indicated some malignancy, or some guilt, rather, though whether his own or another's I didn't know. There had been hints, if that is not too strong a term for the odd muttered half-sentence – again, late at night, in drink, when the talk had veered in that direction – such muttering at once cut off, lips sealed, shake of the head, the disinhibition brought on by copious alcohol no match for the powerful engines of repression at work in him.

One night, I remember, we sat up late in the big room downstairs – he was still in the loft, we had been out to dinner and come back to 11th Street for a nightcap – and the talk shifted to Port Mungo. Jack had a way, when a conversation which had begun to languish then took a turn that seized his attention, of coming up out of his long-legged sprawl across a chair or a couch and sitting forward with his elbows on his knees, back bent and chin cupped in his palm, the other hand hanging in the air, with a finger lifted – or drumming his fingers on the table – I think I had said that the biggest problem faced by artists in cities was light – and all at once he saw something, he came up out of his chair and spoke as if responding not to what I'd said but to the chain of association it had started in his mind.

– It was the light!

– What was?

– It woke her up.

At which point he became aware that he was talking not to himself but to me. He rubbed his eyes, finished his drink, and left soon after.

On three or four occasions he let slip similarly oblique remarks, but they made no sense in and of themselves, nor in any combination I could make of them. Another time – and we were very drunk that particular night, I forget why, so drunk in fact that I have lost the context of the conversation – but he said that she got it wrong, and all I knew, when I woke the next morning, was that that too referred to Peg's death, though who got what wrong I didn't know, nor did I imagine that Jack made it clear when he said it. I once asked if I would ever be told what happened to Peg.

– One day, he said.

– What day would that be, Jack?

– The day I die.

His face split open and out leapt a wheeze of sulphuric laughter. That was Jack. That was my brother. But try and deny the imagination its creative imperative – you cannot. What I did not know I could not help but attempt to imagine. I thought about the mangrove swamps of the western Caribbean, and what I had seen of them during my visit to Port Mungo. There was an old, white-planked skiff moored to Jack's dock which he'd picked up cheap soon after coming to Pelican Road, and in it he and Peg had explored the coastline north and south of the town, and the waterways of the Mungo drainage, and the inshore lagoons.

A couple of days after Vera showed up in Port Mungo she suggested that Peg and I go out in the boat with her. Jack of course would be working in his studio all day. So we set out at dawn, the three of us, we crossed the bay and came out into the open sea, where Vera opened the throttle and the boat shot forward, creating a great wash behind us and shattering the trembling stillness of the early morning. I was far from easy with the speed of the boat, not least because Vera was red-eyed and unsteady, having been up till all hours drinking. The sun was just over the horizon, a pair of pelicans drifted by and Peg was hanging over the bow, raking the water for dolphin and manatee.

Twenty minutes later Vera swung the boat back towards the coast. The narrow fringe of white beach and palms had given way to a dense hedge of tangled mangrove. We came in fast towards it, the bow lifting and the keel bumping, and it was only seconds before we went in that I saw the channel through the mangrove opening before us. The two of them were grinning at me, this an old joke, apparently, and though I'd kept my mouth shut my white-knuckled grip on the seat told them of my mounting apprehension as we hurtled towards what looked like certain destruction.

The channel was narrow and serpentine, but Vera swung the boat along it at speed, and our wash went lapping through the mangrove and raised heron and ibis, which flapped off languidly from the canopy. For a few hellish moments a thick cloud of mosquitoes blotted out all vision and had me dementedly flapping at my face, much to Peg's continued amusement. The channel grew more narrow still, and Vera at last slowed the boat, cut the motor, and all at once the humidity descended on us like a warm wet blanket.

We drifted in silence. On every side I saw spidery, stiltlike mangrove roots branching out from thick-clustered branches before plunging into the soupy waters of the swamp. There was movement within the tangle of roots, sudden cries, now and then a distinct *plop!* as some unseen creature dropped into the water. Peg sat up in the bow with her legs hanging over the side, and turned to see if I was still terrified. I had spent enough time in boats with Jack, when we were young, that I was quite accustomed to daredevil nautical adventures, and Vera was every bit as reckless in a boat as Jack once had been. Suddenly we were through the mangrove and into a lagoon, this body of silver water placid, utterly still. Here the mangrove gave way to mudflats, a narrow fringe of gravelly beach, and a small boggy field of grass and bush behind. Peg called softly that we'd arrived, then stood up. As the bow scraped against the gravel she leapt off the boat and hauled it a few feet up from the shore, with Vera pushing from the stern.

The beach was firm enough but when Peg reached the pasture her bare feet sank into oozing black mud. A profound stillness had settled over the lagoon, deepened and intensified by the sudden screams and chatterings of birds. Peg pulled bottles of beer from the icebox and opened one for each of us, then handed out the sandwiches she'd made the night before. Happily we munched our breakfast and swigged cold beer as the sun climbed into a pale blue sky streaked with wispy white clouds. It was in that place, or in a place very like it, that Peg's decomposing body was later found, submerged face up in a tangle of mangrove roots.

This is what Jack eventually told me about her death. When Peg was sixteen she and Vera had taken the boat out one night. They were both drunk. They wanted to get to a village up the coast because Johnny Hague was drinking in a bar there and had insisted they join him. Jack knew it was a foolish idea, and told them he wouldn't allow them to go. They'd laughed at him. There had been an argument on the dock, and after a few minutes he had thrown up his hands and gone back inside. They took off into the bay and then turned north up the coast. It was a cloudy night.

They were going way too fast when they hit the coral head. Vera was knocked unconscious. When she came to she found herself alone in the boat, drifting on the open sea and with no idea where she was, nor what had happened to Peg. The motor had stalled but there was no damage to the propeller, and she was able to start it up again. For hours she went round in circles shouting for Peg until she had almost no gas left. As Jack described all this I could see her in my mind's eye, leaning far out over the side of the boat, growing increasingly desperate, screaming her daughter's name into the darkness – but no answering cry. The wind was already rising when she got back to Pelican Road and told Jack what had happened.

They went back out and searched for several hours more. The weather grew worse. Vera was no longer sure where the accident had occurred. The mangrove swamps north of Port Mungo covered many square miles and formed an intricate labyrinth of channels and lagoons, and Peg might have been swept almost anywhere by the current. Five days later a crab fisherman found her. In those five days Jack and Vera had continued to search, as had many others from Port Mungo, but with growing certainty that they would not find the girl alive.

Jack decided at the time of the accident to stay silent about the circumstances of that last trip in the boat, in the belief that no good would come of speaking up. He talked to me about it only once, and as far as I know he told only one other person. Nor did Vera ever admit her involvement in her daughter's death, in fact she vigorously denied it. At the time they said they didn't know who Peg had been with the night she died, and that was why it had remained a mystery.

It is hardly surprising then that my brother did not merely grieve for Peg, but was haunted by her memory and found no peace. I don't think he was free of a sense of his own culpability for the rest of his life: he believed he should have stopped them going out that night. When he came to live in New York I became sensitive to his moods in this regard, and saw for myself the extent to which Peg continued to dominate his consciousness. I knew when she was coming to life in his mind, I could almost feel her stirring, and although he tried to push her down by sustaining his focus on his work, with Peg that rarely succeeded. I have never had a child myself but I do know erotic love, I know all about the bone-deep grinding and screaming of buried living emotion and worse, the utter black despair it engenders – all transient. All healed by time. But Jack's feelings for his daughter were more intense than that, and after she died those feelings did not fade away, as a lover's do, they merely slept, and why? Because his love for his daughter was infected with guilt, and this guilt interacted with it like an unstable chemical, producing virulence and combustion.

I remember watching him once while it happened. He was standing at the window in the big room downstairs, gazing down at the street below. For minutes on end he stood there, silently, and I stood beside him, but he was not with me, he was somewhere else, he was in Port Mungo – when all at once a yellow cab came to an abrupt stop outside the house and provoked a blast of horn from the car behind. Some faint shouting as a fat young man in a black leather jacket clambered into the back of the cab. Jack came awake. He clicked his tongue, he was annoyed, as he always was when his thoughts began this absurd cycle again. It is me, Jack Rathbone, and I am the one who is still here, alive – can I not live a month of my life without being ravaged by these ancient memories? This was the voice of the upper self, which at the sight of a fat man climbing ungainly into the back of a cab all at once dispelled the phantom. He crossed the room and flung himself into an armchair and drummed his fingers on the arm. He banished her memory, and for a while, at least, through the sheer force of his will, he was free of her.

He told me once of seeing her in Central Park. Late autumn in the park: schoolchildren, joggers, a few tourists, people with dogs. Peg was in his thoughts, for in the early days after her death he became adept at rousing her, and found he missed her less if he assumed she was with him, and spoke to her in his mind.

So he was walking through the park, conducting a mental conversation with his dead daughter, when he saw her on the path ahead of him. Lanky striding girl in a tattered hippy skirt, scuffed tennis shoes, faded denim jacket – same leggy gait, same tumble of tangled black hair – and he began to follow her. Jack loved the park, he knew it in all its moods, and that day there was mist in the trees, the squirrels busy among the heaped dead leaves, few people about, sounds muffled and colours muted,

III

greys and browns, Rembrandt's colours. She seemed to be making for the lake.

He stalked her along the path by the water's edge. He kept his distance, still uncertain, but every moment growing more sure, and with a rising excitement, that it was her. Clumps of rushes all brown and dry in the shallows, a few geese still lingering, and drifting on the water the same mist that hung in the branches of the trees on the far shore. Beyond them the towers of Fifth Avenue beneath a grey lowering sky. He saw a man throw a stick, and a dog go bounding into the lake and swim out to retrieve it. The geese lifted honking off the water. The dog returned to the bank, the stick between its teeth, and stumbled out with its coat plastered wetly to its flanks.

He began running to catch up with her, calling her name.

Not her, of course, how could it be her? The face which abruptly turned to see what mad shouting creature pursued her was pitted, black-eyed, Slavic – Jack turned and walked off smartly in the opposite direction. It had happened before, he told me, this seeing-a-ghost, and I suspect it may have happened since.

IO

It was a little over a year ago now that I came downstairs after my bath one evening and discovered an unfamiliar smell in the sitting room. I made myself a drink, and when Jack appeared I told him someone had been smoking. He took his time, I remember. He hovered over the drinks tray, laying his long careful fingers on the neck of the bottle I had brought up for him. Jack's disinterest in his own appearance may have accelerated with the years but occasionally, and without intending to, he achieved a certain careless elegance. After days in his studio he would become filthy, and when at last he noticed this he took to his bathroom, and then discovered in his closet fresh clean clothes, folded and ironed by my housekeeper, Dora. Then he presented a picture of elegance. So he did that night, as he loomed over the glass of wine he had poured, and lifted it to his nose.

When he had settled himself he told me he had been busy all morning with what he called the large canvas, a painting begun months before but as yet indeterminate. It was late October, so yes, a year ago, raw and damp, bad for his joints, and he was not in the best of tempers. He had stopped work at noon and eaten lunch at the kitchen table. He had asked Dora if there were any messages. Dora has been with me for many years. What an odd look she gave him, he said – full of foreboding, full of dire warning that what she was about to tell him he might not wish to hear. We both knew this look of Dora's. Jack told her to just please tell him who had called.

– Anna.

It took me a second or two.

– Your Anna? Anna Rathbone?

He nodded.

Anna. The other daughter. Whom he hadn't seen in twenty years. He told me he picked up the phone and sat gazing at Dora with his hand over his mouth as though to keep from saying something he would later regret.

I never knew Anna in Port Mungo, but I certainly remembered her from the dreadful days immediately after we got the news about Peg. She was four years old then. She travelled to New York with Jack and they stayed with me. Vera arrived a few days later. We were all in a state of shock. Anna was silent and withdrawn, like a little ghost. She sat gazing out of the window, clutching a rag doll, her lips pressed together as though she had been forbidden on pain of death to breathe a word. Particularly frustrating from my point of view was that Jack was hardly more forthcoming. There had apparently been some sort of accident. Peg's body had been discovered in a mangrove swamp. She had been missing for some days. The cause of death was unclear, as were the circumstances. There was no boat, so no indication of how she'd got there, and an open verdict was recorded. I felt sure that Jack could at least make a guess as to what might have happened, but when I tried to discuss it with him he glared at me then left the room without a word.

Matters were not improved by the arrival of my older brother. Gerald could at once be identified as one of us, as a Rathbone, I mean, for he was a gaunt, hawklike sort of a man, although unlike us he bore the marks of professional success: he was imposing and ponderous, he wore an expensive dark suit, his manner was clipped and grave, and he had a way of taking off his spectacles when he wished to frown. What was he doing here?

114

Extraordinary thing, but having somehow learned of Peg's death he had flown to New York to sort things out; on the assumption, I suppose, that none of us was capable of it. It seemed he was most concerned about the welfare of little Anna. I have always believed children to be tougher than they look, it was certainly my father's attitude towards the three of us, and I saw no reason why Anna wouldn't get over the shock of her sister's death provided she had an adult or two looking out for her. Jack felt the same. Gerald most certainly did not.

We were in the big sitting room downstairs, which in those days was very different from what it is today. Much more cluttered. It was just the four of us. Anna was there for the first few minutes until it became clear that this would be a stormy meeting, and Dora was called to take her upstairs. Vera took almost no part in the proceedings. She had not yet sobered up and had little to contribute to discussions of child welfare and the like, the only welfare which concerned Vera at that time being her own – I mean, her alcoholic welfare. And for the first time I noticed something which would become more apparent in her later sobriety, namely that real damage had been done in the years of heavy drinking. I didn't trouble to analyse it precisely, but she couldn't think straight any more. There were holes in her memory. Her logic was off. She lost words, proper nouns in particular. So Vera took almost no part in the proceedings, which left Jack to fight for Anna by himself.

He was hardly in better shape than Vera, but for all that he was capable of a furious resentment that his brother should presume to come to New York and tell him what was good for his own daughter, and he lost no time telling him so. That's when I suggested Anna be taken upstairs.

– How do you know what's good for her? said Gerald, coldly. This isn't even your house.

I was astonished by his animosity. Gerald was older than us by several years. We had never been close to him, but nothing had happened as far as I was aware to account for the hostility of his tone. Jack was not strong, but he came back at him with some gusto, he said he had a damn sight better idea than Gerald did, this wasn't even Gerald's *country*.

– Then perhaps she should live in the same country as me. Be a part of a proper family. That child has every right to a respectable upbringing.

I think Jack must have made some mocking remark about the English and their cult of respectability. Gerald grew calm, I remember. He waited for Jack to finish.

– All I'm saying, he said quietly, is that nobody is looking after that child apart from a housekeeper who goes home at five o'clock.

– And?

– My dear man, you think that's adequate?

– My dear man, this is a house where music and conversation and books are taken seriously. That child comes from a family of artists. She'll suffocate in Surrey.

The argument continued, and at one point Gerald said that my household had 'no structure', that it was 'sexually irregular', which aroused my own indignation but Jack could not contain his hoot of laughter. After a while it got more personal still and Gerald came close to suggesting that if Jack had raised his daughter differently she might still be alive. That's when the words 'criminal irresponsibility' were uttered.

– For god's sake, Gerald! I cried, angry myself now.

– Shut up, Gin, he said, you know nothing about this.

That was certainly true. I was mystified by the impression he was giving of having information about events in Port Mungo of which I, for one, knew nothing.

You may imagine Jack's reaction to all this. But he did not lose control. He did not throw a punch at his brother. He did not come at him with the sharp end of a broken bottle, which I was afraid he might, given the state he was in. He turned instead to Vera, and for the first time that afternoon she spoke up. She said to Gerald: Just cut it out.

Her nodding silence to that point seemed to lend her a certain authority, when she did choose to speak. Then she turned to Jack and said she thought Anna should go to England with Gerald, at least for a while. I think Jack knew then he was beaten. He was not strong enough to resist his brother's will, and I think he also recognized that he was in no condition to be a father to Anna. But he resented it intensely.

Gerald wasted no time. The meeting broke up soon afterwards, and he went out into the hall and told Dora to please pack up Anna's things, as she was leaving. It was a pathetic sight, the child silently coming down the stairs with her hand in Dora's, clutching the little bag containing her few scraps of clothing, her rag doll stuffed in on top. She had no idea what was going on. Gerald dropped to his knees and spoke softly to her, telling her she would be going with him now, to live with his family in his house in England. Jack and Dora and I stood in the hall watching this. Gerald stood up and Anna gazed about her, looking for her father. Jack stepped forward and she ran into his arms, and he lifted her up, holding her close. For several interminable seconds he held the child, whispering to her, and then he set her down and with a cold, sorrowing glance at his brother he turned and went upstairs. He was so very weak. A broken reed, I remember thinking. He was letting his own daughter go, giving her up. All at once she began to scream – 'Daddy!' – and Gerald picked her up and carried her swiftly out the door and down the steps. It was terribly distressing for all of us. I went back into the sitting room. Vera was standing at the window. I stood beside her and we watched as Gerald flagged a cab and lifted the little girl in, then climbed in after her. I became aware that tears were streaming silently down Vera's face.

– Darling, I said.

She turned to me.

– Poor Jack! she whispered.

It was some days before he could talk about any of this. By then Vera had left, vague about where she was going but promising to be in touch. Her own feelings about the loss of her daughter were blurred by alcohol. Gently I asked Jack how he felt about losing Anna. He had decided to be tough about it. A shrug, a snort. Well, we've lost that one. We've lost a good one there. And I understood then without his having to tell me that he had resolved not to pursue the child. Almost, it seemed, as if to intensify his pain – he had lost one daughter, what of it if he lost the other? – so he let her go. And when Gerald moved to formally adopt Anna, Jack did not contest it. I had frankly no desire to have her living here, but I too was saddened at the thought of her growing up in Surrey. I did say to Jack later that it was possible we hadn't lost her at all, because if she was really one of us – a Rathbone, I mean – then no amount of Surrey would keep her down.

The night of Anna's visit Jack and I went out to eat at the Spanish place round the corner. The *maître d'*, Luis, was always very fond of Jack. He took us at once to our table, which was in the corner at the back where it was private and quiet and dark. The candle was lit. The wine appeared. Above our heads hung framed posters of bullfighters. Jack put his glasses on to study the menu. I knew my brother too well to ask him outright what had happened with Anna. Instead, studying my own menu, I murmured that I thought she must want to make terms with the past.

– You've done it, I said, but she hasn't had the chance.

– That's not my responsibility, he snapped – that was up to Gerald. Why didn't he tell her what happened?

– Because, my dear, I expect he didn't know. Because you never told him. Who have you told? Apart from me.

I lifted to my lips a large starched napkin. The lighting was dim, the waiters hovered near by, speaking to one another in low tones. Jack, still frowning, drank off a whole glass of red wine, and I could see it kindling the beginnings of a rage in him. No more, or he would be unable to work in the morning. I continued to dab at my lips, and his eyes glittered at me in the candlelight. Curtly he told me she hadn't made the trip to see him and Vera. Apparently she had been in the city some weeks, and was living with a friend in an apartment on the Bowery.

– What's she doing here?
– Nothing. Working in a bar.
– I suppose, I said, that you busied yourself with her bone structure.
– Well yes, he said, I did, actually.

He had the good grace to acknowledge my astuteness with a quick display of teeth. He fell silent again. I grew impatient.

– Jack, for God's sake have another glass of wine.
– No, he said firmly, absolutely not.

But of course he did, and then he was ready to talk.

She was punctual. Dora, stony-faced, brought her into the big room downstairs and Jack rose from the chair by the window and went to her with outstretched hands. I broke in here, I couldn't help myself, I wanted to know how he *felt* – excited, apprehensive? – this was his daughter! Yes, yes, all that, but what was remarkable, he said, was that there was so much of her sister there.

– Peg?

He stared at his plate. I waited for more. There wasn't any. With the years Jack had grown increasingly ill-at-ease talking about his feelings. It was a feature of age, also of the deep sadness he had carried with him since Peg's death. So she looked like Peg, then? Yes. Though where Peg had been sunburnt, he said, and, oh, restless, volatile – Gin, you know what she was like – Anna apparently was very different, she was a wintry creature from northern Europe, an altogether cooler character. But still, the resemblance was strong. Jack gazed off abstractedly. What was going on in that complicated brain of his? I asked him to please tell me what she looked like. Oh, she was as tall as Peg, he said, skin very pale, black hair chopped short, black jeans and a black sweater under a leather coat. Long white hands, and on the back of the left one a tattoo in black ink, the image of a scorpion.

Thus did my brother describe the daughter he hadn't seen for almost twenty years, and in his description I too faintly caught the phantom outline of Peg, but in the negative, somehow. As though leached of all colour and life.

No small talk. They held each other's hands for some moments, and she told him she'd wanted to come and see him for years.

Jack asked her if she remembered the house.

She did.

– You remember when Gerald took you away from here?

She did.

– That was the last time I saw him.

– He said he hadn't any choice. Is that true?

No answer from Jack. He told me he'd felt unequal to the task of giving her an account of how it was for all of us then – me, him, Vera, Gerald – and for her too, of course, a four-year-old child living in a house of artists, all of us still in profound shock from her sister's death – he would do it if she wanted him to, and he thought Anna understood this.

– So why didn't you come and see me before? he said.

But he knew why. After Gerald adopted her he had made it abundantly clear that she was never to have anything more to do with her father, this for reasons that until recently were not clear to me.

– Does he still hate me? said Jack.

The pathos of it. They were standing by the window in the sitting room. Jack waved her to a chair. You feel the largeness of the room because there's so little in it now. One good rug from Oaxaca on the bare boards, two big paintings, Jack's *Narcissus* and one of Vera's early canvases, big strong paintings against the high white walls, and the minimum of furniture to make the room habitable; after Jack moved in I tried to keep my clutter elsewhere. There was a large mirror in a hardwood frame over the empty fireplace. It was also rather a cold room, and this we liked too, it was good for Jack's arthritis.

Anna sat forward with her elbows on her knees, her hands hanging between her thighs, shivering, her black scarf trailing down to the floorboards. She gazed at Jack with a frowning intentness utterly lacking in self-consciousness. She hadn't taken off her coat. Her hair was chopped and spiky and she rubbed at it with a hand that might have been Peg's, once, he said, apart from the scorpion. She had four small silver rings up the side of her ear. A high-templed white plate of a forehead, unblemished and unlined.

– Gerald's dead, she said.

– Yes, of course.

Somehow this had slipped his mind. I remembered my older brother's righteousness on that earlier occasion, his strident anger towards Jack. None of his anger was directed at Vera, she could not be held responsible for anything. As Anna pushed a hand through her hair Jack saw that her fingertips were stained yellow.

– Smoke if you want, he said.

The tension had grown acute but Jack wasn't aware of it until suddenly it broke with him telling her to smoke. He got a smile from her then, the first proper smile, more of a grin really, lop-sided and matey – grey discoloured teeth revealed, one of the canines badly chipped – as she dug in her leather satchel and produced her tobacco and rolling papers. Jack fetched an ashtray. He stared at her for several moments, and then realized how uncomfortable he was making her.

– Is it very cold in here? he said. I'm afraid I don't feel it any more.

– It's bloody arctic.

She fired up a ragged cigarette and sank back in her chair. Suddenly there came a volley of coughs, she doubled over, and Jack stared at her in some alarm, thinking that her pallor perhaps signified something more sinister than a lack of sunlight.

– Sorry about that, she muttered.

She picked a shred of tobacco off her tongue and examined it, then wiped it on her jeans. Just like Peg, he thought.

– Was it a shock? Gerald, I mean.

– It was a relief. He had this awful tumour. Worse for him, being a doctor, he knew what was going on, he was like, cancer is cancer.

Gerald said things to Jack that I have never forgotten, but none of that concerned Anna. She understood that a chasm of mistrust and anger had separated the brothers, but for her it had no relevance. She was here, now, with Jack, and she barely troubled to hide her impatience with this ancient history.

But this was not right, either. There was something else happening here. Jack watched her as with lowered eyes she pulled at her ragged roll-up then tap-tap-tapped the ash into the ashtray. He liked her candour. Jack used to say that he too was impatient with imprecision and insincerity and indirectness, that he too valued the cold-bucket-of-water of unvarnished honesty.

– Why are you here? he said.

– What, New York?

– New York, this house –?

He told me he already suspected why she had come, but she was not yet able to admit it. She thought she ought to, she said.

– Anyway it was time.

– Why was it time?

Eyes on the table again. Some evasion going on.

– It's complicated, she said.

Jack waited.

– Can I tell you about it later? she said. In a few days, I mean. It's just such a *mess.*

No tears, but a most dismal expression, and Jack leaned over for her hand. There was the grin again, the lift of the chin, the long white tobacco-stained fingers pushing through the spiky hair, all this accompanied by a bit of sniffing and coughing, and he suggested they have lunch.

Over the course of lunch it became clear that she had indeed come, as Jack suspected, to find out what had happened to her sister in Port Mungo. Apparently the subject was never discussed in Gerald Rathbone's house. I began then to sense how very strained it must have been for the two of them, this awkward girl come to see the father she hadn't ever really known, and come, what's more, with this serious and terrible question to ask – and Jack, no less awkward, no less a stranger to whatever was required to handle such a fraught encounter with any sort of grace – his inability, too, to be warm, despite the fact that he was growing more pleased, as the shock of her presence diminished, to have his daughter with him again, he who had assumed he had lost both his daughters twenty years before. All this going on, but these two odd suspicious characters unable to articulate what they were feeling, instead circling each other like clumsy wary animals until at last Anna cleared her throat and made her proposition. And I remember the look Jack gave me as he told me this, how his eyes gleamed in the candlelight, almost vulpine, I thought. I asked him what she'd said.

She'd offered to sit for him. To be his model.

– What did you say?

– What do you think I said?

– You said yes?

– I think she needs the money.

She left shortly after five. He said he watched her from the window of the big sitting room as she emerged on to the sidewalk and went off down the block towards Seventh Avenue. She strode off into the dusk with the leather coat flapping about her, he said, her satchel slung over her shoulder and her scarf wound tight around her neck! Thirty years between us, more, he'd thought, but there are days I stride the sidewalks of Manhattan like that, that I lope through the streets like a wolf.

Then he had turned back into the room. The smell of tobacco hung in the air and he enjoyed it, he said, he who had become as fastidious about cigarette smoke as me. It reminded him of the old days when everybody smoked and artists smoked more than anybody else. And it reminded him of Peg, who'd smoked from the age of seven and smoked like a man, cigarette hanging from the corner of her mouth, eyes half-closed, face wreathed in blue fumes. And I saw then what was in store for us. Anna Rathbone, by coming into our life like this, and rousing the past, was rousing her sister; and Peg, once roused, invariably laid waste to that most fragile of organs, I mean her father's heart.

II

U ntil ten years ago, when he came to live with me, and at last accepted that routine and moderation were the only way, for him, to a productive life, my brother lived in a state of the most delicate equilibrium. Periods of hard work would be followed by periods of dissipation. He travelled extensively but he never gave the impression that his life fulfilled him. It seemed, rather, merely to distract him from private matters about which he never spoke. During the Crosby Street years he was never at rest, never at peace, and I began to feel that he was in a state of perpetual flight, though from what he was fleeing I had no clear idea, unless it was the memory of his daughter.

His sexual life in this period was obscure to me. There were various women for brief spells, but I suspect he may have purchased a good deal of his sex. If there was any thread of continuity it was Vera. During the years in Port Mungo she had used Pelican Road as a kind of depot to which she would always eventually return. Jack had accepted this. He seemed able to ride the emotional turbulence of this loose chaotic arrangement, perhaps it suited him. I don't know.

There was the five-day reunion in the summer of 1982, in the Crosby Street loft, but then she'd drifted off again, and quite where she'd landed after her trip to London I didn't know, nor did I know whether she had visited Gerald in Surrey and had an opportunity to renew her relationship with her daughter. Nor, frankly, did I care. That she was out of the picture was enough for me, and I was sufficiently foolish to think she was out of it for good. Not so. Whatever the attraction between those two it had not yet played itself out, despite all that had happened. Back she came two or three years later, and did Jack take her in? Of course he did. I heard about this only through a third party, the sculptor Eduardo Byrne, who was my lover at the time.

I should probably declare here that I do not have a particularly impressive record in this department, I mean with regard to love. With my brother occupying such a large central role in my life, it was hard, as you might imagine, for anybody else to measure up. Julian was the first – Vera's friend, the poet, who'd come with her to Victoria Station that damp fall day in 1957. And what a day that was! – end of an era. It was only when the Southampton train had finally disappeared, and me still standing on the platform gazing after it, that I allowed the awfulness of Jack's departure to come sweeping up from somewhere deep inside and overwhelm me. I had to sit down. I had to have a drink, even though it was not yet lunchtime. Julian was very good, he saw how distressed I was and he took me into the station bar and bought me a large whisky. We stayed there until half past two in the afternoon, when they threw us out. We had eaten nothing, and I was not steady. I may have been a little hysterical. I took him back to Kennington Road where I allowed him to undress me and take me into bed, or to be precise, into Jack's bed. And that is how I lost my virginity, weeping in my brother's bed, overcome with grief because he had left me.

Julian was a nice enough man but he soon began to annoy me. He was courteous, thoughtful, and deferential, and I dislike those qualities in a man. Jack was never interested in what I thought. If I wanted him to pay attention to me I had to make bloody sure it was worth his while. Julian opened doors for me and bought me drinks and asked me how I was feeling, and as a result I became distant and chilly rather quickly, which oddly enough he seemed to like, for he promptly redoubled his attentions. He was such an utter Englishman, and I sometimes wonder whether it wasn't just this that drove me across the Atlantic, I mean an impatience with utter Englishmen. What I will say for Julian is that he taught me how to do sex, and he was gentle about it. This I did appreciate, even when I realized that he would much prefer that I behave like the man in bed, and let him be the girl.

My subsequent romantic history was at best sporadic. After a brief phase of rampant promiscuity – it felt rampant to me – I became extremely selective. But even so I was often disappointed. None of them had that – what will I call it? – a kind of bracing self-involvement that swept one up and carried one along, made one tingle with vitality even if there was a bit of brutality too. Not physical brutality, rather a roughness of manner that came of impatience, and kept one on one's toes, and exposed one at times to ferocious ridicule but also opened one to experience that otherwise would never have been available. I think I came to be regarded as something of an ice queen when I was young, but it didn't put men off, in fact I was much in demand, and I began to realize that they liked me because I was stronger than they were, when what I wanted was a man who was stronger than me. Someone like Jack.

It was different in New York because there I found men who had the kind of brutal narcissism I missed, but the problem with most New York men was that they lacked that which even the most wilting of Englishmen seemed to possess in abundance, and that was wit. New Yorkers could talk about themselves all night with far more passion than they could ever arouse in the bedroom, but they spoiled it by bringing a kind of mind-numbing *earnestness* to these flights of ego. No sparks, no sudden flares of wicked irony, no barbed sardonic asides – no self-deprecation – the only real malice I encountered in my early days in Manhattan came from the mouths of homosexuals, who liked me for my ice-queen manners, and who amused me with their conversation, but who in a very real sense were my competition, for we were after the same sort of men. Several years passed in this way, and I was starting to become seriously emotionally isolated when I encountered Eduardo Byrne.

Eduardo was a tough, stringy man, a gristly piece of meat of a man with a face that always made me think of the men who work in the engine rooms of oil tankers. A merchant seaman, that's what Eduardo looked like, and when a merchant seaman struggles into a suit to attend his mother's funeral, that's how Eduardo dressed. He was a sculptor who only late in his career received any serious attention. When I first knew him he had just begun to make money but the manner in which he lived had not changed. He had a loft on Mercer that was even more primitive than Jack's.

One night he came to the house for a game of chess and told me about Vera's return. My concentration immediately went all to hell, and I soon conceded the game. Eduardo then said that I had too narrow a view of love.

– Love? I said. That isn't love. I don't know what it is that those two have but it's not love. It's a pathology they share. The minute Jack begins to recover, back she comes and infects him all over again.

I did not say, that woman is directly responsible for the death of his child.

– That's love, said Eduardo.

– More like malaria.

I may not have been successful at love myself but I knew what it was and what it wasn't. What Jack and Vera had, and the mess it invariably made of their lives, that wasn't it, and I said this to Eduardo.

– Love is always a mess, he said.

Spurious romantic claptrap, this, as though to live in vigorous talkative concord with another human being is inferior to a dreary predictable cycle of fighting and reconciliation, involving spilled drinks and broken crockery and slashed bedsheets and kicked-in canvases and people thrown out into the night and doors being locked against them, and whole buildings woken up, and yes, actual physical violence – tears and screaming – then sobbed apologies and hungover sex – yes, and wild doings at night that end in tragedy. That's not love, I said, it's emotional intemperance, only a fool would think it was love. Clearly Eduardo was a fool, and I told him that too.

He laughed in his knowing way, thick condescending chuckles which implied that I didn't know what I was talking about. His own compulsive promiscuity hardly qualified him to comment, in fact his inability to commit to even the briefest fidelity was making me seriously question the future of our relationship. I had not yet decided whether the sex was adequate compensation. I told him that any responsible person would greet the news of Vera Savage returning to New York with cries of dismay.

Eduardo was right at least in this regard, that one should not be too hasty in predicting the same appalling levels of discord every time, and perhaps this was because their mutual loss had created a new bond between them. I took them out to dinner one evening, and I have to say Jack looked quite healthy. His hair had been cropped short and he sat rubbing his bristled skull and grinning with pleasure as Vera was humorous at my expense. I can usually give as good as I get in conversation but Vera's tongue, Vera's *mind* – which I will charitably call mercurial – was often too quick for me. She too seemed healthy, she was in a tight black skirt and absurdly high heels, it was the cheap-tart look she had made her own in London and which still apparently bewitched my brother. How was my *flock*, she wanted to know. Vera enjoyed pretending that I was employed in an ecclesiastical capacity. She liked to think I was a lady bishop in the Episcopalian church.

– Weeping and praying, I said.

She grinned at me round her cigarette. There was the black slot, and it was hard to be altogether indifferent to her despite all the harm she had done. It seemed she was good for Jack just then, for he'd been sunk in grief for many months and I couldn't remember the last time I'd heard him laugh. Purple Virginia, she called me, and I think that on some level we were actually beginning to grow fond of each other, even if I did regard her as a wicked and dangerous woman, and endured her company only because Jack wanted me to.

Our dinner was pleasant enough. We did not speak about Peg. It emerged that she had been living for some months in a farmhouse near Rhinebeck, but quite what the arrangements were, who was paying the bills, this was not stated. What did impress me during the course of the dinner was the current of genuine tenderness between them, and this, as I say, I attributed to their mutual loss: each recognized in the other the same private pain, and for this reason they were gentle and affectionate.

Later I walked home by way of Washington Square. It was early April, and after the rigours of a particularly bleak winter the air was warm, the trees were in blossom, and not a hint yet of the sweltering humidity of the summer to come. So, a mellow Sunday evening in spring, and I asked myself why I should not be surprised at the evident pleasure they took in each other, given that the Port Mungo years had been a time of such sustained shabbiness, in every sense, and had culminated so hideously. I'd have thought they would prefer to avoid each other, so as to avoid confronting so much in their lives that was ugly.

Not those two, apparently. Were they without vanity, then? Was it to do with the activity of painting – a daily discipline of vision unflinching? Or was it, rather – and this represented something of a shift, for me, towards Eduardo's position – that here I witnessed a form of love I had not recognized before, so robust in construction – so *stormproof* – that it weathered tempests which would have scuppered any ordinary relationship?

So I entertained the idea of love like a ship unsinkable. A ship unsinkable – I circled the idea and I asked it, was it real? Or was it, rather, a wisp of gothic romance, swallowed whole in childhood and rising now to the surface like an undigested scrap of salad leaf? But no, no. I had always seen it straight. Vera was chronically unstable, but she had always somehow convinced Jack to take her in, I think because he felt he was responsible for her frailty. She played on his guilt, and then she left him. The very repetitiveness of the pattern, the fact that it circled round on itself and never went forward, seemed to mark it for an unhealthy relationship, obsessive-compulsive in nature, and quite emphatically neurotic. So enough of gothic romance, and more of clinical analysis, I thought, unless – and I paused on my doorstep, the key in my hand – unless the thing is a spiral, which even as it circles, rises?

How long she stayed with him I'm not sure, but I think it ran into weeks. By all accounts this was Vera in her domestic aspect, a rare sighting indeed. She shopped for food, she cooked for him, she cleaned the loft. This I had from Eduardo, who was a frequent visitor to Crosby Street at the time. We laughed together at the bourgeois tendency of the Rathbone household, neither of us in any doubt as to its prospective duration. He too remarked on their evident tenderness for one another, and I wondered if something else had happened, an event which had served to clear away or otherwise resolve tensions to do with the death of Peg? I did not say this to Eduardo, of course. Not that it would have made any difference to him, for him love required no such design of cause-and-effect as it pursued its erratic course. Experience, and reading, has taught me to look deeper into things. I fired him soon after. I discovered he had four other lovers at the same time as me, not all of them female. We remained friends however.

One day in the late summer Jack called at the house and Dora brought him into the big sitting room. I at once guessed what had happened. Poor Jack. And things had been going so well. He smoked, he frowned, he stared at the floor. He had just come from Penn Station, where he'd put her on a train. Why had she gone? She wanted to work. Ironic, considering their history.

– She can't work in the loft?

He shook his head. They couldn't work in the same space. She had a studio upstate and she wanted to be in it. I asked him if he wasn't getting a bit too old for all this.

Up came his head, he stared at me with an expression of disbelief, which changed in another moment to amusement. Too old? Too *old*?

– What's so funny? I said.

But he wouldn't tell me what was so funny. He sat there with his elbows on his knees, grinning at the floor. At least I had managed to lift his mood. I had by that time, with the dismissal of Eduardo, re-established a certain tranquillity in my own life and I could see no reason why Jack should not enjoy the same. But the very idea amused him, and he left my house still grinning. He loped off up 11th Street, and without turning lifted an arm high over his head and flapped his hand at me where I stood at the front door watching him go.

But a few years later Jack would move into this house, having come round to my view that the best life is the quiet life, and the best pleasures those taken in moderation. It took him that long to accept that yes, he was getting too old for all this.

But once again he was on his own, and finding the loft intolerable in her absence he accepted an offer to take a residence in Italy for six months. By the first of September he had left for Rome and I didn't see him again for almost half a year.

There was a great change in him on his return. Much, clearly, had happened, and all of it for the good. He came to the house one evening and I was at once struck by how well he looked. When Jack had first come back to New York his skin had been burned a leathery brown and his hair bleached out by the sun.

His diet had comprised too much fruit and not enough protein. He'd picked his way along the sidewalks of Manhattan like a man walking in sand. He'd been overly sensitive to the cold and soon experienced the first twinges of arthritis, doubtless brought on by the dramatic shift from the tropics.

But within a year all that had changed. He had adapted to his northern environment and begun to dress, and eat, and move like a New Yorker – that swift abstracted lope along the sidewalk, deftly passing slower-moving pedestrians, darting out through traffic as the opportunity presented. His hair grew darker but his skin got no paler. He ceased to crave the sun, and remembered his pleasure in the harsh wet winds of our childhood summers in the west of Ireland. He taught himself to live and work and cook in the chill draughts of his loft, and took satisfaction in its primitive functional simplicity. Just one year, and he sloughed off the skin of the Caribbean creature he had been and became a new man, a downtown man, at once a recognizable if starkly individuated member of the art tribe, in basketball boots and black jeans and an old black overcoat in the winter, and fingerless mittens for working in the loft when it was cold, and dark glasses and a baseball cap pulled low so that precise levels of toxicity in his system did not read. Thus the new Jack, the New York Jack of the 1980s, the Jack who lost a fall and winter to grief – and also, I suspect, bad cocaine, or worse – and had climbed back into the world only because my hand was there to haul him up.

That was the Jack, more or less, who'd left for Rome the previous fall. The Jack who came back the following March had passed through another transformation. He'd again had the sun on his face, but not the fierce blaze of the Caribbean, it was the gentle golden glow of old Italy which was on him now, and he looked healthier than I'd seen him in years. Part of it, part of the sheen of health, I mean – even his wardrobe was transformed, and in his silk shirt and baggy linen suit he was almost a European dandy, old scarecrow Jack – part of it, or most of it, rather, came from a sense of well-being which was evident in his every word and gesture, and issued from every pore of his glowing skin. The man was in love, no other explanation possible.

– My dear old toad, I said, what's happened to you?

He eased himself into an armchair. There was a small silver ring in his earlobe. I gave him a glass of wine and he sniffed it, and tasted it, with a discernment I had never seen in him before. Clearly some education of the senses had been undertaken, but wasn't that the point of Europe, for New World men like Jack Rathbone?

– So who is she?

– Her name, he said, is Antonella.

He gave the word its full Italian value, the slow, syncopated, full-mouthed inflection, syllable by languid syllable.

– Antonella, I said, repeating his pronunciation. Is she beautiful and is she young?

– She is beautiful, said Jack, and she is young, but she is not here.

When his canvases arrived a week later he showed me what he'd done. I remembered the thick-laid brushwork and deafening colours of the Port Mungo paintings, the raw eye of the primitivist, or the *tropicalist*, rather, assimilating with a fervour driven partly by fascination and partly by dislocation all he saw and felt down there. He was a stranger in a jungle, the man who painted those pictures, exhilarated and alienated at the same time, and he once told me that he'd stayed so long in Port Mungo because no artist could hope for a sharper spur to his work than that.

But a new mood was evident in the paintings of Antonella. And all at once, as though awakening to a reality that had been in front of me for ever, but unseen, somehow, I recognized the anger in Jack's work. Exhilaration and alienation, yes, but above all, anger. So accustomed had I become to the slashes and slaps and stabbings in his brushwork, and the variety of instruments blunt and sharp, hard and soft with which he worked his paint –

sticks, fingers, shells, blades, damp rags, Q-tips, sponges – that I had long since ceased to see the violence with which he went at his canvas, how he practically *violated* it, as he discharged rage with an energy which translated in the finished work as passion, and imbued it with its considerable force. Drawn from where, directed against what, I didn't know, but I could no longer regard his work as anything other than the product of anger: an art of tantrum.

Why? Because it was *not* evident in the paintings of Antonella. Those paintings seemed to have been made by a man from whom rage had been drained off like oil from the sump of an engine. They were lyrical.

He took them from the rack and propped them against the wall, and as I moved down the loft I restrained any display of the delight and astonishment they aroused in me. He propped them up in the order in which they'd been painted so that I saw the movement from the first portraits, in which I could sense him already searching for an idiom in which to express ideas remote from his usual pictorial range, to the last, which were studies of the girl nude: full-length figures which in their aching counter-points of modesty and eroticism were close to perfect, I thought. He was sitting on the couch with his elbows on his knees and watching me intently. I stood a long time in front of the last picture, Antonella facing the viewer, one knee bent slightly so the foot trailed, and one slim hand caught at the hip, and staring out with what might in coarser hands have been mere pouting provocation but was here a display of trust and mild humour in an exquisite girl, no other word for her, and the touch of the painter so deft, so delicate, that it filled one with an odd longing not sexual, not at all, though it was a sexual painting. No, it was some other longing, for some other joy, which I could not define.

At last I crossed the loft and sat down opposite him. I was strongly affected by the work.

– The best you've done, I said.

A long pause, and I felt not so much his pleasure as his relief.

– Nobody else has seen them. Except her, of course. One or two others.

– They're beautiful, Jack.

– Good!

It seemed he'd got what he'd wanted, what he'd feared he'd be denied – confirmation from someone he trusted that the work was as good as he thought it was. He sprang to his feet and stood gazing at the paintings stretched the length of the loft, and even in the cold air of early spring in New York City the glow of an ancient sun spilled out.

– Better get Vera down to have a look, he said.

Jack's Italian paintings were shown in New York in the fall. They won praise from the reviewers, but sales were poor. In the meantime he had returned to Rome but only to discover that the peculiar fires which had sprung to life in the course of Antonella's sitting for him did not rekindle. He did not know why, and nor did she, but they could not pretend it was otherwise. Their love had been specific to a given time, a given shared work – Rome, of course – and it had not survived the separation. Jack was philosophical. He was grateful for the paintings she had enabled him to make. He said they wept when they parted. There had never been an angry word between them, never a misunderstanding, never a lie. She was seventeen years old.

There is one more episode worth relating in connection to the Italian paintings, and it concerns Vera's response to them. I was not present of course, but Jack gave me a full account of her visit. It seems he wrote asking her to come down to the city and see the paintings, and she'd appeared at Crosby Street a few days later. She'd been reading about his sexy pictures, she told him, and naturally she wanted to see them. She was pleased he'd asked her to come. Vera had burned so many bridges in the art world, created so many enemies, Jack was one of only a handful of people who still knew the value of her eye.

She turned up in the late morning. She was wearing dark glasses, she was hungover, and not in the best of tempers. Jack was still in what I thought of as his *uomo italiano* phase. He continued to wear the linen suit, and he was taking his food and drink rather seriously, lingering over the wine list, questioning the sommelier, talking over dinner about Morandi, Visconti, Armani, whoever, just so long as their last name ended in a vowel. The morning Vera appeared he was still a man alive to the nuanced pleasures of table, cellar, wardrobe and bed – I exaggerate of course, but Jack had had a brief glimpse of *bella figura* and had thought perhaps to assimilate a little of it into his own rather starkly minimal mode of life. Vera was suspicious as he embraced her at the door.

– I hear you paint children now.

A bracing dash of acid, this, and Jack recoiled, still drifting, as he was, on tissue of gossamer fragrant with oils of lambent nubility. He soon recovered.

– On velvet, he said. Then I drink their blood.

– Such stamina.

– Oysters in olive oil, you should try it.

– I have, Jack. It turned me into a simpering idiot.

– You want some coffee?

– Christ, yes. You still allowed to smoke in this Temple of Youth, what's she called, Salmonella? Salmonella the fish-nymph of Sardinia?

Not a good start, and he began to realize that for once Vera's eye might be less than scrupulously impartial to all considerations but those of art. She rapidly took in the canvases propped the length of the long north wall of the loft, moving down the line and pausing only once. She sniffed, she followed the curve of a breast with her finger.

– Sweet.

Then it was over and she sat on the couch with her coffee and her cigarette, frowning and coughing.

– What is it with middle-aged men and young girls anyway?

Or need I ask. You want to paint with your dick, Jack, you go right ahead.

– Oh fuck off.

He was starting to understand how badly he had miscalculated. A man cannot address male desire in front of a woman and expect a sympathetic hearing. And his paintings, he saw – and for the first time as though through a woman's eyes, and a woman, what's more, with whom he had a long sexual history – his paintings were nothing more than a hymn to male desire. Or a series of propositions, rather. An argument. A display. An *excuse*. All at once he hated them, he wanted to destroy them, they were shallow boastings, nothing more. Angrily he began to turn them to the wall. Vera wheeled round.

– Don't do that!

– Why the hell not?

– Oh don't be so ridiculous!

She sat there, half turned towards him, laughing at him.

– Christ Jack, you are a touchy bugger. Leave the fucking things alone! They're good, all right? It's sweet work. It might have been sweeter, but then it'd be crap. But it's not. So relax, OK?

He slapped the wall with his palm and went to the window.

– Stupid to get you down here, he said.

– I wanted to come, I'm glad I did. She's succulent. I'd have done the same myself. Not the same, but I'd have done it. I have done it. But come on, Jack, it's like listening through the wall.

– They make you jealous?

She took off her dark glasses. She gazed at him and in her expression was the question: did he really expect her to answer that? She gathered up her bag and her coat. I think in that moment my brother abandoned his newly acquired Italian persona and became standard Jack once more. He got the point, and being standard Jack, he shrugged. They'd hit each other harder than this before. He kissed her at the door and she surprised him by seizing his hair in her fingers and kissing him back, hard and with her mouth open.

– You dumb bastard, she whispered, and left him aroused as she clattered off down the stairs.

This at any rate was how Jack described the meeting. But he would never again paint pictures like those he made in Rome that year, which does not mean that traces of Antonella did not recur in later work. There were passages in several of the large canvases he painted while living with me which showed that Antonella had clearly been assimilated into the evolving manner, this being another way of saying that the prudent artist wastes nothing, and that what Jack learned doing the Italian paintings he incorporated into his later work.

Did it exhaust him? Did it burn up precious resources, difficult or impossible to replace? He was in his late forties by then, and already subject to the arthritic episodes which at their most severe prevented him from holding a paintbrush. There were also occasional recurrences of the obscure fever he'd picked up in Port Mungo. It was not malaria but it was like malaria. Perhaps two or three times a year he suffered an attack which forced him to take to his bed in a darkened room and sweat it out. In the western Caribbean it was known as mangrove fever, and in children and old people it sometimes caused blindness and even death. These in my view were worrying problems for a man of Jack's irregular habits, and they were not my only concern, or rather my concern was compounded by his insistence on living in a decrepit loft in which rat traps had to be put out at night, and which in winter admitted blasts of frigid air through chinks in the brickwork on the exposed south side of the building, and which sweltered in the summer when the plumbing went insane and the place became frankly unsanitary.

Shortly after Vera's visit Jack had a bout of mangrove fever and called me from his sickbed. I went round at once and found him in a pitiable state. This was July, and the city was oppressively hot, but my brother lay shivering under several blankets and an overcoat. He struggled up as I let myself in and croaked that he'd be fine in a day or two as long as he had a few pots of tea to keep himself hydrated. I took his pulse and his temperature, then told him I wanted none of his nonsense, he was coming to my house where he could be properly nursed by Dora and myself.

– No no, not necessary, Gin –

But he was too weak to put up any real resistance. I packed him a small bag and helped him into his overcoat, and we struggled downstairs to the street. An hour later he was tucked up in clean sheets in one of the spare bedrooms, and an hour after that my own doctor was at his bedside. There was little enough to be done other than to keep putting fluids into him, and for the next few days we tended conscientiously to our invalid. By the end of the week he was getting up for a few hours in the afternoon. Then he was joining me before dinner to drink a glass of red wine and smoke a cigarette. He was thin and pale, purged, he said, and glad of it.

– Flushes out the system, a good muck sweat, he said. You should try it, Gin.

– A good muck sweat, I said doubtfully.

But I was glad he was up on his feet again and showing a bit of spirit. It distressed me to see him weak.

– Jack, you find this house comfortable?

– I never gave it much thought. I hate the wallpaper. And those rugs, Gin!

– I could strip the walls.

– Why would you want to?

I didn't need to say more. He did me the courtesy of pretending to think about it, but I knew the answer was no, at least for now.

– Where would I work?

– The attic.

He nodded. He knew the attic had the floor, the walls, the light he needed.

– I don't think so, Gin.

It was another two years before he moved into the house, but I planted the idea that day. I think he went back to Crosby Street with perhaps the first seeds of disillusion with that rickety shed of a place sown in his mind. Perhaps he remembered my offer as it stayed in the high 90s through August and September. Or perhaps in January, stapling sheets of plastic over the windows to keep out the wind, which also kept out the light, he reflected on how it would be to live in a building where the windows fit their frames and central heating kept all rooms at a comfortable steady temperature, and there was always hot water and Dora made lunch every day. And also did the washing. Was I wrong to lure him from his noble squalor? Certainly not. I believe Crosby Street would have killed him had he stayed there much longer.

But as I say, it took him a couple of years to leave the loft. I did not hound him, hounding was counter-productive with a man like Jack. No, I had sunk my hook, I could only wait for him to reel himself in. He made work steadily, if slowly, over those two years. No new collectors appeared so he had almost no income, apart of course from the allowance I drip-fed him. And yes, Vera was around, off and on, and as far as I was concerned she did him no good at all. She disrupted his routines, she compromised his sobriety, she destroyed his peace of mind. Did he care? It's immaterial. He cared, but he could no more turn her away from his door than he could cut off his hand. And she appeared as powerless to break it off as he was. I was at a loss to explain why this should have happened, and could only record it as a phenomenon, and say: it is inexplicable but it is a fact. They exerted an irresistible force of attraction upon each other, and were equally helpless to control it. So the question arises, why, after Jack left Crosby Street, and moved in with me, did they abruptly stop seeing each other?

Jack would never talk about it. But I worried at it constantly, and even began to wonder if it was something to do with me. It was not. It was to do with a story, or a vicious rumour, rather, of such potent malice and falsehood that when Vera heard it, a rupture was created between them which never healed. She discussed it with me only once, shortly before Jack's death. It was not a satisfactory conversation, and it remains a source of great sorrow to me that to this day she insists on believing a falsehood concerning him which is entirely the product of hatred. It originated, of course, in Port Mungo.

12

I n his last years then my brother was not robust. He lived with me for the simple reason that I could provide him with the kind of protective shelter he required in order to make art. And I have an admission to make in this regard. Jack actually produced very little art, the last few years of his life. It is true he went up to his studio every day, and stayed there for hours, and insisted on being left undisturbed, but the results were negligible. It was a long time since he had completed a painting. The so-called large canvas showed no sign of ever being finished. It was not a thing he liked to talk about, he preferred that we sustain the illusion that a good deal of work was being done up there. But it must have been apparent even to him that nothing ever came downstairs except himself. This told me that the man was fragile, and given that fragility I was by no means sure that this odd girl from England wouldn't crash about and upset him badly. Just how badly, in the end, she *did* upset him, I couldn't have begun to imagine. But I protected her, what else was I to do?

They began work the next day, this at her suggestion, as indeed the entire enterprise was at her suggestion. She arrived at the house at ten. Jack made her tea, and they went upstairs. Halfway up the stairs he heard her panting behind him, her breath shallow from all the rough tobacco she smoked. He paused and asked her if she was all right. She said she was nervous. They reached the attic. Ten years ago it was remodelled as Jack's studio: ceiling and interior walls torn out, rafters exposed, windows enlarged, everything painted white. I was rarely allowed up there, and Dora never. The few times I'd seen it I'd been appalled at the squalor.

– Will it just be my face? she said.

No answer from Jack as he organized himself for work. He struggled into his paint-smeared lab coat. He put a high wooden stool in front of the north-facing window and had her sit. He moved her about on the stool until he had her where he wanted her, and then he adjusted the position of her head. He stood over his work table with his back to her, then he dragged his chair over to the window and sat down, so close he was practically on top of her. He crossed his legs, frowning, peering at her, a block of grey paper on his knee. Later I asked him what he planned to do with her. He didn't know yet. At this stage a few drawings, see what happened. See where it went.

He began to draw, pencil lines for the planes of the face, shading with charcoal, highlights with chalk, and she shifted about on the stool, blinking at the light. She reached down for her bag, groped about in it, produced a pair of sunglasses and slipped them on. He stopped working and stared at her. The sunglasses made her opaque, but also somehow naked. All you saw was the mouth.

– I don't think so.

She took them off.

The work proceeded. At last her head was still, and for some minutes there was no sound but the scratching of charcoal on paper. I pictured it in my mind's eye: the grizzled artist humped in his chair with a block of paper on his knee, staring at a pale girl on a stool, this intense silent conversation taking place in a few square feet of cleared space amid a sprawling chaos of painterly debris. Cold light flooding in, bleaching the girl's skin to a more naked whiteness even than its usual skull-like pallor, as the artist's eyes dropped and lifted and stared, then dropped and lifted again. His fingers stuttering across the paper.

– Can I smoke?

– No.

Silence once more. Jack was working rapidly, he had to, he had to do as much as he could before his knuckles got hot. He told me later he had anticipated that once he properly got to know the girl's face the likeness she seemed to share with her sister would collapse, and a face would emerge that was different in a thousand particulars of structure and feature and complexion. But to my dismay – we were downstairs in the sitting room before dinner – it was not so. It was not so. He was restlessly rubbing his knuckles as he talked. There was, instead, a kind of convergence, he said, frowning, intrigued, in that the head he was drawing, the image of it on paper, was beginning to make a match with the image he held in his memory of Peg's head.

Forty minutes he had her sit there and then he told her she could smoke. She stirred to life as though waking from a deep sleep. Jack later said she was the most natural model he had ever had. Almost at once she ceased posing, he said, and behaved as though she were alone in the room, and a conscious human being alone in a room – a room, that is, without a mirror – is more truly herself than at any other time. She blinked and grinned, she stretched her arms above her head, she yawned, then she reached for her bag and hauled out her tobacco.

– Can I see? she said.

He tore several drawings out of the tablet and pinned them to the wall. She stood in front of them and Jack stood beside her. She appeared, in his drawing, to be frowning, but the eyes were glazed, they suggested a sleeper's vulnerability, or the lazy indifference of a cat.

– Shall we go on? she said.

– I don't think so.

He was gruff now. He would not meet her eye. He did not tell her that his hand was beginning to claw. He did not tell her that he was getting angry. Having to stop work because of pain always made him angry. He hated to feel weak. He worked as long as he could bear it, and when he had to stop it made him angry. It wasn't Anna's fault, but she couldn't know this.

It seems the second session was much like the first, although towards the end of it he became aware of a rising agitation in the girl. They had discussed nothing at the end of the first session. He had made it clear when the session was over, had paid her, and she'd left. I'd been out all day so again I missed her, but how very commercial Jack made it sound, when we talked that evening, and I remember asking him was there any *warmth* expressed between them?

– Warmth? Sure.

– How?

– All perfectly cordial, Gin. Quite warm enough. Sits well, when she settles down.

– Jack, she's your daughter.

– I expect we'll get around to all that soon enough.

Anna clearly wanted to get around to 'all that' sooner rather than later, and at the end of the second session she spoke up.

– Jack, she said.

He was washing his hands, she was rolling a cigarette. He grunted.

– Can we talk now?

– Sure.

My brother was intimidating when he was irritated, and I had to admire the girl's courage, that she would say what she wanted even as Jack stamped about grunting and glowering. He sat down and they faced each other, him in his work chair and her on the stool. I thought she would be direct and she was.

– Where's my mother?

– You don't know?

– I think she might be upstate.

– I haven't seen her in years.

– Me neither.

I was not surprised to hear that Anna had had no contact with

146

her mother since Gerald took her away. So other than what our brother had told her – and that, I imagine, was not flattering – she knew nothing about Vera. But by the end of an hour's conversation with Jack she apparently saw her mother in a new light. Not only was she an artist, not only had she led a rackety, wandering sort of a life, but she'd never buckled to the power of a man nor conformed to anybody's expectations of how she should behave. When Jack told her how they'd run away to America seven weeks after they'd met, the girl had hooted with pleasure. I think she believed her generation was the first to produce feisty women, and certainly she wouldn't have come across many like Vera in Surrey. Jack told me this was all to the good, if it made her realize that everything Gerald had told her was wrong. Jack intended to wean her off Gerald's version of the past.

– She'll tell you all about herself now, I told him. She'll tell you more than you want to know.

– Why more than I want to know?

– My dear, I said, you live like a monk. You need me and Dora, but you don't need anybody else.

That had been true till Anna arrived. Now I saw he wanted to pour it all out. He wanted to tell her everything.

He'd spent an hour telling her the flight-to-America story, and when he'd finished he felt sure she must be eager to get away. But she wanted more. She wanted to know why they hadn't stayed in New York, if that was where the future of art lay, why they'd gone south, fetched up in Port Mungo of all places. What she really wanted, I think, was to hear more about her mother's adventures, and Jack said there was much he could have told her, because incidents he hadn't thought of in years were rising into consciousness in some detail. He suggested they go down to the kitchen and have a cup of tea. Or a drink. They needed it, he said.

It was warmer down there, and they settled at the table with a bottle of wine and an ashtray. The initial chill – the hesitation, the mutual distrust of these two prickly creatures – this had dissipated, and a kind of wary affection had sprung to life between them, all in the space of a morning.

– Jack, she said.

– Anna.

– Are you successful? I mean, have you had a good career?

There was no point being anything other than honest. No, he said, he had not had a good career. He told her about the big show in SoHo and all the good press he'd had. But his sales were lousy and eventually the gallery had dropped him. He'd worked too long in isolation. He told her how he'd created a style of painting called *tropicalism* – was she still with him? – she was nodding away but he wasn't sure – he had her come into the big room and stand in front of his *Narcissus*.

She stared at it for a long time.

– So do you still have exhibitions? she said at last.

– Oh sure. There's always shows. But they're small shows. I don't give myself anguish about it any more.

– Are there many tropicalists?

– No. School of one.

There was a pause here – and then they both shouted with laughter. It was lovely honest laughter, he said, it erupted quite spontaneously, and they cackled away at each other till Anna started to cough. He told her she must have had enough of him for one day, and although I think she would have preferred to stay, she understood that it was Jack who had had enough.

– What are you doing tonight? he said, as she was leaving.

– Going out with some guy.

He closed the door behind her and leaned against it, suddenly deflated, and aware of a grumbling in his wrists and knuckles.

They had agreed not to meet for a few days, as Jack wanted to get on with the large canvas. But when he went up to the studio he found himself drawn instead to the sketches he'd made of Anna's head. He sat and stared at them for a long time. He thought about the years in Port Mungo. She was a silent, dark-haired little thing who could settle with a heap of shells and a boxful of sticks and be occupied at the back of his studio for hours. She never seemed to mind the heat, and she never cried, and when he and Peg went to the beach to drink beer they would take her with them and watch her toddle along the shore, then all at once stop, and peer down, fascinated, for minutes on end, at a dead crab, or a dead jellyfish, or a dried-out branch of seaweed. She would squat down on the sand and extend a tentative finger, and touch the thing, whatever it was – pull her hand away – touch it again – and so her small deliberate researches proceeded. He remembered how much he had missed her when Gerald took her to England, and he remembered too the brisk, brutal way he had then forced himself to forget her. Jack always said he was a bad father to his older daughter, that he knew it even at the time. He chose to be a bad father to Peg, he said, because he did not believe a man could be both a good father and a good artist.

But now he wanted to be a good father to this lost girl of his, though he did not know how to, nor even if she wanted him to. Why? Because he saw Peg in her. And again he roused her image, and tried to glimpse a match with the girl who sat in his studio with a glazed look in her eyes and her hands dangling between her knees. But this time he failed to find the match, and realized it must all be in his imagination. He had simply superimposed a family likeness on to the fading fabric of memory, and grown excited at the resulting chimera.

All this he reported to me that night. We were in the sitting room after dinner. He told me that Anna had asked him if he'd had a successful career.

– What did you say?

– I said I hadn't. Am I right?

I was amused. I myself came to terms with artistic ambition long ago, but I was familiar with the passions that still guttered fitfully in my brother. That night I was indulgent. I reviewed his career, I spoke of the dogged commitment with which he had persevered as a painter in Port Mungo, his courage in holding off coming to New York until he had found his mature style, and the forcefulness with which he had then claimed his place in the art world, before renouncing it with equal force. So discipline, I said, frowning, as I analysed his artistic enterprise – industry in adversity – the creation of a body of work –

When I talked like that it wasn't long before Jack was in front of his *Narcissus* in a state of rapt astonishment at the scale of his accomplishment. He needed nights like this, there were days enough, god knows, when he sat in his studio sunk in the profound conviction of his own futility, despising everything he had ever done. He decided he had misled Anna. He must rectify the error when he next saw her.

Some days later he watched her leaf through his catalogue, sitting on the edge of the couch in his studio with the book on her knees and her ankles splayed out, long back bent and an air of intense pointed concentration. She lingered for several seconds as she lifted the corner of each page, and Jack told me that as he watched her the emotion rose in him with a sudden *lurching* sensation, threatening tears, but with heat also, and his amplified heartbeat accelerated, almost out of control – this an event he had not experienced for many years, and had known only in relation to Peg, long ago, when she was a little girl.

He'd have liked to tell me that Anna, too, almost burst into tears, looking at his work, but no. All the same she had stared at the reproductions for many minutes, then asked him if she could borrow the book. Borrow it, she could have it, for god's sake –! He didn't tell her he had fifty more in a cardboard box down-stairs. He signed it with a flourish and she carried it off as though he had given her a precious holy object, the relic of a saint.

Oddly enough I had yet to meet her, and I felt that it could not be delayed much longer. Not that *I* wanted to delay it, I was eager to see what this scorpion girl of his looked like, it was Jack who seemed unwilling to introduce us, hustling her upstairs when she arrived in the morning and then out again once they had finished. Or perhaps, it occurs to me now, it was her doing, she didn't want to meet *me*. Yes, and I know why. But finally I suggested we have her to dinner, and somewhat reluctantly he agreed. It was his idea that we have a fourth guest. He was afraid, he said, that otherwise I would bore the girl.

He could be such a bastard.

The dining table is up at the far end of the big room, close to the kitchen. Candles burned from tall slender sticks. A thin blue vase of white lilies stood among the gleaming glasses and cutlery. Anna had already arrived when Jack came down wearing one of his more colourful headscarves. She sat on the couch, frowning and smoking and picking at a bowl of nuts, while I sat in the leather armchair, absently fingering the stem of my cocktail glass, and tried to put her at her ease, though without much success. There are people one occasionally encounters who seem to mistrust any attempt one makes to be warm or affable or civilized, and who project the tiresome attitude that all social intercourse is false, a game, a trap. Anna was apparently one of these. I could hardly get a word out of her, and I had deployed a good part of my artillery. She was wearing a very short skirt and fishnet stockings, and ankle boots with spiky heels. Also spiky hair. Some kohl round the eyes, she'd tried to tart herself up but hadn't got very far. I was relieved when Jack appeared. Anna seemed startled. Perhaps it was his headscarf. She sat up straight and produced a shy toothy smile.

– Here you are, he said.

– Here she is. I was telling her about the pictures.

– That one's your mother's, said Jack.

– I know, she said.

He leaned down to kiss her cheek and she rose awkwardly to meet his lips. She had to steady herself with a hand on his shoulder. I moved to the sideboard and poured him a glass of wine. Anna had a mineral water. He sat down beside her and at once she became talkative. She told us about the friend's place on the Bowery where she was staying till she found something of her own.

– The Bowery, I said. Far cry from Surrey.

This provoked disloyal laughter.

– Yeah, Surrey.

– I feel the same about Surrey, I said, in fact I feel the same about England.

We talked about England. She was curious that we'd spent almost all our lives abroad. Outcasts on a distant shore, as I liked to say. I talked about the class system, and English envy – us and them. I said there was no such thing as envy in America, there was no 'them', it was all 'us' – we the people. I watched her carefully. Small frown, dropping of the eyes, fingers laid flat on the table. I looked at her tattoo and wondered why she'd chosen a scorpion. Did she sting? She picked up her glass of fizzy water.

– Actually that's crap, she said, looking up, looking straight at me.

She did sting!

– Of course it is, I said, laughing.

She glanced at Jack. We heard the front-door buzzer, then Dora coming out of the kitchen and crossing the hall.

– This is Eduardo Byrne, I whispered, as we heard his voice, you must sting him too.

The door opened and in he came. Eduardo, my old friend and once, of course, my lover. Why did Jack invite him tonight? He said he thought Anna would feel comfortable with him: Eduardo, he'd said, is a free spirit. I'd asked what that made me but he ignored the question. He had formulated some concept of the evening and it hadn't been my place to question it. When he'd first come to live with me I told Jack to consider the house as much his as mine. He had certainly done that.

Eduardo took Anna's hand and peered at her closely. He had

152

strong knobbly sculptor's hands, years of oil, paint, dirt and rust bedded deep in the crevices of the flesh, and eyes like a sad old horse that had worked too hard too long, dark liquid eyes under tangled black brows with silver wires in them. His face was creased and leathery, blue with beard even after a shave, and his body was covered with hair. Teeth large and grey, hair crinkled up on his head such that it never needed a comb, same first thing in the morning as it was the night before. Apart from the silver wires he seemed not to age.

– Eduardo, I said, pouring him a drink, tell us what you've been doing.

He released Anna's hand and sat down. He rubbed his face. He had nothing to tell us of himself, he said, producing a shrug, the dark eyes rolling up from under their tangled hedge of eyebrow. About the making of work it is impossible to speak, he said, and about the selling of work it is humiliating, so I have nothing to say.

– Then we will have a lively time of it.

Eduardo then turned to Jack and declared he would have recognized Anna at once as his daughter. She was staring at the floor and Jack was smiling slightly. Neither of them said anything – they were embarrassed! I glanced at Eduardo, who scratched his cheek, then emptied the bowl of nuts into his palm and swallowed the lot. The moment passed.

Dora had prepared her roast shoulder of lamb with roast potatoes, and we had Federico in to serve, one of Luis's young men from round the corner. I did the wine. Hot garlic soup to start. Eduardo was fascinated that Anna hadn't seen Jack since she was a little girl, and that she was hearing her own family history for the first time. He got the girl talking and listened intently, tearing his bread roll into small pieces and placing them on his tongue one after another like communion wafers. He asked if she knew her parents ran off to New York after knowing each other only two weeks.

– Seven, said Anna.

– Seven? said Eduardo. I thought two. Two is crazy. But seven is also crazy.

– It was more than two, said Jack. It was more like seven. Who can remember these things?

– Perhaps it was ten, said Eduardo. Or thirty.

– Oh no, said Jack, not thirty. We had to get away from Gordon.

– Gordon the Terrible, I said.

Anna wanted to know what had happened to him. Eduardo, who was possessed of intuition in such matters, realized that her curiosity stemmed from some predicament of her own. He asked her what it was.

He'd touched a raw nerve, this was clear at once. A sick, resigned expression, the mouth working all manner of wry twitches, the body language evasive, ill-at-ease – but yes, her man. His name was Guy and he was married.

Eduardo was sympathetic. We were all sympathetic. The dinner was going well, I thought, as a curtain of intimacy closed round us and we pondered Anna's plight. I poured more wine. Eduardo murmured that he could well imagine the sorts of humiliations she had suffered. Meetings cancelled at the last minute – never being together all night – never being able to call him at home. His constantly divided attention. Anna listened carefully, nodding and smoking, as though her experience was being in some way validated by these rather trite instances of the mistress's predicament. Eduardo certainly knew all about that.

– So why do it? he said. Why go on with him?

A snort of impatience here.

– Yeah, why? I don't know!

Out it came, full of feeling, and the feeling said, I do know but it's too knotty for me, and I can't resolve it.

We all waited, saying nothing.

– Oh christ, I suppose I love him. I've tried to stop, but you can't, can you? You can't just make yourself stop loving someone.

– Sure you can.

This came from Jack, and it startled her. It was not an idea she had encountered before.

– How?

– You make up your mind to it. You kill the love. Every time you feel it, you kill it. It's like drowning puppies. It's not pleasant but it can be done.

– Have you done it?

This was asked dubiously. She frowned as she said it, squinting at him through her cigarette smoke. She'd hardly touched her lamb.

– Oh sure.

– With my mother?

Talk about painting yourself into a corner. It would take him all night to answer that one.

– No, I couldn't.

– Why not?

– I tried, but it was no good. Puppies wouldn't drown.

Nobody but me seemed to register how tasteless this was, this talk of drowning puppies, given what had happened to Anna's sister. She pondered it in silence, picking shreds of tobacco off her tongue and inspecting them. Then she looked up.

– That'll all come out, right? As we talk?

She then talked more about her married man, and astonished us all by admitting that he was in gaol, waiting to stand trial for stabbing a man in a pub. She said she'd gone to visit him in Belmarsh, one of the big London prisons, and saw his wife and kids in the waiting area. She'd had to come away. That was the worst of it, she said. She couldn't even get him to herself when he was in gaol!

But she didn't cry, and Jack said later she had never cried as a little girl. Her chin would come up and she'd press her lips tightly together, and though her eyes were brimming she would not let the tears flow. So she hadn't changed in that respect.

The evening was a success, I think. Jack's guess that Anna

would be comfortable with Eduardo proved correct, for it was clear she appreciated his thoughtful interest, and also that she had warmed to Eduardo himself – this a man who, after a lifetime of chiselling his character to the stark complexity of one of his own black bronzes, could effortlessly display to an impressionable young woman all the brooding allure and dark romanticism of – *the artist*. They went home at half past ten, Eduardo offering to walk her across town to the Bowery. As Dora cleared the table my brother and I retired to the far end of the room.

– So?

I said I was impressed with her. I said I thought she was a remarkable girl, to have come here as she had so as to find out about her sister, though I was worried by this story of the man in gaol. Whether Jack glimpsed the precise drift of my thoughts I do not know. He might have, you could never tell with him. It was late, he was tired, he said goodnight and went up to bed.

I was not tired at all. In fact my mind was seething. I had seen the girl's resemblance to Peg, though it was certainly not as strong as Jack supposed. But it did strike me as rather an eerie coincidence that her punky haircut should resemble the mess Peg had made of her hair the last time she was in New York. But not a very strong likeness, even if Jack apparently thought it was, and this was what disturbed me. I had thought that my influence, and the atmosphere of this house, were powerful forces for good in this regard, our tranquil routines, I mean, and the slow, painless extraction of poison which I effected each evening as we murmured to each other over our wine. In one way the girl was having a tonic influence on him, for he was displaying more enthusiasm for his work than I had seen in a long time. But it alarmed me that this was a direct consequence of his perception of a likeness to her dead sister, and I was still fearful that the rekindling of ancient emotion would eventually have a negative effect, and that sooner or later he would unravel, go to pieces, I had seen it before; at which point I

156

would have to put him back together again, and all my work would have been for nothing.

But I understood my brother well enough to be sure that were I to attempt to obstruct him I would not succeed. He would have his way regardless of my feelings in the matter. For Jack had this in common with Vera, and it largely accounted for the turbulence of their years together, and Peg's disorderly childhood – that he was stubborn, and selfish, and had a will of iron. I had come up against Jack's will on more occasions than I cared to remember, and I had certainly seen him stubborn, oh yes, and selfish in the extreme.

I have said that my brother could be selfish. But what he did next astonished me beyond anything I had seen before.

It happened three days later. He had made his decision, he said, and felt that to delay it any longer would be foolish – this a decision he had not thought fit to discuss with me. He had an appointment with Anna in the morning. She was punctual as usual, he said, and they worked well for an hour. Then he told her to smoke, and as he took off his lab coat he broached the topic. He asked her if she had found somewhere to live. Anna's room-mate had gone out of town so the pressure was briefly off her, but she didn't want to ruin the friendship by overstaying her welcome. When her friend came back Anna wanted to be able to tell her she was moving out.

– You can, said Jack.

– I don't have a place yet.

– Come live here.

There, it was out. A long pause here. No rushing in to thank him, or to say it was out of the question, too kind but she couldn't possibly – none of that English nonsense, instead she frowned, she began to think, he watched her thinking, she glanced at him and nodded slightly then out came the bag of tobacco. When she'd rolled herself a shaggy one and set it alight she asked her one question.

– What does Gin think?

– She thinks you should live here too.

– All right then. Thanks.

And that's how simple and dishonest the transaction was. They worked for another hour and then he showed her the empty bedrooms and told her to decide which one she wanted.

She certainly wasted no time moving in. Nor was she heavily burdened with luggage. She appeared shortly after six o'clock with a canvas shoulder bag and a hard black guitar case, and Jack soon had her installed in the room she wanted, the one at the front of the house overlooking the street. He told her to come downstairs and have a drink when she was ready, then left her to herself and closed the door quietly behind him. When I got home a little later I was presented with a *fait accompli*, and it was all I could do to keep my temper until I'd properly digested what he had done. I went upstairs reeling.

When I came back down I was sufficiently in control of myself to say to my brother that he was looking pleased with himself. He pretended to be unconscious of the irony, saying why wouldn't he be pleased, having his daughter back under the same roof? I told him quietly that he should have talked to me first, but Jack had no time for any of that, and briskly told me that with Anna in the house there would have to be changes.

– Changes?

Dear god but he was behaving badly. I am not fond of changes, as Jack knew better than anyone.

– We will have to try and entertain her, he said.

– I should have thought it was the other way round, I said, but at that moment Anna appeared in the doorway. Jack at once rose to his feet and padded towards the drinks table.

– What will you have, my dear? he said.

Anna was well-mannered enough to thank me for letting her stay with us, and I had to put a good face on it. A little later I gave her a set of keys and explained about the locks on the front door. Then I said something about dinner, and Anna told us she would not be eating with us.

– But why ever not? cried Jack.

He had assumed we would all be sitting down together, but it seemed she had made other plans. She was having dinner with Eduardo. Jack did not trouble to conceal his irritation, nor I my pleasure. A few minutes later she went back upstairs, and soon after that we heard her coming down again, and the front door closing. I glanced at Jack.

– So where would you like to eat? I said pleasantly.

That night I lay awake like an anxious parent, listening for her key in the door. New York locks can be difficult, and I did not want her waking the house. I soon recognized that this anxiety merely masked a deeper one, which had to do with Eduardo. But he was old enough to be her father, and an old friend of the family, so surely no danger there –? None the less it was a worry. I never heard her come in, but there she was at breakfast, pale and waxy as ever, and completely unforthcoming in response to my one polite, noninvasive inquiry as to her night out.

And that's how she got into the house.

13

Having Anna with us soon changed the way Jack and I rubbed along together, this was one of the first changes I observed. When we were by ourselves in the big room downstairs we both listened for her key in the door, her step on the stairs. And although I did not admit this to him for some time, I began actually to enjoy her presence, and was disappointed if she were out! Jack was worse, he was soft and doting, quite unlike himself, and I think even Dora was infected with the new atmosphere in the house, like us she was susceptible to the inimitable vital perfume which fills the air with the mere presence of youth. Anna was an unusual youth, dour and serious and to my mind profoundly mysterious, I think because she communicated so little of what she did outside the house. She implicitly declared that she had a private life, would we please respect that, and of course we did. Of course we did.

I discovered how to navigate the awkward silences she seemed to generate whenever we found ourselves alone together. They never seemed to occur when Jack was present, as he was entirely at ease with her now. But with me the girl was not at ease, and if we were alone together she would soon find some reason to leave the room. The answer was not to try and find a neutral topic to talk about, but rather to talk about *her*. Youth is profoundly obsessed with its own dilemma, which crudely put is the problem of going forward with the appearance of sure-footed confidence into what looks like a morass of uncertainty and risk. One day I asked her if she had any plans. She seemed startled by the question. She had a job of some kind in a bar, which kept her out several nights a week, but beyond merely surviving in New York we had heard of no specific schemes or goals or ambitions. I suspected at the time that she was here solely to get to know her father again, possibly her mother as well, but for some reason was reluctant to say so. I had no patience with any of that. What is it, I asked her, that you want to *do* here?

As I say, she was startled, and I felt I had intruded on her privacy. But I persevered. Was there a career she wanted to pursue?

Expression of distinct relief. Oh that's what you mean. What else would I mean? Shyly she told me she wanted to do something creative.

– You want to be an artist, Anna?

– Yes.

– A painter like your father?

– No, not like him.

This came out with what to my surprise sounded like disdain, contempt almost. Certainly with a charge of fierce feeling that I couldn't interpret at the time. Perhaps she believed that painting was dead, I thought, and wanted to be a conceptual artist. But when I said this she said no. I didn't know what to think, but at least we had managed to have a sort of conversation, and it was easier between us after that.

For the first time in many months Jack began to work in the afternoons, not on the portrait of Anna, that was the morning's work, but on the large canvas, which he had begun to call *A Dream of the Lower Waters*. As soon as I heard the title I knew the painting would be a reworking of his old motif, what he called the Narcissus posture: a figure leaning over a surface in which he finds a distorted reflection, and the reflection clawing up at the leaning figure through a web or latticework of some kind. It had not escaped me that there was a grim correspondence between this and the macabre picture I held in my mind's eye of the Port Mungo fisherman who'd leaned over the side of his boat one day, out among the mangroves, and discovered to his horror a drowned girl gazing up at him from a tangle of underwater roots.

These fresh energies of Jack's I attributed entirely to Anna's presence in the house. I saw that she was beginning to assume the role of muse to her father. She continued to sit for him in the mornings, and by now they had established a routine, she came to him three times a week from ten to one. She let Dora know when she would be eating with us and when not, and by the end of the month I believe we had all adjusted to our changed circumstances. As for our having to entertain the girl, I was not aware of making any particular effort myself in that direction.

I was surprised to learn that Jack had not yet talked to her about her sister's death, nor had he decided what he would say when he did. But he had at least told her something of the early years in Port Mungo. I asked him how she'd responded, and he said he didn't know, she gave away so little. More to the point, he said, he'd also been waiting to hear what she thought of his catalogue. The day after he'd given it to her she had come into the studio and gone straight to the large canvas, and frowned at it as though she had formed ideas about his work overnight and was testing them against the work in progress. Since then of course she'd moved into the house with us, but still she'd said nothing about the catalogue. I knew it was troubling him, so I made a point of asking him every evening if she'd mentioned it yet. I was still a little angry that he'd failed to consult me before inviting her to live with us.

– Not a word.

– Must be awkward.

– It's extremely bloody awkward. I feel as though she's

come upon me fast asleep, and she's inspecting me, and I'm naked.

– Jack, it's your work she's looking at, not your body.

– It feels the same.

I suppose I understood this, but why didn't he just ask her? Oh no. That wouldn't do. He didn't want to put pressure on the girl. So he continued to fret. But the work went forward, and I understood that by this time he had completed a number of sketches and had begun a full-length study.

– What size? I said.

– Sixty by twenty-four.

That was big. Or tall, at least. I wondered who'd stretched the canvas. Jack used to have an assistant but he'd let him go, there simply wasn't enough for him to do. I asked him if he was stretching his own canvases now.

– Anna's helping me.

A little later he told me it had been Anna's suggestion that he employ her as his assistant. She was apparently intrigued by what went on in a painter's studio.

– Not surprising, he said, with all the artists in the family. I think she might be one herself.

He described how every morning they'd have a cup of tea in the kitchen then go upstairs. He said he liked to watch her in the studio, for he recognized that the role she assumed there was his role, the artist's role, and that in her imagination the studio had become her studio, herself the one who came into it every day to struggle with her demons and out of such conflict bring ideas to life on canvas, or whatever it was she thought he did up there. He said she strode about quite confidently now, no longer awed as she had been at first – there had been something reverent in her manner, the first few times, as though the studio were a sanctified place, a chapel – but now she strutted about in front of the *Dream* with a vaguely proprietorial air, and he could almost hear her address the painting, very much as he himself would before he started to work, or *interrogate* it, rather, ask it where it all seemed inclined to go – what it was he must do next – this the throb and thrill of the thing, he said, but also the fraught danger every morning: starting again, that is, on work left the day before in a state of incompletion.

As she peered and pondered she seemed to be playing out some such script in her head, and perhaps her imagination was adequate to the task. Perhaps she did understand what it was Jack did in his studio every day. It was another mark of her growing confidence that she often initiated conversation after they had begun working. She stood naked in front of a large drape of black velvet, gazing off blankly as Jack stared and stared, and dabbed and dabbed, then out it came.

– Gerald said my sister should have been sent to England to be educated. He said he couldn't understand why she wasn't.

– Never been a shortage of things Gerald couldn't understand.

It was the quick bitter riposte of a distracted man at an easel. But he saw her flinch, and reminded himself she had had no word of her sister that had not come from Gerald. She was ripe for the dismantling of the construction of events she had been given since childhood, and he knew he must not hold her responsible for received ideas, no matter how grotesque. In the struggle for Anna's mind and heart Jack had the advantage now. He must not show his teeth like this, it did not help.

– Gerald had no idea what our life was like.

– Did she get educated then?

– Sure she got educated.

After a fashion, he might have added; his fashion. He didn't tell her that the girl practically ran wild.

– So she could read and write.

– And she could paint.

At this she turned towards him and he told her sharply to look straight ahead.

– You taught her to paint?

– I don't know that we did much teaching. She just imitated what she saw going on around her.

– Was she any good?

No answer from Jack.

– Do you have any of her work here?

– No.

A long silence now, and not an easy one, the room thick with questions, the most insistent of which was where this sudden anger of his had come from, why such a spiked denial?

– Sorry, he said.

She waited for more but that's all there was.

– It's just I don't know what to say and what not to, she said.

– It's not your fault.

Another silence.

– I drowned my puppies, she said.

– Oh yes?

– Yeah. I finished it.

Throughout this she stood there unmoving, her arms by her side, her head turned away, her eyes fixed on a point outside the window. He was behind the easel with his head down. The atmosphere grew more relaxed. More time passed in silence. I have seen Jack at work with a model, more than once he has painted me. Touch the canvas, lift the eyes, look hard, touch the canvas again. Mix the colours on the glass, rub the canvas with a damp rag, wash the brush. Jam the brush between the teeth, draw well back to inspect, gesture at the sitter with the brush then repeat the gesture on the canvas.

Take another long hard look. Wash the brush, remix the colours, criss-cross dabbing, touch the canvas with a Q-tip, change the brush, stick the old one in a jar of turps, take a swig of tea, and so on and so on and so on –

– I just wish I'd known her, she said. Oh god Jack, maybe this is all a waste of time. It only makes you angry and me confused. We should just say she's dead and leave it at that, not try and bring her back to life.

She poured this out to the window then began to turn towards him, then thought better of it.

– I think we shouldn't give up, said Jack.

– Why?

– I don't think she would want us to.

Hard to argue with that.

Peg in Port Mungo. He wanted to impress on Anna that the girl was born there, delivered into the world, it is true, by an Englishman, but she never knew Europe. The two times Jack brought her to New York she was not happy, she soon became restless and was eager to get home. She was a native of Port Mungo, and knew it in a way that he and Vera never would. She grew up with the children of the town, she was in and out of their houses every day of her life, it was of no significance to her that her skin was white while theirs might be any one of a dozen hues between bone and coal. She spoke the patois that Jack had never troubled to learn, she ate what Jack remained too fastidious to eat, in short she encountered none of the barriers between herself and them that even after years Jack had not crossed. And she ran wild, by which he meant that after a couple of hours of schooling in the tin-roofed building behind the marketplace she had little else to do all day but mess about in leaky boats. Jack saw no harm in it.

And she painted of course. She loved to paint. They let her use their stuff, Jack said, they encouraged her as much as they could.

Anna stood frowning at the window as Jack talked on, and he was aware, he told me later, that while he worked – and he seemed able to work fast when he talked about Peg, though he was not sure what prompted what, the painting the talking or the other way round – he was aware of a flow of reactions across her face, still turned away from him in quarter profile, as she took hold of this picture of her sister's childhood. Did it conform to what Gerald had told her? He tried to see it as she must have, through Gerald's eyes, and glimpsed a dark primitive world where a white-skinned girl scampered half-naked with the native children and grew up without benefit of civilization or culture.

– Was she a bad girl?

Curious question. It said much about her, I thought, when Jack told me, and the unresolved complications of her view of herself, I mean this evident attempt to make sense of her own life through an understanding of her sister's. Jack tried to tell her that the concept of badness was not easy to apply in a place like Port Mungo. She was always home before dark, and I think this may have been the only rule they had. Night falls fast in the tropics.

– What about my mother's drinking?

Here Jack heard the distinct rumble of his brother's ponderous moral lucubrations.

– What about it?

– Did it affect her?

They let her drink a beer with them when she was eight. When she was seven they let her smoke. There was smoking and drinking in the house every night, no point trying to hide it from her. She was curious, she wanted to know what it was all about, this thing her parents did with such ritualized enthusiasm every night, and Jack had long been anticipating the day he could sit out on the deck with his daughter, the pair of them drinking beer as they talked about whatever it is that fathers and daughters talk about.

Another lengthy silence.

– Were you a bad girl? said Jack.

Good big grin in response to this question. The English certainly have this distinction, their dentistry is the worst in the world. Already yellowing with tobacco, those chipped irregular teeth like a set of tilting tombstones in a neglected country churchyard, and the girl barely into her twenties – it was extraordinary that she should be so beautiful, and her teeth so bad. I certainly thought her beautiful, and I know Jack did too. Was it merely youth that lent her beauty in our jaded old eyes? Perhaps, but I think not. That fine head, the swan's neck, the gaunt towering frame – the architecture of the creature was so very fine, her flesh so white and her hair so black that it gave me the best sort of pleasure simply to watch her, she reminded me of Jack at that age. I noticed one evening after dinner how his eyes followed her as she moved around the room, and I was aware that mine did the same. Was she aware of it? She didn't show it, but she must have known what was happening. It was not good, something ghoulish, surely, these two old crocodiles feasting on the beauty of a tall pale girl with bad teeth –!

– Quite bad, she said.

– Oh?

– Nothing very dramatic. I didn't like to worry them.

– You were discreetly bad.

– I suppose so. Were you bad?

– I was wild till Vera came along.

A little later they were sitting over coffee in the kitchen, talking comfortably, intimately, the lunch things not cleared away. Jack asked her if she remembered which room she had stayed in when she first came to the house as a little girl. She didn't know. He told her it was the same room she'd chosen two weeks ago.

– That's so weird, she said.

– Why is that weird?

– To not remember the room, but to recognize it. I must have recognized it, right?

– That's not weird. What's weird is that you should want to move into the room you lived in when your world had just collapsed.

– I guess I felt safe there.

– I guess you did.

She sipped her coffee. She pushed her chair back from the

table and crossed her legs. She flung an arm over the back of the chair, turned towards the window and coughed. He stared at her frowning profile. She reminded him of a photograph he had seen somewhere recently. She turned back and looked straight at him.

  – Did my sister kill herself?

Poor dear foolish Peg – I could hear Jack saying it – she had her mother's knack for finding trouble though not her skill at getting out of it. Too ready to follow, too eager for the good time, never any pausing to consider the consequences. It was her nature, and this being so, Port Mungo was probably the best place for her in all the world. But it was no paradise, and Jack was always emphatic about this, there were forces at work on the river that were darker and more complex than the sunny surface of tropical life would admit – oh, all this oblique stuff, which raised more questions than it answered, yet I imagined it flickering through his mind as he and Anna stared at each other in the kitchen, silent but for the ticking of the clock above the cooker and the muffled roar of the city beyond.

  – No.

  She dropped her eyes and then her head. She was sat square to the table, an elbow planted either side of her plate and her forehead clamped in the heels of her hands, with her fingers sticking up through her hair. Without moving a muscle, without lifting her eyes, she asked him was he sure. She asked the question in a hollow tone, black empty yawning hole of a question, the way she said it: Are you sure? So hollow it wasn't even a question. It was just what had to be said.

  – Yes.

  The hands flopped on to the table, the head came up. She looked suddenly exhausted. She cast a quick fierce sidelong glance at him.

  – Gerald said she did.

*   *   *

This now becomes painful in the extreme. When Jack told me what she'd said – *Gerald said she did* – I'd felt a distinct lurch of horror, and it was all I could do to conceal it from him. He was watching me carefully. He asked me what I thought the girl was talking about. I said I had no idea. He said he didn't either, but he hadn't pursued it, he'd let it go, he simply hadn't the mental wherewithal to attack yet again Gerald's skewed idea of what had happened in Port Mungo.

But I did know exactly what Gerald was talking about, or rather, I knew what Gerald thought he knew. It was the terrible day he took Anna away from my house. That afternoon I'd gone to the Park Plaza Hotel, where he was staying, but without telling anyone. So much of what had happened earlier in the day was mysterious to me that I felt I couldn't simply let him carry Jack's child off to England without at least hearing why he was doing it. So for the hour before they had to go to the airport we talked in his room, and Anna played with her doll on the carpet between us.

It has the feeling of a nightmare for me now, the hour I spent in that hotel room at the Park Plaza. There is a lurid, unreal quality to it, and I remember it in some detail. Gerald was not surprised to see me. He was brisk and urbane as he met me at the elevator and brought me into his room and had me sit in a wing chair, while he sat across from me on the other side of a glass-topped table with his back to the window. The room faced north and I had a fine view of Central Park. The autumn foliage was changing colour and what seemed an endless carpet of red and yellow and gold was spread before me as far as the eye could see. Gerald took control of the conversation at once. He asked me how I thought Jack had changed in the years he'd been away, and I knew what he was getting at, like me he'd realized Jack had deliberately destroyed in himself the forms of polite social behaviour we'd been taught as children. Gerald said that presumably he regarded them as vestiges of the English way of life, and abandoned them so as to embrace – what, exactly? – a pure primal existence which allowed him to fulfil his creative urges? This was how Gerald expressed it, and his words dripped scorn and condescension.

Certainly I had glimpsed something of what he was talking about during my days with Jack in Port Mungo, and again when he and Peg visited me here in the city. But I'd thought it a matter of manners, merely, and I said this to Gerald. What does it matter if his manners are uncouth? He's an artist, for god's sake.

My brother took off his spectacles and rubbed his eyes. As he did so there was a good deal of frowning, and he asked if I didn't suspect it went much deeper than that. How, deeper? I said. Oh, this foolhardy adventure of his, this idiotic romantic notion that for his art to flourish he must remove himself to some backward place where he wouldn't be distracted by the complications of urban life. What a delusion that always turns out to be!

I pointed out that Jack had worked hard in Port Mungo. I found Gerald's attitude patronizing, and I was irritated. He said he didn't doubt that Jack had been working hard, but in the absence of institutions and art galleries and museums and so on, in other words with nothing of the culture to guide him – could he have improved very much? He replaced his spectacles and said: Gin, what nature can teach us is quickly exhausted.

I didn't believe him capable of judging such a thing. I asked him if he was saying that Jack's life had been a waste.

– If he thinks he can make worthwhile art outside the western tradition then yes, his life's been a waste.

– That's why you're taking his daughter away?

Now we'd arrived at the crux of it. He stared out of the window. As with the artist, he murmured, so with the man.

Suddenly I thought of Vera, who early on had recognized the limitations of Port Mungo, its dreary sameness, day by sun-drenched day, the utter monotony of the tropical existence and all that this monotony brought in its train. She'd found in travel, in exploration of the Caribbean islands and the mainland of Central America, an antidote to the lassitude she was wise enough to fear –

Gerald's thoughts seemed to have travelled in the same channel as my own.

– He couldn't keep Vera down there.

I watched him carefully. He was coming to the point. He told me then exactly why he was taking Anna away. In Vera's absence, he said, in his loneliness and frustration, Jack had indulged a primitive physical reflex. A primitive physical reflex, Gin!

And that was when at last I saw what he was driving at. With utter disbelief I then listened to him saying that Jack had recognized under his own roof a girl just coming to sexual maturity. And had gone to her room at night.

– No, Gerald!

– Listen to me!

He was not specific. He could not tell me when it had begun, but said he knew what it looked like once it had begun. He had seen it in his practice, he said. It was not as rare as I might think. A lot of it in Suffolk. The pattern was invariable in such cases. What cases? Paternal incest.

– Rubbish!

– Listen to me, Gin. The girl adored her father. He would have spoken quietly to her in the darkness and made the arguments such men always make: there is nothing wrong with this, it's nice, it feels good. And then when it was over: but you must not tell anyone.

I was shaking my head, I denied absolutely what he was saying to me. He continued. You can imagine it having the structure of any clandestine relationship, Gin. You can imagine him convincing the child that it was their special game, this secret thing they did and teaching her how to enjoy it. How could she resist him, what defences did she have, once he had corrupted her? He was her father. He had the right, or so he would tell himself.

Still I refused to believe a word of it. I stood up and listened with mounting horror as Gerald talked, his tone as clinical as if he were describing the progress of a disease, which I suppose in his mind he was. On he droned, his voice level and cool, explaining that her conscience would disturb her more and more, and yes, she would tell him it was bad, what they were doing. But how could it be bad, he would say? She must not care what other people thought, because other people were stupid, they didn't understand –

– Who told you all this? I cried.

Little Anna looked up in alarm and I sank to the floor and knelt beside her and told her that everything was all right.

– It doesn't matter who told me.

I suppose I should simply have walked out, but I was strangely transfixed by these hideous lies. I sat down again. She was entirely in his power, he said. Her shame put her in his power. And as the months passed this squalid drama played out perhaps every night, perhaps every few nights, perhaps only once or twice a month, it doesn't matter, the effect was the same. The girl would have become very deeply depressed. Feelings of utter worthlessness. The sense of being dirty, filthy, all the time. Her mother was present, for part of it at least. She knew what was going on, at some level, so she drank all the harder to keep the knowledge of what Jack was doing to the girl at night well below the surface –

– That's enough, Gerald!

– That's why she killed herself. And that's why I'm taking Anna away. To protect her from him.

We were both suddenly drained, shocked, *shamed* by what he'd said. It was hard for us to look at each other, as though we too had been contaminated by this foulness. I stared out of the window at the rotting, dying leaves.

– Who told you this?

174

He would not say, but all at once I had the answer.

– Johnny Hague told you!

His eyes flickered to mine and I knew I was right. Oh thank god. I was flooded with relief. Oh thank god. I tried to explain to Gerald that Johnny Hague was not to be trusted, that all this poisonous stuff issued from a love affair gone bad, that Johnny hated Jack and had spread malicious rumours about him, there wasn't a grain of truth in any of it – Gerald wouldn't listen! He had no more time, the car was waiting downstairs, they had a plane to catch. I implored him to hear me out. No, he would not discuss it any further. He had told me why he was taking Anna away and now they must leave.

So I sat in that hotel room high over Central Park and watched as he carried Anna off, knowing that it was Gerald's mistake but that I could never say anything about it to Jack because he knew it too and yet had *done nothing*.

The day Jack told Anna that he didn't believe her sister killed herself she didn't come back to the house for dinner. I suspected she was staying at Eduardo's place. Jack and I sat in the sitting room that evening, the pair of us deflated and depressed. All at once Jack stirred, and stood up, and told me to come upstairs with him, he was going to show me the portrait. Strange, he said, as we climbed the stairs, how it had begun to draw him back at night, this was not the first time, despite his having concluded the painting was turning out a failure. He felt a rare ambivalence towards that painting. It was all wrong so why did he keep going back to it? He did not turn it to the wall, or destroy it, but kept it out, rather, and chalked up its attraction to some mystery of the art-making process, and god knows, he said, he had not come to the end of mysteries in that department, no artist does.

We reached the studio. I have said that Anna was beautiful. But at the same time she was gaunt, and gauche, and it was all there in the picture. And it occurred to me, as Jack carried it to the window, and stood it against the sill, so it was framed by the night-sky, that the power of the painting had its source in the very contradiction that rendered the girl beautiful – her beauty only apparent, I mean, because it was conflicted, because the glacial stagnation of a classical kind of beauty was here disturbed by subterranean clashes and fissures: Anna, in crisis, became beautiful, when otherwise she would be merely gawky – was this it? I said this to Jack as I gazed at the painting, and he said he wished he could ask Vera the question, no doubt she had already thought the same thing about someone else and reached conclusions for which he would spend five years groping.

It was an unfinished full-length portrait of Anna standing against a hanging drape of black velvet. It reminded me of a Venus I once saw in the Louvre, a Cranach I think. Her body was slightly torqued from the true, one bent arm lifted, pressed close to her head, the hand clamped to the back of the neck. The other hand was pulled behind her back, as though chained or cuffed to the wall. Jack turned off the lights and we moved to the other side of the room. The low glow of the city suffused the studio with gloom, in which the pallor of the painted skin seemed to absorb what little illumination spilled in from the outside and then gave it back into the ambient dusk with an effect not unlike moonlight, the cold pale radiance that came off the girl's painted flesh. Naked, she was like a long white flower, a slender androgynous creature straight out of the pages of romantic mythology –

And I remembered a night in Port Mungo. Jack and Peg loved the wild weather, and this one night we heard the wind rising offshore, and by the time we had made our way to the beach the palms were already flapping and flailing, taking the brunt of the gale not with their trunks but their leaves. Peg flung off all her clothes and ran into the surf, where she tossed and plunged like a dolphin. It was midnight. The wind died as suddenly as it had arisen, and then the moon emerged from between high clouds pushing west towards the mountains. The sea slackened to a light chop which broke foaming on the sand as the night-sky turned dark blue and filled with stars. Peg rose up in the shallow water and waded in towards the shore, lanky slim-hipped creature with her skin bleached out by the moonlight, and it was the same body I saw in Jack's studio that night.

14

It had been raining steadily for two days. The sky was dark and small lakes had formed in the streets, forcing pedestrians to pick their way along the sidewalk with some care so as to avoid being befouled by passing traffic. My cab splattered along Houston Street like an amphibious landing vehicle. I had him make a left on Lafayette and put me down at the door. How pleasant to get out of the filthy weather and into the wood-panelled warmth of a familiar cocktail bar. Eduardo was already there. A warm embrace, a tender kiss: I was fond of that man. I had loved him once. He had money now but the manner in which he lived had not changed at all, his loft was part lumberyard, part bodyshop, and a Franklin stove his only concession to comfort. He had long since left Mercer Street and now occupied the ground floor of an ill-serviced building next to a garage on a forgotten street south of Canal, close to the Holland Tunnel and within earshot of the West Side Highway.

– So, I said, as I struggled out of my raincoat.

– So.

My old friend was unshaven, in a creased leather coat and a baseball cap, having come from his loft, where his work, he said, was going as well as could be expected considering he had an important show next month.

– How are you feeling?

He spread his arms wide and his shirt stretched taut across the bony chest, the hard belly.

– Never better.

I wanted to talk to him about Anna of course. After the last session with Jack she had left the house and not come back. That was three days ago. We assumed she was with him, and he confirmed that yes, she was. This arrangement was far from ideal from our point of view, but there was nothing to be done. I tried not to show my concern, though he must have been aware of how we might feel. I think he simply didn't care. He began to pick away at this aspect of the girl being here, that her enquiries into her history should bring her to America. That traffic, he remarked, normally goes the other way. I was not sure what he was getting at, Eduardo's mind had at times a labyrinthine cast to it, but there was meat enough in the subject of Anna in America to keep him rumbling and mulling for the duration of a dry martini. It occurred to me that he was avoiding the conversation he knew we must have, so I interrupted, and asked if she ever talked about Peg; and to bring the girl's sister into the conversation like that was to startle a man who could spend an hour thinking about the contents of a pocket of an overcoat not worn since the previous winter.

– She was quite upset when she left us. You *are* looking after her, aren't you?

– Oh sure.

– We just found out Gerald told her Peg killed herself.

He frowned. He picked the olive out of his glass and put it in his mouth. Then, with his eyes on me, he slowly chewed the olive. I felt my words disappearing without trace into the voluminous folds of his mind.

– Did you know that?

He nodded.

– How does she feel about it?

– She doesn't talk about her feelings.

– Not even to you?

He shook his head. There was something he wasn't telling me and I wanted to know what it was. I leaned across the table.

– Eduardo, I said in a low voice, she's a good girl.

He lifted his big bull head and wiped his mouth, nodding very slightly. I sat back in my chair. Now I understood what was going on. Eduardo was attracted to trashy women, this I have always known. Anna had a loose, louche way about her but she was sound all the way through, not a trashy bone in her body, or not that I was aware of at the time. He must have discovered this too late. He'd made a mistake, that's why he agreed to come out and have a drink with me.

– So what happened? Something's happened.

A quick furtive movement from those bagged and tired eyes. I was right. I suppose I should have been angry with him but what good would that have done? I had no illusions about Eduardo Byrne. I had never approved of this affair with Anna, nor had Jack, but we had not been asked what we thought.

– I've got a problem.

– I thought so.

– It's this boy.

This was exactly what I'd been afraid of. Eduardo was a goat.

– Go on.

– He might show up in the loft.

– And what if Anna's there?

– It's a problem.

For a moment he assumed such a hangdog expression that I couldn't help but laugh. Men are pathetic. So canine in defeat. Either they whimper or they bark and snap. Not Eduardo though, not for long. Up came his head, faint gleam of – what, lecher triumphalism?

– Eduardo, come on. You want to hurt her? You know what she's dealing with.

– But I cannot control him! I never know what he will do next!

A smile darted across his face at the thought of this un-controllable boy of his, and I realized that my old friend had not changed. I should have known this, and been more strenuous about keeping Anna out of his clutches, for clearly she was only one of the several lovers Eduardo was currently fielding. This we didn't need. At this delicate juncture in the unfolding relationship of Anna and her father, with the crucial question of Peg's death having just been broached, this sort of sexual complication was the last thing we needed. I was feeling very cross with him indeed but I didn't let him see it, I wanted first to understand the situation. So I ordered more drinks and drew it out of him as you would a splinter from an infected wound.

A month ago he'd met a boy who worked in a restaurant near his building. The boy would come to the loft any hour of the day or night, and if Eduardo didn't open the door to him he threw stones at the windows and shouted details of their sex life, demanding to be let in for more of the same. All of which was nothing to me, other than that Anna might be there, and given what she was going through I didn't want her damaged. She was vulnerable, I told him. She was coming to terms with a traumatic event in her early childhood which had had the most serious consequences. Eduardo thought I was being overprotective, but all the same he was worried; not because she was fragile, rather the reverse. He had recognized a steely quality in Anna, he said. She was like her father, she had the seeds of a fanatic in her. It was a Rathbone thing and it made her dangerous.

– Dangerous!

He nodded. I was astonished. I had gone to Eduardo intending to urge him to do no emotional harm to the girl, and here he was telling me that she was the dangerous one!

She was reading in the big room when I got back to 11th Street, and I was relieved she was in our house and nowhere near Eduardo's loft. All at once I saw that her movements had already acquired a heightened importance for me, and when I told Jack my news later that evening he absorbed it wearily. His contempt was withering. His opinion of Eduardo had never been high and now he condemned him out of hand, not for what he was doing but for the harm it could do to Anna. He said nobody had the right to a pleasure which if discovered might damage another person. I said practically every adulterer in the United States fitted that description. Marriages and families were routinely destroyed in just that way.

– Quite, he said.

But it was one thing to make these judgements, another to see your daughter being drawn into a situation of deception and betrayal which had the potential to devastate her, and be unable to do anything about it. We had both intuited this much at least about Anna, that she was not yet a hardened and cynical player, and though Eduardo might have detected steel in her she was not in his league, and everything she'd said about her man in prison was quite enough to indicate that her heart was still a girl's heart, simple and trusting. She may have drowned her puppies, as she'd told Jack a few days earlier, but neither of us believed she was grown-up yet, not in matters of sexual love, and still less in the kind of complicated manœuvres with which Eduardo Byrne had long been amusing himself in New York City.

I told Jack that Eduardo knew what was at stake and must be left to handle it. He accepted this but only after we had a rather heated exchange. I think had he not been so distracted by what he was doing in the studio he might have taken control of the situation and done something about it.

We heard her coming in at dusk on the Tuesday evening. The house had been like a tomb. We only became properly aware of the extent to which she animated it when she was absent. We'd missed her, and I know Jack blamed himself for her absence. He did not say as much but it was clear he suspected that a lack of finesse or sensitivity on his part had driven her off. It is one of the grimmer aspects of growing old, how profoundly one experiences loss. One no longer has the confidence that what-ever is lost will be replaced, nor much faith in one's ability to attract a replacement. Loss begins to seem absolute, and creates a dismay that smacks of death.

We listened to her coming in through the front door and crossing the hall. Had she just come back for her things? Had she seen all she wanted to of Jack, believing all this time – courtesy of Gerald – that he had sexually abused her sister to the point where the girl had killed herself? But why, if she thought her father capable of such a thing, would she make herself so vulnerable as to stand naked in front of him day after day?

Then the door opened, and I knew she was back to stay. So did Jack. And he experienced an emotion, he told me later, of which he had long since believed himself impotent, and so powerfully that he rose to his feet and crossed the room and took her in his arms.

She clutched him tightly, stiffly, and when they broke apart there were tears on his face. Then she came to me and I too was hugged. I remembered a painting of the prodigal's return, though Anna of course was no prodigal. But so effectively was I persuaded that my fears were without foundation I cast about for the fatted calf. The best I could come up with was champagne.

– Splendid idea, said Jack, and went off to the kitchen. Anna and I sat down across from one another, and I was beaming like a fond old hen.

– You've been at Eduardo's?

– Yeah.

– You must know, dear Anna, that the last thing Jack wants is to cause you pain. You do believe me?

– I think I'm just a bit confused right now. Gerald told me one thing about Peg and now Jack says it's not true.

– Of course you're confused. What does Eduardo think?

This startled her. Up came her head. We heard a faint *pop!* from down the passage to the kitchen.

– He's on your side, she said.

I thought: I should bloody well think so.

– Meaning?

– He says my father's trying to tell me the truth but he's afraid of what I'll think if he makes Gerald look bad.

Shy grin here, a glimpse of those yellowy tombstone teeth. Like a death's head, I thought later. When I had to shelter her from the law. Here on West 11th Street, house of widows. Vera and Dora and Anna and me, the girl telling lies and me the only one who saw the thing clearly.

– He does want to tell you the truth.

She was about to ask me a question but just then Jack appeared with a chilled bottle and three flutes and our attention shifted to him. It seemed he had made a decision and wanted to waste no time putting it into effect. He sat down and stared at Anna and said he wanted to tell her how Peg died.

Anna stared at her father.

– Go on then, she said.

So Jack described, much as he'd explained it to me, Peg and Vera's last outing in the boat. The poor visibility, the collision with the coral head, the weather turning bad, the mangroves –

Anna sat staring at the floor with her elbows on her knees. She let out a gasp when he finished. It had taken no more than a minute or two. There was a long silence.

– Who was driving the boat? she said at last.

– Your mother.

– Was she drunk?

– Yes.

Another gasp. Not of surprise though, rather as if these hefty doses of unadulterated truth were going down like shots of some powerful liquor.

– So why did Gerald say she killed herself?

– Someone in Port Mungo told him. Someone unreliable.

Silence. She frowned, it was enough, she had nothing else to ask. At last she lifted her head and grinned at us, and said how much better it was to know a thing, no matter how dreadful it was, than not to know and have to imagine it. What you imagine is always so much worse, she said, and we both agreed with this sentiment with some alacrity. Jack poured the champagne and we promptly drank it in a spirit of celebration. I had a chance then to study our returning prodigal, and again I was astonished by that certain quality I had detected in her before, I mean her ability to absorb experience raw. Here was a young woman who had just taken on board some catastrophic information but had remained on the surface as placid as ever. It was hard not to think of the cliché of the still waters. I suppose it was what Eduardo referred to as her steely quality, which according to him was a dangerous Rathbone trait.

15

S pring was in the air. Jack said he noticed by the light falling on the building across from the studio that the arc of the sun was higher in the sky. He knew the city would be lashed by at least one more storm, but still he was glad to see a sign that winter was almost over. He'd resumed work on the large canvas.

He had woken early the morning after Anna's return and knew what he must do with it. Perhaps he had been dreaming about it. He did dream about his work, and often had fresh impetus afterwards, whether or not he had looked at it in weeks. He got up and went straight to his studio. He hauled the trolley over to the wall and began poking through the pile of cans and tubes until he found what he wanted. He went to work and stayed at it for four or five hours, then hunger drove him downstairs to the kitchen. Anna was at the table. She may have attempted a conversation, I don't know, Jack was intent only on eating something and getting back to work: he was having a good day, and his joints were quiet. He fried two eggs and took them upstairs with a piece of toast and a mug of tea. He worked all afternoon and then had a bath and a short nap. When he came downstairs again it was evening and he found me home but Anna out.

We talked for a while but the conversation was desultory. I saw he was slipping into that state of mind where the world, the real world, I mean, of other people, receded, and the picture being painted would expand until it permeated his entire existence. I was familiar with this pattern. I recognized the beginnings of a period of immersion, and an end to the anxiety that gnawed at him all the time he was not properly at work. Peace of mind was possible for him only when he was painting, all else was depression and anxiety, not in any melodramatic sense, simply those feelings were the background noise of his mind when he was attending to life outside the studio, which he felt as a kind of exile. It was his good fortune to be painting again, because dear god, he would say, there was no taking it for granted any more, the years devoured the blithe confidence with which one went to work, the years displayed the fragility of one's competence, and the looming grey wall of failure against which one struggled, that got higher – all this the psychic encumbrance of an artist of a certain age entering a room and preparing to go to work.

So to feel a rising confidence in his ability to work unafraid, this was the good fortune to which he awoke the morning after Anna came home again.

Ten days he had now. All the days in all the years he had gone to work – ten more. A storm was approaching. Ten more days before the storm broke and he was stopped in his tracks, and although he had far from exhausted the productive surge was hauled bodily out of the studio by circumstance and responsibility and the rest of the grim machinery which all his working life he had tried to push to the periphery of things but which came back relentlessly, provoking the familiar dull useless anger. The days are numbered, he would say, glaring at me as though I were attempting to steal his days, they are finite, he could calculate them if I wanted him to, how many more paintings he might reasonably expect to complete, assuming the competence could be sustained till – what? – seventy-five, eighty? Would he be able to make good work at eighty?

Would he be alive at eighty?

During Anna's absence, he had been too distracted to paint. In fact since becoming absorbed by the portrait of Anna he had paid less and less attention to the *Dream*, and was losing touch with it. Nor had he any idea when he would once more have the vacancy of mind he required to resume work on it, there was no possibility of immersion while Anna held his attention. And when he was cut off from his work for more than a few days another more serious question would begin to form, that being – what is the point? He mentioned this to me once and I remember saying: what is *what* point? – and he realized then, he said, why Vera had been right to discourage me from continuing to paint. For if I could not understand the question, so he bluntly told me, I had no business setting up as an artist. What is the point, he tried to explain to me, of life – of one's actual existence, day by day – if one has no creative work to do? He could see that the idea worried me. The idea that life, or oneself, should have meaning only as a function of the creative work one did – he saw that I could not live like that, and it was my failure, he said, that I lacked that – what, disposition? – genius? – curse? – which drove the best of them and which they clutched more closely to themselves than anything else. Houses, money, marriages, children – all will be abandoned, he said, if only we are permitted to keep making art. He said this was the meaning of the Narcissus myth, and it had inspired the many variations on that myth he had painted over the years, including of course the original *Narcissus in the Jungle*, which still hangs in the big room downstairs.

But he had his ten days, and painting had this effect on him, it made him strong, strong enough, certainly, to confront the memories he seemed so very apprehensive about at other times. Peg rose up in his mind as he worked, a companion all shining and cleansed of mangrove slime, and Jack murmured to her as he moved about in front of the canvas, darting at it with small cries, then standing back, staring, turning away to the trolley and groping among the heaped tubes, and he thought: dear Peg, she got lost in it just as Vera did, and it's not a gift, no, you have to earn it, the freedom to make yourself a slave of painting. To stare unflinching into your own self as though into a mirror and ignore everything else.

For ten days he worked well and happily and Anna was not at the centre of his thoughts. When he saw her in the evening he was not altogether there. He knew that I would have explained to her what happened when the work took over, and that I would have formed with her the same bond of amused complicity I had formed with Dora during earlier protracted periods when he had absented himself in all but body from the life of the household. We treated him as a sort of ghostly familiar, an entity more spirit than flesh, a thing to be seen drifting about the house at certain times of the day or night and even spoken to, but without any actual living connection to us. Anna was surprised by the change in him, but as I say, I was able to explain all this to her.

Perhaps more-spirit-than-flesh is not quite right. Perhaps it was the other way round, more flesh than spirit. He ate, he drank, he slept; his absence was that of the spirit, rather, for the spirit was up in the studio, in the canvas. We cohabited with one of the undead, the ghoul who made art in the attic.

Then the storm broke, and it was catastrophic. Anna had found a job in a restaurant and was working as many shifts as she could so as to put some money together, though what she was putting it together for she hadn't told us, her rather nebulous career in art I suppose. I assumed she went to Eduardo's loft when she got off work, and I dreaded her discovery of this boy of his, though I had to conceal my apprehension when she was with us in the house. Jack was in his studio all day, and I had the impression the work was still going well despite what I'd told him about the messy situation Eduardo had created.

One evening we were having our cocktails when someone came to the door. We were not expecting a visitor and were not in the mood for company. We could tolerate each other but that was all. We heard Dora shuffle across the hall, and then a familiar voice. Eduardo. I rose to my feet.

– What happened? I cried.

He sank into an armchair and softly struck his head with the heel of his palm.

– She found out.

– Jesus *Christ.*

This from Jack, who strode to the far end of the room and leaned against the wall with his back to us.

– How? I said.

– She showed up this morning –

– Anna did?

– Yes, and the boy was there –

– Oh no.

– I did not know she was coming! She did not tell me!

Inarticulate groaning and cursing and hammering of the wall from the other end of the room.

– Go on.

– I was in the studio, so he opened the door –

– And it was obvious?

– Oh yes. He was wearing my bathrobe.

At that point Jack seemed utterly to lose control and came striding down the room enraged, and what he would have done next I do not know because we all became aware that somebody else was at the front door, with a key.

Anna.

Afterwards, I remembered with particular clarity seeing her in the doorway of the sitting room, our Anna, apparently calm, staring at Eduardo, who, having turned towards the door, now pushed himself heavily up out of his armchair and stood facing the girl, who then moved swiftly towards him, her face white and her lips pressed tight together, and holding out her hands to him – and me thinking, it's going to be all right after all – and Eduardo offering her his hand, his right hand, and a second later a sharp loud cry of pain – fuck! – as he pulls violently away, his hand crumpling like a leaf and blood flowing, and him staring at it with his jaws and eyes wide, the blood pouring from between his clawing fingers as though he is trying to cup a bowl of it in his palm and cannot, for it is streaming through his fingers and splashing on to the polished hardwood floor.

– Fuck! he shouts again, as he gropes for a handkerchief and clamps it to his palm, and at last looks up, astonished and disbelieving and in pain, and stares at Anna, who has moved to the window where she stands with her back to the glass, returning his stare, her mouth slightly open and her eyes bright, leaning against the sill and gripping it tight, her thin chest heaving.

Later still, when Eduardo had been taken off in a cab to St Vincent's, and Dora had mopped up in the sitting room, the three of us sat in the kitchen and talked. She told us everything, how she'd decided in the morning to buy Eduardo some flowers and take them over to his loft and surprise him, he was working so hard for his show. She'd walked down Broadway, feeling good, she said. West along Canal, south on Washington and west again on Eduardo's block. She'd been buzzed into the building and knocked at his door.

– This black kid opened the door, I knew him from the restaurant. He was squeezing oranges. He stood there with this piece of squeezed orange in his hand, it was dripping on the floor, and he was giving me this creepy smile and he was like, was my name Anna, because Eduardo had told him all about me, and I kind of woke up because of the dressing gown. It was the one he gave me to wear when I stayed over.

– Then what?

– I had to get out of there. I still had his fucking flowers! I just threw them into the street. Then I went into this bar on North Moore and had a whisky. I thought it would calm me down. Then I had another one. Then I started to get angry, so I walked around for a while and then I went to a movie. That's about it, really.

She gazed at us without any hint of remorse, or shock, or

anything at all that I recognized as an appropriate reaction to what had happened.

– So when did you think of cutting his hand?

– During the movie.

– And the razor blade?

– I just thought of it.

– How did you know he'd be here?

– I was watching his building and I saw him come out and I followed him.

Gingerly she reached into her leather jacket and extracted a razor blade bound with black electrical tape so only the edge was exposed. It was still smeared with blood. She set it down on the kitchen table and wiped her fingers on a paper napkin. We stared at the gruesome object.

– You may have cut some tendons, I said.

– Good.

There were no tears. Her anger was still fresh. There was a sort of cold purity to it, it seemed a thing of impersonal passion rather than felt emotion, if that distinction means anything. Herself an agent of abstract retribution and her palmed razor blade the instrument. Later Jack said he thought this as robust a display of sound mental health as any he had seen in a long time. I was far from convinced. I was made profoundly uneasy by what Anna had done, and particularly by her own attitude to it, this frigid stance of righteousness.

– What do you propose to do now? I said.

– I never want to see him again.

– OK.

– I never want to think about him again.

– That won't be so easy.

Up came her head, the eyes hard and bright. She looked older than her years, in fact she looked ageless, it was her core I saw there, bedrock self, and it chilled me.

– Why not? Get on with my life. Bad episode, all over now. I can live without men.

Fearless and defiant, in a way I admired her for it; but not entirely realistic.

– I do think that you should talk to someone about it. With us, if you like.

– So I can talk to you about it if I want?

– Of course.

– All right.

Another silence. That seemed to be it, as far as Anna was concerned. I opened a bottle of wine. Anna wanted to know if Eduardo had always been such a bastard and I had to tell her that yes, he had, and that I wished I'd warned her but I honestly didn't think he'd pull a stunt like this with her. I said I was sorry and she said that it was OK, and we were all just beginning to calm down when there was a tap at the door. Dora put her head into the kitchen and gave me to understand that she had something to tell me, so I got up and went out into the passage.

– You have a visitor, she said.

At this hour? I at once thought of the police. Dora was behaving rather strangely. She was giving me her ominous face.

– Who is it?

– It's Anna's mother.

16

Rapidly down the hall she came, shouting at me, unkempt as ever, in a flapping shapeless overcoat, her hair flying in all directions and her high heels ticking on the floorboards. Anna knew who she was even before Jack rose to his feet with a cry of joy. I was of course taken completely by surprise, not just by her presence here on this of all nights, but by the blazing intensity with which she now stood panting in the kitchen doorway and gazed at Anna. It was a remarkable encounter. They liked the look of each other, this was clear at once. Vera opened her arms, grinning fondly as she prepared to swamp the girl in a shaggy bear hug, and Anna, smiling shyly, her eyes alight, wrapped her long arms around her, spread her fingers across her mother's back and held her close.

– Look at you, you're the image of my Peg, Vera murmured, holding the girl at arm's length, gripping her shoulders, to inspect her. I had never seen Anna like this before, flushed with pleasure and confusion; and how rare it is, I thought, to be so overwhelmed by another human being that we lose the power of speech and blush like a child. We sat down and Vera briefly gave her attention to Jack and me.

– Dear god, Veer, said Jack, how like you not to be in touch for years and then just show up on a Saturday night.

– You're at home, aren't you?

Anna was hiding her face, busying herself with tobacco and

rolling papers, then Jack was getting Vera something to drink and Vera had resumed staring at Anna, eating her up with her eyes, the grin still there, the sportive gods of humour very much in evidence. Vera once told me her philosophy of life, this was in the old days. When in doubt, she said, the only thing worth asking for is more. More? Just more. Whatever's on offer. The Philosophy of More, she called it.

– Here, give me some of that, she said, once Anna had rolled her cigarette, and the tobacco was passed across the table. Jack handed her a glass of fizzy water with ice and a slice of lime, Vera glancing at me as she took it, and our eyes met. Oh, it was hard not to like the woman, in spite of all the damage she had done, to Jack, to Peg – but all of it so long ago, all water under the bridge. I say this, though in truth I could now *afford* to like her – I had Jack, and she didn't. Her eyes were back on Anna as she rolled a cigarette and licked the paper. The razor blade wrapped in black tape still lay on the table. She picked it up and turned it over in her fingers.

– I hear you cut up Eduardo Byrne, she said.

How on earth had she found out? Dora must have told her in the hall.

– I wish I'd killed the bastard.

Vera bit her lip. She was amused, already she loved the girl's spunk, no solemn concern at all for her trauma. Strange to think I was looking at what had once been a nuclear family.

– I'm glad it wasn't me, she said, I wouldn't fancy getting cut up by the likes of you. What about you, Gin?

– Perish the thought, I said.

– Perish it indeed.

– Poor Gerald, she then said to Anna, suddenly serious. What was it like?

– It was quick.

– That's something.

Her levity was gone. She sat smoking, pondering my brother's death. I remembered how Vera's mood could govern a room, as though she were a thermostat which controlled the emotional temperature. She examined her cigarette and crushed it out. I think she was not a smoker any more, just as she was apparently not a drinker. Not tonight anyway.

Anna watched her. She was very still. What was going through the girl's mind? Here was her mother, whom she hadn't seen in god knows how many years. A few days previously she'd learned of this woman's responsibility for her sister's death. Earlier that night she herself had sliced a sculptor's hand with a razor blade. Shock after shock, yet she seemed able to absorb them with barely a break in her stride. The depths to this girl were either immense or nonexistent. I believe the thought occurred to Vera too.

– Bit of a street fighter, are you, then?

Anna grinned at her.

– She's a skinhead, right? She's a sex pistol.

– Oh sure, said Anna, shifting about with pleasure.

– Where are you staying, Veer? You want to sleep here? said Jack.

Vera did not look at Jack, instead she glanced at Anna.

– My bag's at the hotel. They have hotels downtown now, did you know? I'd better go.

– Don't go, said Anna.

– All right, I won't.

So she stayed, and we talked some more, the four of us, had something to eat, and caught up on our lives. It was Vera's habit to take control of a conversation so as to spare the company the prospect of boredom, and always with that spirited force of personality that made one happy to yield her the floor. I suppose it was pure fascination she aroused, you wanted to see more of the workings of her personality, for she was complicated, she was unpredictable, she was entertaining even in her sudden glooms and silences. There was what I can only call a full nature at work in Vera Savage, and such natures are rare, we are seldom fortunate enough to get a good close look at them. She inspired strong reactions, and she inspired love. She certainly inspired it in Anna that night, and while I saw the effort – I realized after some minutes that she was not strong, she was struggling to perform with her customary gusto – I don't believe Anna did. And it occurred to me that if the traumas of the early evening carried some kind of delayed effect, a visceral reaction, I mean, to the ugliness of what had happened, then it would be absorbed at least in part in the welter of impressions and feelings awoken in Anna by her mother.

Later I lay awake turning this prospect over in my mind. At a certain point I knew I would not sleep. I had become anxious. I was remembering how unconstructive Vera's influence on Peg had been. I imagined Anna adopting her mother's cynicism, laughing the whole thing off, refusing to confront her own rather worrying propensity for violence. Vera's life was not one to be imitated. Let Anna look to me, or Jack, better still, if she wanted to be guided, I thought, and see her mother for what she was. Was she smart enough to think this out for herself? Or was she seduced by the buccaneer spirit, as her sister had been? Somewhere quite near me she slept, or perhaps she did not sleep, perhaps like me she lay there with her eyes open, working over experience too heavily freighted with significance to be fully assimilated other than in the silent depths of the night. Jack slept, and so did Vera. Hard to imagine either of them worrying about any of this after midnight. But Anna and I, with complications piling up like wrack lifted by a rising river, our separate minds worked through the hours of darkness to impose sense and order on the events of the last days.

Sunday morning dawned clear, and the large shapeless shuffling threatening dark possibilities of the night had retired to their usual shadowy cloisters, and plain practical problems took their place: far less daunting. With a single phone call I established that Eduardo's palm had been stitched and his tendons were undamaged, but his upcoming show would have to be postponed. Vera was up soon after I was, and the pair of us sat at the kitchen table drinking coffee. We talked about Anna and I asked her to be careful of the girl. I put my hand on hers, I gazed at her in all seriousness, and saw her start to buck. It was the old truculence I saw, the old blind pride stirring to life, but I kept my hand on hers until she quieted.

– Meaning?

– Don't let her see you careless. Things matter. Don't make her hard just because she was hurt.

– I doubt I could make her anything she didn't want to be.

– You know that isn't true.

I sat back, lifting my fingers from hers, and watched her. I thought perhaps she was less a stranger to responsibility than she once had been, perhaps she was at least on nodding terms with the idea of responsibility. Seventy now, she had fought it long and hard, and all the old instincts were still there. But compromises had been reached, truces signed.

– It's one of the two or three things I continue to regret, she said, that I didn't try and hold on to her.

I was curious what the others were. The life she'd lived, and only two or three regrets?

– What's so funny? Gin Rathbone, are you laughing at me? The old bear growl never frightened me.

– I am laughing at you. Two or three regrets, is it? Not bad.

– Not bad be fucked. All right! All right. I won't set her a bad example. I'm not up to it anyway.

I was relieved to hear her say it. Dear Vera. Jack appeared in the kitchen doorway.

– One thing in exchange, she said, turning to him.

– What's that?

– Take me upstairs. Show me the studio.

* * *

199

It was a small price to pay. Actually it was no price at all, having Vera in his studio never did Jack anything but good. Up the stairs went the three of us, himself in front like a bride on her wedding night, he said later, and with more than a whisper of a bride's anxious anticipation about what awaits her above. He opened the studio door and stood back to let Vera go in first, no darting about to set things straight, none of that nonsense, Vera knew her way round a studio. She stood in the middle of the floor in her baggy clothes, she turned full circle, sniffing, in her element. She murmured something about Jack's studios always smelling the same but her attention had been caught, and held, I saw at once, by the portrait of Anna.

She did not go to it immediately. She had a long look at the large canvas first. And it was, as I'd suspected, another variation on the Narcissus posture, this one the clearest depiction yet: a figure leaning out over the side of a boat, reaching down towards a second figure beneath the water, a reflection, whose arm reaches up, and the two hands almost touching. The boat was white, the water black, the figure in the boat a smudged crimson. A third figure much foreshortened stood upright in the bow, holding an oar. They were in a cave of some kind. It was a stark, simple painting, and Vera stood silently in front of it, shifting her weight from foot to foot, suddenly lifting a hand to isolate a bit of brushwork – she had delicate hands, Vera, feminine hands, plump and white, when she troubled to scrape the paint and muck off them – and talking to herself – oh yes, very nice that – or, more ominously – what the hell is that all about? – which had Jack by her side and staring at the offending matter, and seeing what she saw though not agreeing with her, not yet anyway. So she muttered at the painting, Jack hovering behind her so as to miss nothing and then, at last, unable to hold back any longer, the tension too much for him – directing her to a passage he was happy about, some accident of texture and gesture he liked, and that she'd recognized all along.

– Narcissus crossing the Styx.

– Off to hell, said Vera. Just like you, eh Jack?

A flash of glee from under her frown, and away she went again – yeah, very nice, like it a lot, sweet – while Jack glowed and swelled like a candled halloween pumpkin. All this she gave him before she pleasured herself.

She stood quite still in front of the full-length nude and there was no mumbling now. There might have been a quiet sigh. Jack came to the window and stood beside me, looking down into the garden, and up at the sky, which had clouded over, it was flat and grey now. He knew the painting was wrong, he knew she knew it too but she was held by it as he was, he couldn't abandon it and she couldn't stop looking at it. Suddenly he grew impatient, and said he felt like smoking a cigarette. Vera's presence often had this effect on him, she was his downfall in ways both great and small.

– Oh leave it alone, for christ sake, he cried, you know it's no good.

She ignored him, she took her time, and when she did come away it had only been a minute or two but it felt much longer. A minute or two is an eternity in front of a bad painting, particularly if you're the one who painted it.

– So?

She sank into the big chair and crossed her legs. I suddenly saw she was tired. Up for barely an hour and already tired. She seemed unable even to lift her head and look at Jack. He let her sit there as he paced about, doing the talking, explaining his ambivalence towards the picture, even telling her what it looked like in moonlight.

– How is it when she sits?

– She goes empty. We made a deal.

He hadn't meant to say this and it was the first I'd heard of it too. But she had to know. He didn't know why she had to know, only that she did.

– What sort of deal?

– She'd sit if I told her about Peg.

She nodded. Not surprised. He said later that this was how it always used to happen when the two of them were alone together and Peg's name came up. They seemed to move to another place, or on to another plane, rather, where more massive significance attached to things, and large last dramas played themselves out, matters of life and death, and laced through and around them their own lives, hers and his, their mistakes, their malfunctions, when personality and circumstance were horribly out-of-true and damage was done to the innocent. Only one real innocent in their story, of course, and Jack had no idea whether Vera had resolved the painful inarticulate confusion she had more than once displayed, and which she had seemed unwilling to sort out and had instead – he presumed – pushed down, blocked out. Drowned. But now her silence was not restless, he did not hear the psychic machinery grinding. She was tranquil, slumped in the big chair with her hands unmoving on the arms, her head quite still and her eyes on the portrait of Anna.

– The odd thing is she wants to know and at the same time she doesn't.

– Why odd?

– She said she came to America to find out.

All at once there were smoky black knots of complication, of unspoken guilt, and resentment, and remorse and rage, all of it to do with Peg's death. I watched closely from the far side of the room. Did each blame the other? Did she hold him responsible? She was opaque. She stood up and again approached the painting. Jack grew uneasy.

– Are you going to tell her? he said.

It must have occurred to him that Vera intended to talk to Anna about her sister's death, tell it from her point of view, whatever that was.

– Somebody must. She came to you.

– Let me tell her.

I was on the point of saying, but you've told her already! – when something passed between them, some complicated understanding. Jack was relieved, at least that much was clear, and I guessed that the responsibility of telling Anna was his alone.

– You know what it is?

She was standing square in front of the picture now, hands in her pockets, her back to him.

– It's not her, she said, it's not even Peg. It's you, Jack.

Why hadn't he seen it? Why hadn't I? I saw it now!

– Haunting. Portrait of the artist as a young man. Right, Gin?

She turned to me, impish fires springing to life in her tired eyes. She was right, it was Jack as a boy. I had seen that thin white body often enough. It was Jack at seventeen, as he was when he first met Vera. He paints himself over and over again, I thought, it's all he ever does. Even his jungles are self-portraits, he told me so himself.

– Haunting, she said again.

– Fuck off.

That got a laugh out of her. We went downstairs a few minutes later. She wanted to get back to her hotel. On the doorstep I asked her to check out of the hotel and come stay in the house. I said I wanted her to be comfortable and I meant it.

Now she was touched, and it was all getting too mawkish for words. But she didn't say yes there and then. She said she wanted to see more of us while she was in the city, and she would call the house later. Then off she went, down the steps and into the street as Jack and I stood watching in the doorway.

I didn't see Anna until late in the morning. As expected she was suffering from a compound hangover induced by the events of the previous day, partly alcoholic, and partly emotional. She told me she had been sick in the night and I wasn't surprised. There she sat at the kitchen table, in her floppy pyjamas, her eyes full of sleep, and asked me if her mother was in the house.

I was still profoundly uneasy about her reaction to what had happened. I wanted her to confront the violence she had done. I felt we must deal with it now, and that Vera must help. I told her Vera had gone back to the hotel and would call the house later, and then I asked her how she felt about what she'd done to Eduardo. I saw as if through a pane of glass how the pain flooded up and was then forcefully pushed down again. Her face puckered like a child's, then turned hard. Her eyes briefly filled with tears but not a single one spilled down her cheek. Was I right – did I *have* the right? – to question the manner in which she chose to regulate her emotional life?

– It's too soon, I said. Let's have a few quiet days.

I think perhaps she had not yet thought about the immediate future. I think the idea of a few quiet days filled her with dismay, the prospect, I mean, of having quietly to digest this recent ugliness. Again I saw the hurt bewildered child rise up behind her eyes, and like a child she asked if we could all have dinner with Vera tonight.

– You call her, I said.

She took the number and padded out of the kitchen and I knew that for a few days at least she would be fragile. Good that she had us to support her.

Later I was pacing about the sitting room, waiting to hear what was happening about dinner. We hadn't seen her all afternoon. It was time for cocktails and still no word. I asked Jack if he thought she was all right. He was sure she was. So many complications now, and all to do with Anna. At least now we had Vera as well. Vera would help us see her through it, and eventually Anna would laugh about it. Her mother had always found it easier than either of us to see life in its comic aspect. I said this to Jack.

– Vera pretends that life's a comedy, he said, but deep down she knows it's tragic. That's because she feels.

– Toad, don't be profound. I'm not in the mood.

– It's the sign of a generous spirit.

– What is?

– Sparing your companions your tragic view of existence. More people should try it.

By nine that night it was clear Anna had forgotten our dinner plans. I told Jack I was going to check her room. Up the stairs I went, along the corridor, and knocked on her bedroom door. No answer. I went in. It was as I suspected. In fact it was as I dreaded, for I had grown more and more certain that she had gone.

The black leather bag she had slung up on top of the closet was not there. Her underwear drawer was empty, as was her bedside drawer, except for a subway token. Nothing hung on her hangers. I sat on the bed a moment before going back downstairs.

– She's gone, I said.

I picked up the phone, and while I waited for the hotel to answer, I said: You're not surprised.

He shook his head and walked to the window.

– Is Mrs Savage still with you? I said.

Jack turned from the window and faced me from across the room. I nodded as I heard the answer, then hung up.

– She's gone, too.

Anna did not make contact for more than a week, and so we had only our imaginations to provide any picture of where they might be. The house seemed very empty. We both, I think, felt abandoned, spurned. Vera had left her phone number and we rang it several times, but there was no answer, nor was there in the days that followed. Could they have gone to Port Mungo? It was, in a way, plausible, but no. Ageing painter takes lost girl to jungle paradise where lost girl was born. In the Nature's Womb healing and redemption occur. Lost girl emerges whole, artist dies happy. Credits roll to the sound of violins.

Thus my thoughts as I paced the big room, and Jack shifted about in an armchair, frowning, tapping his fingernails on the side of his wineglass.

– Dear god I wish I still smoked, he said.

Unable to contact any public authority – to say what, that she'd gone off with her mother without telling us? – unable to do anything but wait and fret – these are the kind of hours, said Jack, that the gods of anxiety intended for the smoking of a great many cigarettes. But he resisted, and he continued to resist, and so, day after day, we moved about the house in silent despond, and the weather mirrored our mood. I told Dora what had happened, and she, dear woman, as always was a rock. No word from anybody. Even in New York, where communication fizzes through circuits of connection as dense as the root systems of a potato patch, inexplicable lulls do occur and one grows oddly becalmed. The phone doesn't ring all day, nothing appears in your mailboxes and you wonder if the equipment is faulty – but no, it is just systemic lull. The city, as though to echo and amplify the deafening silence from mother and daughter, became silent, too. There were mists, those salty mists which drift into New York in the early spring and remind you that this is after all an Atlantic seaport, and though it has since become the capital of practically everything you can think of, in the beginning what mattered was the harbour and the ocean. And so, fogbound with no signals reaching us, our thoughts turned in abstract circles which soon became knots, tedious knots, knots of tedious solipsism.

Jack spent many hours in the studio that week and seriously considered buying a pack of cigarettes. He said it was like the first days after giving up. The sense memory of tobacco came flooding back at all hours – he said he could *taste* the bloody things! What old association was this now clamouring for closure? He allowed himself to be absorbed by the conflict –

to smoke or not to smoke – he said it kept his mind off Anna. Then there was the portrait. If he stared at it a few more hours would he learn anything new? Marks, daubs, the work of his own hand, what trace there of anything outside his own consciousness? The lingering vapour of another being, perhaps, but the vapour faint already and growing fainter with every minute he gazed at it. And if cigarettes tempted him, what of old photographs – should he haul them out and render himself weakly liquid staring at faces of people frozen in time, with their mistakes still waiting to happen? No. No. And he came to see this as the work he would make of those misty days, this his performance art, to smoke no cigarettes, to look at no old photographs, to be as spartan, as minimal, as severe in his appetites as it lay in his power to be, which meant one glass of wine a night, no more. Fruit and salads, one glass of wine, there was madness in the house, he could feel it, he said, he was vulnerable to it, and to remain immune to it he must seal his psyche tight: become Fort Jack, this was how to stay sane and healthy in a time of unease and disorder – and yes, I thought, hearing all this, and profoundly bewildered by it, there is madness in the house, and I know where it's coming from. But I said nothing.

So the strange days passed. Jack became ever more silent as the ascetic mood deepened and his blood-sugar level dropped. Dora was like a ghost moving through fog at the periphery of vision. The house was quiet. The city was quiet. Even the park was quiet, Jack said, he walked there most days. Somewhere Vera was talking to Anna. She was answering her questions. She was telling her the story of Peg's death, and I didn't know why that made Jack so anxious. What did he have to fear – that she was telling Anna the story she had once told Johnny Hague?

I asked Jack why he was worried. He was leaning against the window frame, watching the street – he seemed always now to be watching the street, I did not have to ask him why, and he nodded. His answer was curious. Anna had come to New York to find out about her sister, he said, but he had wanted to prepare her before he told her. Not merely by establishing the context of their lives in Port Mungo, but by allowing her to get to know *him*. Only when she properly knew *him*, he said, would she properly understand the circumstances surrounding Peg's death. This I could understand, I suppose. My brother was not young, and with the years he had accumulated layers. He could not reveal himself to the girl over a weekend. He had facets, dimensions, carapaces – selves – a thousand moving parts constitute the coherent machinery of a mature human being. Let her get to know him, this was his idea, and then she could begin to make sense of her sister's death.

It was growing dark outside, and I asked if he wanted his glass of wine now, but no, he didn't. Nor did he want the lights on. The shadows thickened in the sitting room. What he feared, he said, was that Anna would get a botched version from Vera, who would long ago have constructed an account that lessened or even entirely eliminated her own responsi-bility for the accident. She would then have clung so tena-ciously to her account that she would now be genuinely unaware that it was untrue. Vera disliked uncertainty or ambiguity, he said. She always needed the *gesture*, and could not tolerate any delay in the making of the gesture. When she painted, he said, it was not hard to see the same impatience, the same inability to linger over a decision, the pressing necessity to decide the thing at once and then move on. That's how she would have made a picture of Peg's death, a few bold strokes to give it a shape, a form –

All this I heard, there in the near-darkness, as Jack paced the floor with his fingers twitching and clenching, and I could not tell him what I feared – that the few bold strokes she made for Anna would be the same ones she'd given Johnny Hague. And I had begun to suspect that that was precisely what Jack feared too.

*   *   *

We talked no more about it that night. I think we were both exhausted. I had certainly had enough. In the old days we would have gone out and got very drunk, and Jack would have evacuated the complicated contents of his brimming heart as I listened sympathetically and made sense of it all, and in the morning we would not remember much except the feeling that painful matter had been spilled, though whether it had been swept away in the spilling was another question. But we did not behave like that now, Jack and I. Not simply because getting drunk was far more expensive, physically, than it once had been, but because we understood that it would serve no purpose. Things truly important to people of our age are not susceptible to alcohol, alcohol changes nothing. It is good for everything else however.

So our state of suspense continued. We would not be able to move on, or to move back, rather, to our normal life until Anna returned and we learned what Vera had told her. How sad it was, I thought, that this guilt of his was without any real foundation in reality. Poor Jack. All these years, tormenting himself with the question – if I had done this, or that, would she be alive today? Useless thinking, but impossible to abandon so long as some undying spike of powerful emotion attached to the idea that Peg might have been saved, and himself the one who could have done the saving.

And then I asked myself: and Vera's position in all this? Was it her doing, the undying spike of emotion that kept alive my brother's guilt? Did she collude in this guilt, connive at it, stimulate and sustain it? And with that thought the figure of Vera rose up in my mind, loud, talkative, alert, fearless, engaged – yes, drunk – yes, selfish and irresponsible – and I stood her beside my brother, my serious, complicated, fierce, driven brother – my self-deluded, narcissistic brother – and I thought: there is only one person in the world who can live with Jack Rathbone, and that is me.

*   *   *

We began to wonder if Anna would ever come back. She had left nothing behind, only her guitar, which I'd found in its hard black case under the bed. I'd opened the case, and found it was an expensive-looking instrument with mother-of-pearl inlay in the neck. I ran my fingers across the strings. We had never heard her play it. Surely she would come back for it. I watched my brother wandering around the house, distracted, and I was suddenly reminded of the days after Peg's death, when he was in that same state of grief and loss. He was in mourning for Anna just as he had been in mourning for her sister twenty years before, and finally I understood why he so fervently insisted on the girl's resemblance to Peg. It was because Anna had *replaced* Peg. She had brought her back to life, and a deep pain in Jack had at last begun to ease, and in his soul he had felt a sort of peace, relief, calm. All this she had awoken in him. I had seen it with my own eyes, although I had not properly understood it until this moment: Anna had become a double of her own sister, sufficiently like her that Jack was able to flesh her out, emotionally, as it were, to the scale of Peg. The full-length portrait was his declaration that just such a substitution had occurred.

But for this – what? – this simulacrum, this *ghost*? – to die, figuratively – what did this mean? How could a ghost die? What did it mean to talk about the death of a ghost? But this it seems is what my brother was mourning, during those empty days, he was mourning the death of a ghost. Is he going mad? I thought. Is he mad already? I began to be seriously concerned.

The household, as I say, was in a state of suspension and there was little I could do but wait and watch – wait for Anna to come back, or at least to let us know where she was, and that she was safe, and watch Jack. Watch *over* Jack. Watch over him as you would any grieving person, vigilant, ready to step in with balm and comfort as required. It was as a result of this watching that I realized that the man was bereaved, and that he'd been thrust into emotional territory he had occupied before.

Every night I took him out to one or another of the restaurants in the neighbourhood, usually the Spanish place, but he grew less communicative with each passing day. I asked him if he was doing any work. A shrug, a baleful glance flung across the table as he picked listlessly at his food. Jack had that same power Vera had, he could create an atmosphere around himself, and his silences now were freighted with spiritual significance. A kind of gloomy majesty attended him in his despondency, and while I was perfectly capable of puncturing the mood I did not. My task, at this point, was simply to be vigilant until the crisis passed.

I was curious about a couple of things. I wanted to know what was going on upstairs, between him and the portrait of Anna. Was he glooming over it like some decrepit obsessive in a dingy romantic novel? Or had he turned it to the wall? I asked him if he'd turned it to the wall. Loud bark of laughter, and diners at nearby tables turned to see what had so amused the tall silent man in the corner. This was the most vivid manifestation of life I'd seen in him in days.

– Barely ever look at it, Gin. Don't need to turn it to the wall.

I didn't believe him for a moment.

– Still think it's wrong?

– It's not the picture that's wrong, it's her. There's nothing there.

– What do you mean?

For a moment I thought he had penetrated his delusion: there was nothing there *of the sister*. But I was wrong.

– There's nothing to her. Well, is there, Gin? Did she ever say anything that stuck in your mind?

Plenty, I thought, but I was more interested in his own thoughts. I made an ambiguous noise and said nothing.

– Empty, really, like a child. All those black clothes – just a frightened kid from Surrey. All Gerald's fault. No impress of experience, do you see? Locked up tight in her narcissism. She won't amount to anything.

Shaking his head, he attacked his lamb.

– It's there in the painting? I said.

– It's there in the painting, he said, chewing vigorously. Or rather, it's not there.

Devalue the object of desire and the pain of loss diminishes. That at least is the theory. The poor man must have been hurting very badly indeed if he'd been reduced to this. There was some truth in what he was saying, but it was not apparent to him. He was speaking the truth even as he was telling himself lies. The other matter I was curious about was to do with Vera, and what he'd been thinking about her these last few days. I asked him.

– Do you think her mother's reached the same conclusion? I said.

– Pah!

Clatter of cutlery, more turning of heads. Jack glared at his neighbours and the heads turned away.

– Listen, he hissed. You know her. She's a devious woman. This isn't about Anna.

– It isn't?

He shook his head, drank off some red wine, ran his tongue around the inside of his mouth, and went at his roast potatoes with a will. You'd have thought he hadn't eaten for a week. Something was released in him, some pent energy, and he needed fuel.

– It's about me.

I wiped my mouth with my napkin so as to conceal the smile that sprang to my lips. Locked up in narcissism indeed. Anna was worthless and Vera was using her to plot against him, was this it?

– How is it about you?

– Oh come *on*, Gin, you're not such a fool as that. Of course it's about me. Everything Vera does is about me, you know that. She didn't fool you too, did she?

His eyes blazing at me in the candlelight, mad, quite mad. What to do, encourage him to spill it all, or pin this nonsense to the floor where we could see it for what it was?

– You think she's going to pour some fiction into Anna's ear so as to turn her against you, so as to get back at you for what, exactly –?

– Oh Gin.

This was murmured by a man who seemed to have nothing more on his mind than clearing every last morsel of food from his plate and draining every last drop of wine from his glass. I waited, feeling the first stirrings of annoyance. He was cocky in his madness.

– All right, I said, enlighten me.

He finished eating, wiped his mouth, though the supercilious smirk remained. This wasn't Jack, this sneering paranoid – madness cheapens people, I suddenly thought, makes a man one-dimensional, a tawdry caricature of himself. Then I saw something else in his face, and it was as though the current had suddenly been reversed. The madman's anger crumbled like a cardboard mask, revealing only pain.

– She blames me for Peg and I can't bear it any more. It's too much for me, Gin.

I was on the point of saying – oh, but that's absurd – but I did not. Instead I waited. All I saw was turmoil, and I knew I was right: he blamed himself, and he had struggled with the guilt for twenty years, and now he was too old to bear it any more. He was more fragile than he appeared. I had protected him from the world for years, but now the world, the past, had slipped in under my defences and a blade was at his throat. All this I saw in that old man's panic.

– But *how* does she blame you? Jack. Listen to me. What is it that she blames you *for*?

He couldn't answer. He was overcome with emotion. He lifted his napkin to his lips. How was I to help him if he wouldn't tell me the truth?

– Jack, she's older too.

Piece of string to a drowning man, this, but he seized it all the same and hauled himself up on to a dry place.

– That's true, of course. She might be kind –

At that moment his jaw fell open, his expression was transformed. He was gazing beyond me, and rising to his feet, absently thrusting his napkin onto the table. I wheeled round in my chair to see what it was he was looking at, and there in the doorway of the restaurant, her eyes raking the place, stood Anna.

17

She hadn't seen us. Then she saw Jack, standing over the table with his arm lifted, a beacon of hopeful welcome. She moved towards the corner where we sat in the shadowy recess we had always occupied – until, that is, she came into our lives and moved us near the bar where she could smoke. Lips pursed, frowning, she negotiated the narrow channel between the tables, and diners glanced up incuriously as she pushed through to the corner where the two elderly parties had been having rather an emotional dinner. I half rose off my chair, aware that I was wreathed in smiles and filled with a pleasure stronger by far than I would have liked – in fact I was very displeased with the girl – and annoyed with myself for being such an old fool, but delighted all the same to be an old fool now that she had come home. Had she come home? I glanced at my brother. My delight was as nothing to the silly fondness turning his crusty features to the consistency of custard. She sat down and looked from him to me and back to him, grinning.

– Hi, she said.

Jack's long fingers had closed on hers and held them fast.

– You are a wicked child, he said, to run off without a word like that – and dear god there were tears in his eyes, in the candlelight you could see them glistening!

– Do you think they'll let me smoke? Everybody's stopped eating.

– Smoke, smoke, said Jack, smoke your little lungs out, just don't go off without telling us again.

– You weren't really worried.

– I was out of my mind.

– Gin, was he out of his mind?

She turned to me and whatever apprehension she may have had about facing the pair of us, it had quite evaporated in the warmth of her reception. She was softer in her manner than I'd ever seen her. It seemed entirely sincere.

– He was, I said. We both were.

– Well I'm sorry.

– So where were you? Account for yourself. More wine, I think. Where's Luis?

– Hasn't touched a drop since you left, I murmured, the pair of us now complicit in the joke of Jack going out of his mind with worry.

– I was at my mother's.

– Wrong. We phoned your mother several times. No answer.

– We thought it was you. We decided not to pick up.

So it was going to be all right after all, I thought. If she believed the worst of Jack she wouldn't be behaving like this, playful and affectionate, almost flirtatious. The relief was washing over him like a shower of rain. He looked ten years younger. Luis appeared and at last he let go of her hand, and ordered more wine: a good bottle this time. Luis saw we were celebrating, and without a change of expression produced an ashtray from his pocket and slid it onto the table.

But what was to happen now? Now that we'd all expressed how nice it was to see one another again? What had she learned from Vera, and how had it affected her feelings towards Jack? And how were we to begin to talk about any of this?

– I didn't know my mother taught you how to paint.

The tact of youth. But Jack was far too well-tempered to bridle for even a second.

– That's what she told you?

216

– Yeah.

She grinned at him through a cloud of cigarette smoke. Jack lifted his wineglass and for a few seconds his proud head with its blade of a nose, and the soft love in the hooded old eyes, was the head of my father. It was many years since I'd seen such tenderness in him.

– It's true, he said.

He was so tender he was honest.

– I took a lot from her, he said. I mean I stole a lot from her. I took it when she wasn't looking.

– She told me.

– What else did she tell you?

I was silent as this went forward. We were serious now. Jack laid his hands flat on the table and was staring at them, frowning, as though they displeased him in some way. Anna was suddenly off balance, unsure of herself.

– She said you took her canvases and worked over them.

Dear god I hadn't heard that one before! Jack continued to stare at the table. A few long seconds ticked by. He lifted a hand, as though about to make a solemn declaration, then laid it gently back down on the table. He regarded Anna with an expression of mild injury.

– I only did it once.

Even so!

– Well, twice.

– That's very bad, right? For a painter.

She knew nothing!

– It's pretty bad, said Jack.

Then he explained how he was desperately stuck in his work, and he'd gone into Vera's studio and found a canvas on the easel, and for the first time in weeks something had moved in him, so he took the canvas into his own studio and carried on where she'd left off, and that got him going again.

– She was pissed off, right?

– Oh, she was pissed off, said Jack.

I wasn't as brave as Anna. I didn't ask him how he could have done it again. I presume in identical circumstances, with identical results. It must have been worth it. Perhaps he felt justified by his vision of a family partnership in art. But it was quite enough for one evening, and he didn't ask her what else Vera had said about him. The point was, Vera had spared him. She had not turned the girl against him, and she so very easily could have done.

– What are your plans? I said.

– Can I stay at the house a bit longer?

I glanced at Jack.

– I think that might be possible.

– I've got an idea but I don't want to talk about it yet in case I jinx it, do you know what I mean?

Yes, we knew what she meant, and we left the restaurant soon after, doubtless to the relief of Luis, what with all the smoking and shouting that had come from our table. How strange it was to come up the steps to the front door the three of us together again, and how different our mood from what it had been just two hours before. And Jack, instead of mourning a ghost, was emanating a profound contentment. He was himself again, and this was a source of no small comfort to me, for I had been seriously concerned that he was losing the ability to distinguish the fictions of his own mind from the truth.

The next morning I came downstairs to the kitchen to find Anna on the phone to her mother. She hung up. She told me that Vera had travelled down to the city with her.

– Gin.

– Yes.

– I know I've upset your life but I'll be gone soon.

– You're very welcome, Anna. I mean that. You must stay here as long as you want to.

A little later I called the hotel from my study and asked Vera if we could meet.

*   *   *

We met in a busy coffee shop at Broadway and Chambers which displayed in the window framed photographs from the 1950s of various holders of the Miss Subway title. It was a nice day in early April. The morning was pleasantly cool, the sky a cloudless blue. By day Chambers Street is crowded, teeming, the traffic dense and noisy. Vera was sitting in a banquette with a pot of tea and an English muffin in front of her. It made me smile. I thought her more a neat-scotch-rare-steak sort of a woman. I said so.

– Gin, it's ten in the morning.

– And?

She allowed me my joke.

– We had a lovely time with Anna last night, I said.

– She told me.

– I wanted to thank you.

– Why?

– I think you know why.

– Tell me.

So I told her. I said that Jack's relationship with Anna was very important to him. He'd be badly upset, I said, if the girl were to take against him. Vera regarded me coolly. In the light of day I was able to get a good look at her at last. Extraordinary that all the hard living had failed to ravage her utterly. She could pass for fifty, or less, and it was only when she turned her head to the window and the sunlight flooded her face that I saw the work of the years stitched into the skin around her eyes and mouth. The jaw was firm, the teeth were white, more or less, minus the one still missing in the top row to the left. Her hair was threaded with silver now and heaped in an untidy bun pinned with combs and pencils. Silver rings on her fingers, several with turquoise stones from New Mexico. She had been sober for some years. She wore a baggy black sweater under a denim jacket with various pins and brooches on the breast.

I wondered was her lover a man or a woman. Women our age

often tire of the male. We opt instead for the tenderness and candour and faithfulness of our own species. It's all we want, really. That, and to be made to laugh.

– I'm glad you appreciate it, she said.

– I hate to see him distressed. He's quite frail.

Then to my astonishment she bridled.

– The hell with that, she said, *frail!* – and she leaned in towards me, tapping a fingernail smartly on the tabletop.

– I didn't tell Anna everything I know about your brother, she said, but I don't see why I shouldn't tell you.

– I know my brother.

– Gin, you know nothing.

I was certainly startled by this turn in the conversation. I had wanted simply to do the woman the courtesy of thanking her for her discretion, but it seems I'd enraged her by referring to Jack's frailty. I was on my guard at once. I thought: she may be sober but she's as volatile as ever. I didn't think I wanted to know what she apparently now intended to tell me but I had little choice in the matter.

– Jack's not *frail*, she barked.

– He spent twenty years in Port Mungo raising your daughters while you were running around.

– That's what he told you?

– I saw for myself.

She eyed me silently for a moment or two, then glanced out of the window. Pedestrians streamed by. Some blocks away a siren wailed. She wheeled back, and spoke fast, barely drawing breath, the Glasgow thick in her voice and the eyes sparking, the fingernails tapping an angry tattoo on the table. She told me that Jack only ever wanted one thing from her. Knowing she was better than he was, he took whatever she had, and for him that's what life was all about, she said, stealing ideas from other people because he was a third-rate artist himself.

– And I suspect you know it, Gin, she said, but you two

have this myth of Genius Jack. Well that's a crock. He dragged me down there because he couldn't bear to see me succeed up here. He was all eaten up with jealousy, and I truly think he found it absurd that a woman could have more talent than he did and that's why he wanted me down there in that dump, so I'd be invisible. Why do you think he wanted babies? It kept me quiet while he got his painting lessons.

There was a grain of truth in all of this, but not much more. I knew Jack's history. She hadn't finished. She got restless, she said, of course she did, what woman wouldn't? She had lost her way, turned into a lush, and screwed up a promising career.

⸙ But if you think Genius Jack stayed down there all that time out of discipline or perseverance or whatever you're wrong. He stayed down there because he was scared to show his stuff where it mattered, and that's the only reason he was around for Peg, fear. That's right. Simple as that. And if you think he did well by Peg then think about this, Gin. If it wasn't for him she'd still be alive.

She stopped as abruptly as she'd started. We stared at each other for several seconds and her words hung in the air between us like a bad smell. I didn't know where to start, I was reeling.

– So his work's no good –

The appalling tension she'd created slackened off markedly. She was brutally dismissive.

– Everybody knows that.

– And the shows? His success, his name?

– He got lucky. He came back here with that neo-primitivism, or neo-tropicalism, or whatever the hell you want to call it, and it struck a chord. There was a lot of rubbish out there then, and a lot of money too. He was very clever. He convinced a lot of people he was Gauguin come back from the dead. It was a hoax, and if you had an eye, Gin, you'd have seen it.

– Sour grapes.

– Oh don't be so ridiculous. Jack wrecked my prospects long before that.

– I thought you had more . . .

I couldn't think of the word.

– So did I. You think I'm proud I let him derail me? He knew what he was doing. He used me, Gin, he took whatever he could get –

It astonished me, and it saddened me, to hear her blaming Jack for her own failure. I was silent. She was staring out the window again. Then she hauled her bag up into her lap and groped around inside it, and though she kept her face down I could see the tears falling. The stories we tell ourselves so as to go on living and not go mad. She hated Jack because he had succeeded where she had failed, and she blamed him for that failure. Suddenly up came a tear-streaked face with both eyes blazing.

– Don't you feel sorry for me – I know you, Gin Rathbone!

– I don't think it's Jack you're blaming here.

– No, you think it's all me. You're wrong. I'm not too happy with how things have turned out but I do OK. I just thought you should know your brother's a fraud, worse than a fraud.

I gazed at her. I shook my head sadly. There was a reason she'd made such a mess of things, as an artist, as a woman.

– You're just like him, aren't you? she suddenly said.

She spoke in a tone almost of wonder, as though a light had been lit in her mind. I saw at once what was happening.

– So I'm a fraud too.

Here she snorted with laughter.

– You don't have an attic full of bad painting to show for it.

I rose to my feet.

– I'm sorry you feel this way, Vera, I said, I only wanted to thank you for keeping your feelings to yourself while Anna was with you. The effort was clearly too much for you.

– Gin, you can be such a pompous bitch, you know that?

– Goodbye, Vera.

With that I left, and not until I was out on the street did I allow the rage to rise, and for a moment I could not move, I stood there on the sidewalk, and the crowd parted round me as though I were a rock in a stream. Then I looked for a cab.

There is something *viscous* about a lie. One knows it for the lie it is, but all the same – something sticks. I have said that there are two large pictures in the big sitting room downstairs, Jack's *Narcissus* from Port Mungo, and Vera's massive *Vandal at the Gates*. Each has a wall to itself. The house was empty when I got back, and I went into the big room and stood, first, in front of Jack's painting, then in front of Vera's. Then back to Jack's. For fifteen minutes I went back and forth. At the end of that time I had convinced myself that Vera's scabrous critique of my brother's work was motivated by envy and nothing else. All the same a whisper of doubt troubled me, until this idea of viscosity occurred to me. One knows a lie for what it is, but all the same, something sticks.

How pleasant it was to have Anna with us for cocktails again! She came in just after six as I was pulling a cork. Jack had not yet appeared. She flung herself into an armchair and blew air at the ceiling.

– Jesus I'm knackered.
– This will revive you.
– Gin.
– Yes.
– I have something to ask you.

But at that moment Jack appeared in the doorway. He had been in his studio all day and hadn't changed his clothes, or even washed, as far as I could tell. He looked utterly unkempt. He stood a moment, regarding the happy scene.

– I should like a glass of that, please, he said.

Then in he came, and there we were again, together as we had been before all the trouble started. Jack sat down and gazed at Anna, grinning. I don't believe I had ever seen quite that sort of a grin on my brother's face before, all teeth, I mean, distinctly canine. There was an odd fixity about it. It lasted too long, and I saw Anna grow uncomfortable. She glanced at me. The moment passed. We decided to have dinner at the Spanish place, which seemed a declaration that we intended to go on as though nothing had happened. The evening passed off smoothly enough, although Jack was very quiet. I was a little surprised by this, for I knew how profoundly relieved he was to have Anna with us again, and I'd expected him to be animated.

I woke up at two in the morning. Utter silence. I turned on the bedside light. I am a good sleeper, this never happens to me. I knew at once what had awoken me. It was not a sound but a thought. It had occurred to me earlier in the day and been repressed, then it had thrust up into my sleeping mind. Not surprising that I'd been unable to deal with it, nor that when my defences were relaxed it would announce itself with enough clamour to sit me bolt upright from a deep sleep.

I padded down to the kitchen and made myself a cup of tea. I knew I would not sleep, and at half past four I took a pill. I woke up some hours later, rather groggy. After a shower and a cup of coffee I called Vera's hotel but she had checked out. I called her house upstate. There was no answer. I sat thinking what to do for ten minutes, then packed a small bag, and asked Dora to please tell Jack and Anna that I might not be back till tomorrow. By eleven o'clock I was out on Sixth Avenue looking for a cab to take me to Penn Station.

An hour later I was on a train going north up the Hudson. It is a trip I have taken often, and normally it gives me great pleasure. I consider it one of the best train journeys in the world, although I have little with which to compare it. But this day I barely glanced at the river, or rather I glanced at it, stared at it, but I barely saw it. My mind was elsewhere. When I got off the train at Rhinebeck I had only the most sketchy idea where Vera's house was, but the taxi driver at the station knew at once who I had come to see, apparently she was well known locally.

The house stood on a bluff with a distant view of the Hudson far below. A short switchbacked driveway gave off a quiet road that wandered into the hills high above the river, near the site of a skirmish in the revolutionary war, marked by a plaque at the side of the road. A pickup truck was parked beside a large barn, and off in the trees on the far side of the barn I glimpsed a number of wood and metal structures. Art. Sculpture. Somewhere a dog was barking. The day was cold and the sky was blue, with bulky white clouds kicking across it high above the river. The back door of the house opened and Vera stepped out on to the porch, wiping her hands on a rag. Seeing me emerge from the taxi, she leaned on the railing and in her expression I detected no ill-feeling but amusement, rather. And curiosity. As I crossed the yard she shouted at me, had I come all this way to apologize?

– I never called anyone a pompous bitch!

– Gin, I'm sorry about that. You're not a pompous bitch most of the time.

– It's a bit damn windy up here.

She took me into a kitchen with a long table down the middle of it. The windows on the north side had sheets of clear plastic stapled over them. She made me a cup of coffee. She didn't ask me what I was doing up here, nor did I tell her, not straightaway. Somehow it didn't seem strange to either of us that I was there. We sat at the table with our fingers wrapped round our coffee mugs. I felt as though I were in some rustic restaurant that lacked the benefits of central heating.

– I know why you're here, she said.

– I thought you might.

She was silent. We heard somebody moving around upstairs. Her eyes flickered to the ceiling.

– Do you know that Anna wants to go to art school? she said.

I remembered the girl saying she wanted to talk to me about something. She probably wanted me to help her out financially.

– No.

– She showed me some of her work.

225

– Any good?

She paused. She was tentative.

– Promising.

We watched each other as another of her artistic judgements hung in the air between us. This one was less contentious than the last.

– I think she needs some help from you. A loan.

– I thought she might.

– You're a good woman, Gin.

– I'm very fond of her. So is Jack.

– Yes. Jack.

We were back to it. She sat staring at the table and I just plunged right in, and told her what I knew about the night Peg died. I tried to present it as neutrally as I could, the drunken boat trip, the clouds concealing the moon, the coral head waiting in the dark water – and then I asked her the question that had woken me in the middle of the night. What had she meant when she said that if it hadn't been for Jack Peg would still be alive?

She was staring at me. She looked stunned.

– Gin, that's a complete fiction.

In her own kitchen, sitting across the table from this woman I had known all my life, I was not combative. I had lived with my brother's past for so long it was as familiar to me as my own. I knew that his account of his own experience was not rigorously objective, but what account is? Any version of as dense a weave of events and feelings and intentions and effects as a *life* will inevitably be flawed, its stresses and emphases reflecting not the truth – as if there were such a thing – but rather the shapes of bias and denial crafted by memory in the service of the ego. Jack was no different, locked as he was in the Narcissus posture of the dedicated artist, and I had always taken the pinch of salt, though in fact the appalling guilt with which he had for so long been struggling suggested a mind *unwilling* to distort or erase the past so as to live with itself more comfortably –!

But now I asked myself if I had been deceived. The history

suddenly seemed unsound, the entire edifice unstable. The wind rattled against the windowpanes and I glanced out at the sky, and across the valley the bare trees on the hills above the river. It occurred to me that a clarity of vision was possible here that was not possible in the city, I mean not just visually but intellectually, or spiritually even. There was less noise, less static, somehow, in the atmosphere. Vera was talking and I began to pay attention once more, and in that cold kitchen, with the wintry sky outside the window, and in the silence of this high place, her words had a terrible stark ring as she spoke about how badly Jack had treated her and Peg in Port Mungo. In the city truth is an elusive bird, as flighty in its way as falsehood is sticky. Too much noise in the city, too many clashing accounts of any given phenomenon, so one learns to be tentative and circumspect. Sceptical, ironical, stoic, detached: this is the urban posture. Up here her statement was stark and sincere and I had no desire to contradict her.

– Go on.

So she told me. I knew my brother for a driven man, I knew what he had sacrificed in order to make his art. Had I ever properly attempted to imagine how it was to live with such a man? I thought I had, in Port Mungo I thought I'd seen what his dedication cost those who lived with him – that ingrown negative energy – but I hadn't seen it properly, not in view of what Vera was now telling me. She spoke of Jack's cruelty. How sneering and critical he was about her work, and later about Peg's. How difficult he made it for anyone else to work under the same roof. I thought of the vision he had so often talked about, of the art partnership, the American Studio – surely it wasn't possible that the man who dreamed that dream could be destructive of the work of others?

But it was, apparently. He could belittle Vera in front of other people, call her a wash-out, a has-been, a never-was. Alone with him in Port Mungo she found it difficult to sustain any belief in herself.

– Why didn't you go?

– I did go.

– But not for good. Why couldn't you go away and not come back? If he was so dreadful.

– Because of Peg and Anna.

– You couldn't take them with you?

No, she couldn't. She didn't know how to look after children. She was not a motherly sort of a woman. She drank too much. She wanted to travel, she wanted to paint. She had no money. As a child Peg was happy. She knew to keep out of her father's way during his working hours, and if she did go into the studio she knew to keep quiet. And certainly she was better off in Pelican Road than she would have been bumming round the Caribbean with her mother. So Vera travelled to get away from Jack, and came back for her children.

I sat at her kitchen table and did not know what to say. I thought: but she too has her bias. Doesn't she exaggerate? Men and women argue! Terrible things are said in the heat of anger! – men and women when angry with each other do not speak a truth-seeking language, they speak adversarially – they prosecute, they defend, they make a case –

I made this case to Vera but she shook her head. It wasn't quarrelling, she said. Again the quiet tone, the words falling in a silent room like rocks into water, one by one. My brother was a cruel man. Selfish, unreasonable, demanding, he stayed in Port Mungo because there he could play the tyrant, and she, beaten down, without money, made frail, and rapidly slipping into alcoholism, she could neither challenge him nor abandon him, not while he still had Peg and, later, Anna. And Peg belonged to him, he had made this abundantly clear. He had looked after her, fed her, sheltered her: she was his. And when she grew up she was still his. Peg took my place, said Vera, quietly, and I became the weak one. The child. You understand what I'm saying?

This was difficult to listen to. Again we heard the footsteps on

228

the floorboards above. She sat up and turned towards the door, but nobody appeared. She looked at me and blew out a lungful of air.

– Shall we go out? Or are you too cold to move?

– A walk would warm us up.

So we walked along the road and got the blood moving in our veins, and the conversation of the kitchen table seemed somehow less awful out in the open air. How little I knew my brother after all, it seemed. He was cantankerous, yes, and stubborn, and selfish, but no more so than any serious artist, or so I had thought. Life with Jack was quite tolerable, and I said this.

– You don't threaten him.

This was true. I didn't threaten him, I indulged him. I supported him. I had supported him all his life. I thought about the paintings he had made since coming back to New York, during the years in Crosby Street, and then in my house, and I saw again that they were filled with rage, but more than that, a sort of bravura, and an empty bravura at that, they didn't *say* anything: these the paintings that coincided with the gradual collapse of his career. The Port Mungo paintings, the work of his so-called tropicalist period, those at least had fed off the colours of the world rather than the colours of his mind, or of his angry, isolated soul. We walked on in silence. I recognized that we had reached the point where we must talk about Peg's death. We were at a crossroads, I mean we were literally at a junction, where Vera's road met a road coming in from the east, and where the roads met, a grassy island with a bench overlooked the river. The view was astonishing. We sat in silence for a minute or two.

– Tell me about Johnny Hague, I said.

– Johnny looked after me.

– Was he your lover?

– Gin!

She said my name sharply, with annoyance, as though to say – listen to what I'm telling you. She said she needed someone to look after her. At times she needed a doctor, often enough there were bruises and cuts after some squalid drunken fight in Pelican Road. Johnny patched up her cuts and he patched up her spirit. He was tender and protective. He loved her. And yes, he was her lover, for some years, early on, but later he was simply a good friend to a woman caught in a ghastly fix, trapped in a destructive relationship and an addiction to drink and unable to get clear of either.

– He knew Gerald, she said.

– I know.

– They were at King's together.

– He told me. Was he addicted to morphine?

– He had it under control.

It seemed to go with the territory, to be of the character of Port Mungo, somehow, that the doctor would be addicted to morphine while his friendship, or his unrequited love, rather, sustained a woman driven to alcoholism by an artist too obsessed with his work to pay her any attention.

Suddenly I saw Peg as a scapegoat: an innocent, whose function it was to draw off all these toxins and pacify or even *purify* the community with her death. She purified it to the extent that Jack and Vera became free of Port Mungo after her death, free to come north and begin again, and Anna too – Anna fortunate to get away from Port Mungo before she too was crippled by the squalor and disorder of their lives down there.

– And Johnny, what became of him?

– He got out in the end. He came up here to see me. I have no idea how he found me, I forgot to ask. Probably through Gerald.

I asked her how that visit had been. He was a funny, dear man, she said. He wasn't young any more. None of us is young any more. But still the same old Johnny, dreamy, muddled, idealistic, good-hearted, self-indulgent. A gentleman, she said, if that means anything at all these days. Unsettled, looking for a place, unable to stay in Port Mungo, which apparently was becoming unrecognizable as the western Caribbean attracted more and more visitors, and resorts sprang up along the empty beaches. Johnny had stayed in the farmhouse for a few nights. They'd talked about the old days.

Silence, there on our windswept crag high above the Hudson River. Then she began to speak again, staring straight ahead and her hands flat on the boards of the bench. That's when she told me. It took a few minutes. Calmly and quietly she told me how Peg had become so depressed that she went into the mangroves one night and swallowed a bottle of sleeping pills. She told me how Johnny had been in the bar of the Macaw when Jack came in about ten days after her body was found. He was in a bad way. He had been drinking for days. He had to talk, and whatever antagonism existed between the two men was forgotten in the extremity of Jack's desperation and his need. He began to spill his feelings at the bar, and Johnny took him to a table at the back of the room where they would not be overheard.

What Jack had then told him, Johnny had immediately passed on to Gerald. Since then he had said nothing to anybody until the night he'd sat at Vera's kitchen table. What he'd told her was this: that one night Peg and Jack had sat up drinking – Vera was away, somewhere down the coast – and the more they drank the more distraught Peg had become. Jack's memory of that part of the evening was more or less intact. But what happened after midnight, about that he was confused. What he *thinks* happened was that he had at last been forced to agree with her that her life had become an unspeakable horror. And such was the state of drunkenness they had reached, he said, or such the state of *clarity*, rather, a certain kind of drunkenness can create in the mind, the alcohol rousing a kind of higher sobriety – he had agreed with her that she would be better off dead.

Vera stopped here.

– Jack told Peg, I said slowly, that she would be better off dead. Told his own daughter she'd be better off dead. Why?

– He didn't know if he said it or not. He said it was possible, given all that had been said already. I don't have to tell you why. You know why. Gerald told you.

– Oh dear god.

Over the hills on the far bank of the Hudson a hawk hung in the sky, far off in the distance. Tiny bird drifting on the currents of the wind. The bare bleak facts of the thing, coughed out in a Port Mungo bar by a drunken man incapable any longer of keeping to himself the evil he had done. I doubt he ever told anyone about it again, said Vera, and Johnny Hague, whom he had chosen, perversely, to hear his confession, spoke of it only twice: to Gerald, and to herself. And who had Vera told? Only me, she said.

– Not Anna?

– No.

– Anna doesn't know?

– No.

– Why didn't you tell her?

– Better she think it my fault than that Jack –

– Jack what?

She wouldn't say anything more. So I repeated what Gerald had told me in his room at the Park Plaza twenty years before, and she disputed none of it, not even her own guilty awareness of the changes in her daughter, and the suspicions she repressed, or drowned, rather, in floods of booze, until the day Johnny Hague sat at her kitchen table and told her what Jack had told him in the bar of the Hotel Macaw.

– That was the end. I had to stop drinking, I had to get straight. I couldn't see Jack after that. Not until last week, or whenever it was.

– Because you'd heard about Anna.

– I couldn't miss Anna, could I? And you two were keeping her to yourselves.

– I should have called you.

– Yes you should, said Vera hoarsely.

– So you're telling me that it started, I said, this thing between Jack and Peg, before Anna was born, and went on after? And she killed herself because of it?

– Yes.

That was quite enough for me.

– I don't believe it, I said. I don't believe a single bloody word of it. Not a bloody word!

18

I caught an early evening train. I got into Penn Station after dark and found a cab. There was nobody in the sitting room or in the kitchen. It was Dora's night off. I poured myself a drink. The silence in the house was not comfortable. I paced about downstairs, responding to a restlessness, or a disturbance, rather, in the atmosphere of the house. Something had happened – this thought struck me all at once, and with considerable force. While I had been away, while Jack and Anna were alone, something had happened here. No, it was me. I was rattled, anxious, and desperately weary. I had been numb on the train, unable even to begin to assimilate what I had heard that afternoon. I remember once thinking, with regard to Peg's death, that there are no mysteries, only secrets. Only people who keep secrets. Nothing had changed. People were still keeping secrets.

I tried to read the newspaper. Normally I enjoy having the house to myself, for me solitude is a pleasure. On those rare occasions when I am alone here I indulge the pleasure of possession – the house is *mine*. Not shared, mine. Not this night. This night the house was by no means mine, others had taken possession of it, in a manner that was not yet apparent to me, and had then gone out. Or were in their rooms, though they had not responded when I went upstairs and called them. Nor was there anybody in the studio, I had seen no lights on up there when I got out of my cab. For some reason there was a large kitchen knife on the window-sill, and nobody had drawn the blinds. I drew them now. Then for some minutes I sat down with the paper, until I heard steps descending the staircase.

I became unaccountably alarmed at that descending footfall. I was unable to say a word. I sat frozen in my armchair, half-turned towards the door.

Why could I not call out?

Anna appeared in the doorway.

– Oh hi, Gin.

I stared at her, the tumult still working in me.

– Anna.

She flung herself into an armchair and would not look at me. She chewed her thumbnail. When she did lift her eyes to mine I was unable to read her expression. I felt we were back where we'd been when she first moved in, awkward with each other and unable to make conversation.

– Is everything all right? I said.

– Not really.

– What's the matter?

No answer to this. A kind of morose shrug, eyes averted once more, then out with the tobacco and the rolling papers. I felt I was in a dream. With trembling fingers she assembled an untidy cigarette and lit it.

– Gin.

– Yes, Anna.

– Jack's dead.

I don't suppose I shall ever forget that moment. How to describe the – lurch – the mind makes when it is given information so utterly unanticipated – the lurch into a void, as though one has stepped off the high ledge of a building, and in one's freefall, clutching at the oddest twigs –

– But I've only been gone a few hours, I said.

How could he be dead when I'd been away so short a time? My words made no sense to Anna either. I was sitting forward, staring at the girl. I became aware that my mouth was open. I shut it.

– Where is he?

– Upstairs.

But I didn't move. I suppose I was in shock. It took a minute for me to organize an appropriate question.

– What makes you think he's dead?

– I better tell you what happened.

– Have you told anyone else?

– I was waiting for you.

So she began to talk, as I sat there attempting to make sense of this girl telling me that my brother was dead upstairs. I didn't know what she was saying. I interrupted her.

– Is he in his bedroom?

– No, he's in the studio.

I told her to go on. I suppose the reason I didn't want to go upstairs was because then I would have to confront it, whatever it was she was talking about. Down here in the sitting room it was not real. I think I expected to see Jack appear in the doorway at any moment. Then it would be clear that this was all some new oddness on the part of this odd girl. She was telling me that after I'd gone Jack had asked her to pose for him again. He wanted to work on the portrait. She didn't really want to but it seemed so important to him that she'd agreed. She went up to the studio in her bathrobe, as she'd so often done before, and when he was ready she'd slipped it off and stood in front of the hanging drape in the pose he had taught her.

I nodded my head. This was all clear enough.

But he was behaving so strangely. He was muttering to himself and she couldn't understand what he was saying. He would suddenly turn towards the window and stand very still, as though listening to somebody speaking to him from the building across the street. She grew more and more uncomfortable but when she moved he shouted at her to stay where she was. After this she became frightened.

Then she was disgusted.

– Why?

This was not easy for her. Her fingers were knotted together and twisting round and round. Her head was down, she was frowning. Her eyes flickered to mine and then away again. From where she stood she couldn't see him properly, she said, he liked to put the easel close to her and at an oblique angle. But out of the corner of her eye she could see what he was doing.

– What was he doing?

– He had it out.

– What?

She made a gesture. She was lying.

– No, I said.

– Yes, Gin. *Yes.*

She was suddenly so angry!

Then what?

Then she put her bathrobe back on in spite of him shouting at her not to move. Couldn't she see he was working? She tried to leave the room but he stood with his back to the door. She'd shouted back at him.

– You shouted back at him?

– I really shouted at him.

– You weren't afraid of him?

– No! Dirty old man. Christ.

All she saw, she said, was a contemptible, pathetic, dirty old man. Then what?

– He started crying. He kind of slid down the door. Pathetic. I just stepped over him and came downstairs. Got dressed. I called my mother but she said you'd left.

– Did you tell her what happened?

– No.

I began to think about going upstairs. My breathing was

coming very fast now. I felt hot, and rather nauseous. I had to sit still a little longer.

– Then what?

– I got a knife from the kitchen drawer and sat down here waiting for you.

– So what makes you think Jack's dead?

It took an effort for me to say it. There didn't seem to be enough oxygen in the room. This conversation had shifted from being entirely unreal to being too real and now shifted back into unreality.

– I went back up.

– Why?

– I don't know. I got bored, I guess.

Twenty minutes later I went upstairs with Anna. Climbing the last flight up to the attic I was not strong, and more than once I had to pause for breath. At the door she waited for me. We stood a moment outside the closed door to the studio, the only sound my panting.

– OK, I said.

She opened the door. It was dark, only a dim glow seeping in from the outside. There was a strange unpleasant smell. On the far side of the studio there was something on the floor. Anna hit the switch and for a second or two the room was flooded in brilliant white light.

– Enough! I shouted, and she turned it off.

The thing on the floor was my brother Jack lying in a pool of blood: flat on his back, naked from the waist up, hands clawed. Long skinny white body. The wounds were under his elbows, each of them now a clotted crusty mess. His eyes were wide open and so was his mouth, as though he were utterly astonished. His large feet splayed off to either side. Like a huge dead bird. Above him hung the portrait of Anna, and he seemed to be staring up at it. In the clawed fingers of his left hand was a razor blade wrapped in black electrical tape.

*   *   *

239

Much later, after the police had come and gone, and the medical people, and the body had been taken away to the morgue, Anna and I sat downstairs together. I had made a number of phone calls – Vera, Eduardo, Jack's doctor, one or two others – then Dora had come home and found strangers in the house, and on being told why they were here she became hysterical for five minutes. Then she pulled herself together and made coffee. We could hear her sweeping the stairs and the hallway now. For several hours I had acted the competent householder as I'd dealt with the cops, and then the doctor and the paramedics. Anna had stayed with me throughout, and remained as calm as I was. Not even the sight of two men in white jackets bringing Jack's bagged body down the stairs to the gurney in the hall disturbed our grave unflappable demeanour. Now we sat each with a large whisky and our demeanour had not yet begun to show any sign of crumbling.

– How did you do it?

– Do what?

There was no need for her to pretend with me but I didn't say a word.

– Do what, Gin?

More silence. Dora appeared and in an unsteady voice asked if there was anything else we needed. I told her there wasn't. She went back into the hall, closing the door behind her. We heard the vacuum cleaner. The studio was locked. I didn't know if I could ask Dora to wash the floor up there. Perhaps I would ask her if she knew anybody who'd clean the studio, then she could say if the task was too painful for her. After that I would have to see to his things. So many paintings he had up there! I read somewhere that you can never get blood out of the floorboards, not completely. They always stay pink.

– I guess I should feel sad or something, said Anna, but I don't feel anything.

– You will.

When I'd told Vera she had shrieked with dismay. Eventually

she could not speak any more. She said she would come down to the city tomorrow.

So Anna and I sat glumly in the sitting room.

– I was glad when Gerald died, she said. He was suffering such a lot.

– You think Jack wasn't suffering?

She got up without a word and ran out of the room. I thought of Rothko then. Jack's hero. I was living in New York when he died, and I remembered how he'd cut himself with a razor blade, not his wrists but the brachial arteries under his elbows. So there was a derivative quality to Jack's death, it lacked originality. Say the same about his paintings, I suppose. I began to laugh. I was feeling a little giddy. I think I may have been close to hysteria. I wondered how she'd managed it, how she'd convinced him to do it, I mean, or perhaps what happened was that she'd convinced him to let *her* do it – a ritualistic sort of a thing, ritual vengeance. Ritual parricide, long contemplated, deliberate in execution: all that would come out, I thought. Not publicly of course, not in a court of law, I mean here in the house, where she'd be safe. For we would have to protect her, Vera and me, and Dora too, we women would have to keep her safe so nobody would ever know that Jack Rathbone did not commit suicide, no, he was put to death by his own daughter. Thinking this, I began to feel the grief rise in me and as it did I became aware that in the toilet down the hall Anna was being violently sick.

Then all at once I could hear Jack laughing! – somewhere up at the top of the house, the lovely wild laughter I remembered from my childhood, and dear god it did for me, it did for me utterly, and as the floodgates opened my poor heart burst and the pain poured out of me like a river –

ACKNOWLEDGEMENTS

No man is an island, apparently, but by the middle of a book most writers get to feeling distinctly peninsular. In this we are deluded. We go into the room alone, and we stay in the room alone, but what happens there to a great extent depends on the web of support we enjoy outside the room. Here are the names of some of the people who, during the writing of this novel and its aftermath, have given me love, help, encouragement – recreational companionship – and to them I give my heartfelt thanks: Maria Aitken, Pempe Aitken, Max Blagg, Marti Blumenthal, Liz Calder, Peter Carey, Catriona Crowe, Jack Davenport, Gary Fisketjon, Michelle Gomez, Edward Hibbert, Sonny Mehta, Andrew O'Hagan, Alexandra Pringle, Deborah Rogers, Edward St. Aubyn, Betsy Sussler, Lynne Tillman, Colm Tóibín, Binky Urban, Stewart Waltzer. And of course Helen, Steve, Judy and Simon McGrath.

A NOTE ON THE AUTHOR

Patrick McGrath is the author of a story collection, *Blood and Water and Other Tales*, and five novels, *The Grotesque, Spider, Dr Haggard's Disease, Asylum*, and *Martha Peake*. He lives in London and New York with his wife Maria Aitken.

A NOTE ON THE TYPE

The text of this book is set in Linotype Janson. The original types
were cut in about 1690 by Nicholas Kis, a Hungarian working
in Amsterdam. The face was misnamed after Anton Janson,
a Dutchman who worked at the Ehrhardt Foundry in Leipzig,
where the original Kis types were kept in the early eighteenth
century. Monotype Ehrhardt is based on Janson. The original
matrices survived in Germany and were acquired in 1919 by
the Stempel Foundry. Hermann Zapf used these originals
to redesign some of the weights and sizes for Stempel. This
Linotype version was designed to follow the original types
under the direction of C. H. Griffith.